Rachael King has worked for various media, including *Rip it Up*, *Staple*, *Pavement* and 95bFM, and as a researcher for television. She played bass guitar in several Flying Nun bands until the mid-nineties. In 2008 she was the Ursula Bethell writer in residence at the University of Canterbury. This is her second novel; her first, *The Sound of Butterflies*, was a bestseller and in 2007 won the NZSA Hubert Church Award for Best First Book of Fiction at the Montana New Zealand Book Awards.

Magpie Hall

Rachael King

V

A VINTAGE BOOK published by Random House New Zealand, 18 Poland Road, Glenfield, Auckland, New Zealand

For more information about our titles go to www.randomhouse.co.nz

A catalogue record for this book is available from the National Library of New Zealand

Random House New Zealand is part of the Random House Group
New York London Sydney Auckland Delhi Johannesburg

First published 2009

© 2009 Rachael King

The moral rights of the author have been asserted

ISBN 978 1 86979 288 6

Random House New Zealand uses non-chlorine-bleached papers from sustainably managed plantation forests.

Cover design and artwork: Sarah Laing
Text design: Laura Forlong
Author photograph: Peter Rutherford
Printed in Australia by Griffin Press

For Peter

One for sorrow,

Two for joy,

Three a letter,

Four a boy.

Five for silver,

Six for gold,

Seven a secret never to be told.

The Magpie Song (Anon)

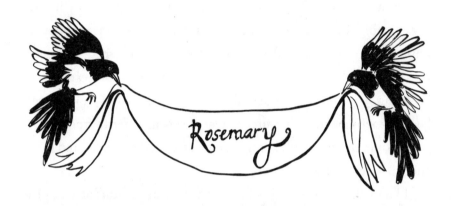

Rosemary

There were two rumours surrounding my great-great-grandfather Henry Summers: one, that his cabinet of curiosities drove him mad; and two, that he murdered his first wife. I don't know if either of these is true — all I know is that the cabinet went missing soon after Henry's death, and the woman's body was never found.

After the Canterbury earthquake of 1888, he bought a damaged country estate among the South Island's farming gentry. When he had finished rebuilding the house, it was unnecessarily grand, with arched leadlight windows, turrets and a tower, a miniature Gothic castle transplanted to the New Zealand landscape. Henry named the estate Magpie Hall and the magpies were there still, perching on its chimneys, keeping guard. After his wife Dora supposedly drowned in the river, he went on to remarry, and her disappearance became a stain on the family history that faded over time.

Growing up, this was as much as I knew about Henry and Dora. Later, all I had to build their story were the clues the house gave up, some vague memories and a letter from my grandfather.

In Gothic romance novels there is always an imposing country house, and quite often a young, naïve heroine — frequently orphaned — haunted by the ghost, literal or otherwise, of a woman who has gone before her. There are letters, libraries and attics, someone imprisoned somewhere. Always a mystery of some sort, and often two potential lovers: one fair and intellectual, the other earthy and brooding, with wounds that only a woman, the *right* woman, can heal. Sometimes there is a fire, a great cleansing inferno from which the heroine emerges with her hero, rejuvenated, the past behind them and a perfect future ahead.

I know this because I have been immersed in the stuff of Victorian novels for too long now, writing my interminable thesis. I suppose by coming to Magpie Hall to claim my inheritance I thought I would be inspired; instead all I found was the distraction of my own family's ghosts, and of my own failings, the very ones I had gone there to escape.

I drove inland for two hours through the rain in my beaten up Subaru, over plains and deadly straight roads until the land began to undulate and the hills were broken apart by limestone cliffs. In the back seat, the scraggy bones of my thesis — pages and pages of desultory notes, false starts and ramblings — languished in boxes, along with piles of novels and academic texts and my ancient laptop and printer. I don't know when my love for Victorian novels had turned into a burden.

Hugh, my supervisor, had helped me to carry everything to the car, protesting, but I had to get out before I suffocated. The university was making cuts and the long arteries of the English department corridors were empty. When I sat in my cramped office, I heard doors slam and padding footsteps, but if I stuck my head out there was nobody to be seen. The cuts had made the staff nervous and they shrank inside their offices. Sometimes I would hear the murmur of conversation — once even sobs breaking through the yellow walls — but I filled my floor-to-ceiling shelves with books from the library to insulate myself from the sounds of people's careers foundering and crumbling. It was no wonder they took solace in each other's arms.

Hugh was one of the lucky ones — for now. When I told him I was leaving, he tried to embrace me and I let him, holding myself rigid against his fleshy chest.

'Christ,' he said. 'What about me? God, you smell amazing.' He took a deep whiff of my hair. 'You *are* amazing.' Clinging like a rat in a flood.

'I'm sure you'll cope.' I pulled away, then patted his arm, aware of how stiff I was, how maternal the gesture. 'You'll have Gloria.' My patience dropped away then. 'Count yourself lucky. At least you've got a job.'

Rumbling, grudging laughter. 'Teaching snot-nosed little bastards who just want a few easy credits for their commerce degrees. Lucky me.'

It was never enough. Nothing was ever enough. Not enough to have a wife — a younger woman, devoted to him in every way — two children, a decent, if not secure, job. He had to have me as well. Not instead of his family, although he had given me hope at the beginning, but as well as. He had once talked about taking me back to Wales, where we would live in a cottage in the hills for a year and both finish our projects — my thesis and the tome he had been scratching at for ten years, too scared to complete it because then it would be real, out in the world and open to criticism. Hugh didn't do criticism, unless it was directed by him at others.

Like the fool I was, I believed him.

I tried not to think of his wife as we fucked, usually at the flat that I shared with a burlesque dancer above a tattoo parlour, twice on the floor of his office. I once saw Hugh's wife visiting him with their youngest child, a brown-jerseyed boy just old enough to walk in erratic steps. She had smiled at me as she held the boy's hand while he wobbled past, and something inside me had crumpled. She looked harassed, with red cheeks, hair falling from her loose pony-tail, but she still had the energy to smile at a stranger standing in the corridor gaping at her.

That was the first time I left Hugh, but he had begged me to come back, shown up on my doorstep with a bottle of single malt and some collapsing tulips. He would leave her, he said, when the children were older. She'd be fine: he'd set her up; she could have the house. He'd never liked it anyway. We could still go away, just not immediately.

That was when I first began to really hate myself, just before my grandfather died, and I didn't want to admit what a bastard Hugh was.

Death has a way of forcing your hand and now I was leaving. I was leaving Hugh; I was leaving the claustrophobic walls of the English department and all its distractions. As we walked through the downstairs lobby, laden with the books and notes, russet leaves swirled about our feet, brought inside by the current of students as they hurried through the doors.

I let Hugh finish putting the boxes in the car, then I climbed in without a word and drove away. I watched him in the rear-view mirror as I left. His hand was raised as if he were waiting for me to wave back. He stood like that until I turned the corner and headed south.

❧

The house was shuttered against the coming winter, and the spectre of my grandfather stood on the front step to greet me before dissolving into the shadows. I had left the rain behind, and the weak autumn light descended from the clouds and bounced off the cliffs to the north, playing tricks. The stillness frightened me. I had been coming here most of my life and my arrival was always accompanied by movement and sound: Grandpa waving, one of the dogs wriggling its hips and coming over to sniff and bark hello, always at least one chicken out of its coop, scratching and nudging the earth with a crowing rooster not far behind. The bustle always diverted me from what I felt now — a slight panic, a creeping awareness of the places on the farm I had managed to avoid for twenty years staring at my back, willing me to turn and face them.

The looming presence of the house was exaggerated by the great shadows it cast with the sun behind its turrets and chimneys. Long spikes stretched across the paddocks. The flowers had retreated for the autumn and the ivy that climbed the grey stone walls had been reduced to a tangle. Rotten autumn leaves gathered on the ground in damp clumps and even the macrocarpas that lined the nearby paddocks seemed to have moved closer.

A single magpie perched on the nearest chimney. It leaned towards me, leering. I stood on the gravel and stared at it a while before turning away to unpack my books and bags from the back seat. I had a fresh tattoo on the inside of my left wrist, and it ached with the effort of carrying the weight in my arms. When I kicked the car door closed, the sound was like an explosion in the late afternoon air and the magpie beat its wings, protesting.

Grandpa's old gumboots were stationed at the front door, abandoned sentries. I put down my books to fumble inside one of the boots for the key, still in the same place it had always been.

It was colder in the panelled entrance hall than it was outside. It would have been a formal room once, but now it was filled with the debris of farm life: more gumboots, the humped backs of coats hanging three on each hook, umbrellas and the remnants of firewood. An axe was propped in the corner. A bucket and mop fell over as I brushed past. Stepping into the living room — opening the curtains, flicking at the dust that floated and settled again — I was overwhelmed by the smell of dog hair and mildew, and the perpetual odour of coal dust from the fire that burned all year round. Beneath that was the smell of beeswax from the solid mahogany and oak furniture. The heavy velvet drapes, now loosened from the windows, let in the thin light; the flocked wallpaper was peeling in places, and the thick dark carpet muffled everything. The only sound came from the ticking grandfather clock, which was odd. Somebody had been in to wind it.

Staying at Magpie Hall had always been the opposite experience to life in my parents' house; here, we didn't have to worry about tracking dirt inside or leaving grubby fingerprints on anything. My mother couldn't cope with the dust and the cobwebs, the clutter of books and ephemera. She always looked relieved to drop her children at the door and leave us for the holidays with a kiss on the cheek, getting back to her crisp house in the city.

'It's all the eyes,' she told me once, because presiding over everything, along the top of a bookcase that ran the length of the room, shapes reared up: a magpie, frozen mid-crow; a cockatoo, crest arching in the gloom. A goat's head, the only remains of a failed business venture. Grandpa's old friends, and now mine. I made a clicking sound with my tongue, half expecting them to move, to cock their heads with curiosity, but they stayed there, staring out through shiny bead eyes. In the corner of the room, perched on a thin branch with its body tilted to the light and beak extending in an arc, was Grandpa's prize, the huia. Its iridescent black feathers were gathering dust, nobody to protect it.

Before I could do anything else, I needed to rescue it. I dragged a chair from the darkened dining room and stood on it. I felt wobbling and frail, up on my toes, fingers stretched until they ached. But then I had the bird in my hands, in my arms, and was dropping to the floor like a cat. I blew on the feathers, causing dust and desiccated insect carcasses from the neighbouring spider's web to spray outwards and fall. I placed the bird on the side table, where I would see to it later, and went to look at my inheritance.

Magpie Hall was to be renovated. Carpet ripped up and floors polished; walls knocked down for open-plan living and indoor–outdoor flow; wallpaper torn off and walls relined and painted fresh modern colours. I had seen the plans.

I don't think Grandpa would have liked it. He had left the house and farm to his three children — my father and his brother and sister — and, oddly, to my brother. I think Grandpa had notions that Charlie, as the eldest son of the eldest son, would take over the family business that my father had shunned, that he would take a wife and pass the farm to the next generation of Summers. But my brother was firmly attached to the city life, with a promising career as a doctor ahead of him. Better for Grandpa if he had left it to me.

At least I wouldn't be gutting the house. I would have kept it just the way it was.

But I had no say. I was invited to the family dinner following the reading of the will, and they barely discussed the matter. They knew what they wanted — my parents and aunt and uncle — and only Charlie sat still in the corner, pale, clutching a beer. He felt guilty, I know, that he had inherited so much when his sister and cousins hadn't. After a few more drinks, Charlie had stood, swaying slightly, and said, 'What if I want to be a farmer?' and the rest of the family had laughed him down. But I knew he hadn't meant it as a joke, not in that moment. For one tiny second, I think my brother had imagined a different life for himself.

Around my parents' huge dining table it was decided that they would subdivide the farm — after it had been in the family for generations — and sell it, and that they would keep the house. It would be turned into a bed and breakfast hotel, to earn its keep. My family has never been poor. At the time I didn't understand why any of them needed any more money than they already had, but I kept the thought to myself. Perhaps, too, they had other reasons. Although my father and his siblings had grown up happily on the farm, things had happened there since that they would prefer to forget. We all would. I just didn't think that punishing the house was the way to go about it.

As I walked through those dusty rooms, down the corridor lined with old watercolour landscapes and still lifes, I knew that this would be my last chance to know the house as it was; that soon my family heritage would be watered down, perhaps washed away, forever.

Although some of the antique furniture would remain, for 'character', everything else would be cleared out or stored in the attic. The first to go would be the stuffed animals — the 'menagerie room' we called the study where most of the animals were kept, and where Grandpa practised his taxidermy. But it wasn't just Grandpa's collection — the birds and the stoats and the stag trophies he had spent his spare hours bent over — it was also Great-great-grandfather Henry's collection, which meant there were some rare and very old specimens, of both exotic and native birds and animals, including the huia. My family would have liked to donate it all to a museum, or, even better, to sell it to private collectors, but here at least I had some say. For Grandpa had left the entire collection to the only family member who had taken any interest in the art of taxidermy: me.

❦

I was ten years old. Charlie, two years younger, stood over the magpie, pinging the rubber band of his slingshot. He hid the weapon behind his back when he heard me approach.

'What did you do?' I asked. Blood grazed the bird's eye, but other than that it had no visible marks. I knelt down beside it.

'Nothing. It was an accident. Stupid bird.' He ran off, laughing, his skinny legs windscreen wipers in the long grass. He turned once to yell, 'Stick it up your arse!'

I lay down on my stomach and pushed my face towards the magpie, looking for any sign of life. I touched it, picked up the body in the cup of my hands. It was warm, soft; its head flopped lazily.

'There birdie, poor birdie.'

I pulled it into my chest and kissed it, wanting to comfort it somehow. The close proximity to real death thrilled me. It was the most elegant creature I had ever seen. I wanted to hold it forever.

I knew just what to do with it.

Grandpa was in his taxidermy room, tidying up.

'Now, what's this you've brought me?' Taking the bird from me, seeing the look of concern on my face and handling it with more gravity than he needed. 'Yes, yes,' he said. 'A fine specimen of *Gymnorhina tibicen hypoleuca*. Not a native, mind. Introduced in the 1860s to control the insects that were destroying the crops. Did you know that?'

I shook my head.

'And now they're here to stay. Like old friends. Let's see what we can do for this one, eh?'

We kids had once been attacked by magpies. They had swooped and dived at us as we walked through the eastern paddock to the river for a swim, and a beak grazed my hair before I put my hands over my head and ran, screaming, back to the house.

Grandpa taught us how to deal with the birds. He broke two thin branches off a tree and showed us how to walk tall, sticks erect above us. He found four ice-cream containers and some pens. We drew psychedelic eyes on the bottoms and set off for the river, all of us, marching like tin-pot generals with the containers on our heads, their eyes hypnotising the magpies above and keeping them at bay. We named the pool at the other side of the paddock the Magpie Pool. Charlie proclaimed himself King of the Magpies after that, but I was not at all surprised that one of his missiles had found its mark.

Henry Summers must have loved those magpies to name the house after them; or maybe they were such an integral part of the landscape they were unavoidable.

I felt bereft when Grandpa took the bird from me and laid it out on the table. I sighed, and he looked up and saw my face. He moved aside then, reached for my hand and pulled me to him. 'Do you want to do it? Do you want to bring the bird back to life?' I nodded, of course, but I was scared of the scalpels that lay on his workbench, of what they might do to the bird, so perfect in its death.

Grandpa made an incision from the magpie's throat to its tail

('Airway to arsehole,' he said) and after he had gently peeled back the skin, he let me squeeze the secateurs that cut through the leg and wing bones at the shoulder and hip, and finally the neckbone. The bird had merely shrugged off its coat and now lay naked beside it.

Together we mounted it. The magpie became our project for the rest of my holiday there as we scooped out the contents of the skull with a brainspoon, dried the skin with salt, checking up on it daily until it was ready, fashioned the body from clay and sawdust, chose glass bead eyes and sewed and glued and slowly watched it take shape. We positioned it with wings outstretched, full of life, defiant. We sat on the high stools at the workbench, shoulder to shoulder, bent over the bird. Grandpa's great knobbly hands, with their brown-acorn knuckles, enclosed mine so often as we worked that I came to know their smell and texture as well as I knew my own small pale hands, which were like rabbit paws next to his.

The magpie came home with me at the end of the holidays. My mother tried to make me keep it in the shed, but I would not let it go. It perched in my room and kept a guard over my dreams as I slept. I took it to school for show and tell and all the children wanted to touch it at lunchtime. They sidled up, measuring me, not sure whether to revile or worship me. It was a dilemma they would face all through my school days.

Now, the menagerie room looked as though Grandpa had just stepped out for a cup of tea. The big work table, hip height, dominated the centre of the room, and the tall stools I used to balance on were dotted around it. His instruments were lined up ready to use: scalpels, brushes, brainspoons. Containers of eyes, descending in order from biggest, like marbles, to the tiniest of rodents' beads. Glass cases cluttered with jars and small animals stood with their backs to the walls.

I took a moment for it sink in: this collection was now mine. I owned it. Every parrot and hummingbird, every tui and snarling stoat.

Outside, the day was dulling. A small whirlwind picked up a pile of leaves and scattered them across the vast lawn.

I didn't know how long it had been since Grandpa was well enough to work in this room. My parents tried to get him to move in with them, especially in those last few months, when he was really ill, but he refused to move. He said he was damned if he was going to live out his last few months in a house in the city where he couldn't see the stars at night. But we all had busy lives and nobody could afford to take the time off to care for him indefinitely at Magpie Hall.

He had grown up in this house, as had his father; his wife had died there; he had raised his children, seen grandchildren come and go. The house was far too big for one old man and his housekeeper, with no other dwellings for half a mile — and those the workers' cottages up the hill, where Joshua the station manager lived with his wife and young children. Magpie Hall wasn't built for this solitary life. Standing there, I felt its spaces echo around me, and realised it was the first time I had ever been there alone. And in that moment I understood why Grandpa had left the house to Charlie, in the sweet hope that it would be restored to a new generation, that the cycle that had passed with Grandpa would begin again, that Charlie might start a family there. And although Grandpa wanted to stay there until he died, I know that the silence got to him, that the house had lost some of its life since I had stopped coming as a child all those years ago. Its spaces were thick with regret. Its edges had faded and frayed.

Finally the family employed a nurse to look after Grandpa but we visited him often and in the end he said he preferred to have a near-stranger looking after him. When he couldn't wash himself properly or go to the toilet unassisted, he would rather his family didn't have to do it for him. It was about dignity, he said.

I moved back to my home town after my grandmother died, to take up my university studies and to be closer to Grandpa. I grew up in the right part of town, went to all the right schools. By day it was a pretty, safe place, covered with bright flowers or a sprinkling of frost, depending on the season. Old money lived there, apparent in the huge colonial houses that sat behind brick walls and hedgerows, shutting out the world. By night it became a city where prostitutes were found floating in the river; where teenage girls were raped or murdered; where a young man could be beaten to a meaty pulp for wearing pink sneakers; where tourists were knifed in the town square for talking funny; where the citizens were held captive by boy racers, who circled the perimeter like sharks, engines growling and tyres smoking. The good folk cowered in their houses and waited for the sun to rise. I had left as soon as I was old enough, swearing never to return, so when I did, I chose to live as far away from the town centre as possible, over the hills in the industrial port.

With the bare bulb now illuminated, the animals threw sharp shadows on the walls. Exotic butterflies and beetles were trapped behind glass, and the light reflected off their wings and bodies. Grandpa had told me about them — they were from Henry's vast collection, captured in Africa and Australia and Brazil. The most marvellous part of the story was that he hadn't just acquired them; he had caught them himself. Who knew how much had gone into each specimen, how much it had cost him, in money, danger and sweat? And here they were, colours as alive as ever.

I let my gaze slip to the glass cases. These had been my guilty pleasure as a child. The kids at school didn't believe me when I told them what they contained: not only stuffed animals but jars of creatures preserved in what I supposed was formaldehyde or alcohol, with faded labels written in old-fashioned ink: a coiled thin white snake, with a label that read *Zamenis hippocrepis, Egypt, 1882*; *Squid, Aegean, 1875* stuffed into the jar, its tentacles wrapped around themselves and pressed against the glass. More jars were stashed behind them, three deep. One snake, *Dipsas dendrophila*, from Sumatra, had large scales on its black and white body, giving it the appearance of a fish floating in water. I don't think Grandpa even realised how much time I spent in this room when he was out on the farm. I knew where he kept the key to the case and I hid in the menagerie room with Henry's collection while the family forgot my existence. I opened the doors, moved aside the jars at the front and reached in to pull one from the back: one of the good ones that only I knew about. I would never have shown my little brother what I now held in my hands, suspended in the heavy liquid, turning in the light: a human foetus. Next to the foetus on the shelf, a pair of tiny feet. A baby's feet, soles pressed against the glass, with rosy rings lacing its toes. The label read: *Smallpox, 1885*.

I tried not to think of the story they suggested — the parents' grief, and whether they had knowingly donated their child's extremities to science. Whether they also kept something of it, a grisly memento mori. Perhaps it is bad enough to lose a child, without having to be reminded of it all the time.

What brought me back to look at the jars again and again was the fact that these creatures, human and animal, had lived more than a hundred years before and yet here they were in my hands. The person who had preserved these had the power to bestow immortality.

I pulled out the letter the lawyer had given me at the reading of Grandpa's will. I had read it only once then put it away, too distraught by the death and immersed in my problems. But the letter was one of the main reasons I was here, so I sat on one of the high stools and read it again.

My dear Rosemary,

I am dictating this to Susan, my nurse, as my handwriting is slow and shaky these days. By the time you get this you will know that I have left you my taxidermy collection and the other contents of the menagerie room. The rest of the family might think it strange that I am leaving it all to you, but as you are the only one who has ever taken an interest in taxidermy, it is absolutely fitting that you should have this collection. Much of it, as you know, belonged to my grandfather, Henry Summers. He taught me the art, as I taught it to you. I know you don't do it so much any more, but I hope that this collection will inspire you.

You will find some rather unpleasant items in this collection, my dear. I never showed them to you because I didn't think you were old enough to understand, and by the time you became an adult, well, you'd stopped asking. To understand why they're here, and why I have kept them for so long, you need to know a bit about your great-great-grandfather.

You know that he came here in the 1880s and that he restored this house. He was from a very well-respected family in England, a gentleman with prospects and many illustrious friends, including, I understand, Edward VII himself. He was not a warm person, my grandfather, at least not to me, which is one of the reasons I tried to be more to you. He taught me things, but I never felt it was out of love for me. So, no, he was not warm, but he was a fascinating man, and for that I was proud to be his grandson. You know that he was a collector, and that he visited all manner of countries in pursuit of the strange and the wonderful. He wasn't content, like many men of his social standing, to spend money amassing his collection of curiosities, just by waiting for consignments to arrive from the far reaches of the earth. He went to get them himself. That is what brought him to New Zealand — the search for the moa and the huia, and perhaps slightly less nobly, the search for Maori artefacts. What he didn't count on was meeting a woman, falling in love and marrying, thereby sealing his fate, and all of ours, to be born New Zealanders.

The woman he loved was not my grandmother, who was his second wife. The first drowned in the river. Her body was never found. I believe that he cared for my grandmother, but I don't think there was a great deal of love between them. In fact I think she was scared of him, as we all were. He had a terrible temper and would fly into such rages that we all had to stay out of his way. Towards the end of his life, they got much worse, for no reason, and if it's possible for someone to die of anger, I would say that this is what killed him in the end. He would lock himself away in the room that housed his special collection, his cabinet of curiosities he called it, and nobody was ever allowed to see it. I sometimes listened at the door and heard him talking to himself, and I heard him crying once, and saying the name 'Dora, Dora,' over and over again. Dora was his first wife.

I never understood why he just stopped building up his collection. After Dora passed away, he never left the country again, but threw himself into developing the farm, which was passed on to my father and eventually to me.

He left the cabinet to the British Museum. After he died, my father found it all boxed up, ready for shipping, with instructions that it was not to be opened until it arrived at the museum. Unfortunately it seems that it got lost in transit, and we never found out what happened to it.

What I'm trying to tell you, my dear, is that you now own not just my animals, but the collection of a great explorer and a great man. Unfortunately you do not have the cream of his collection, whatever was in it, but if it were ever found again, it would be yours, too. Or perhaps it would belong to the British Museum, I'm not sure. So spare a thought for Henry Summers when you look at his more gruesome artefacts. I trust that you will know what to do with it all.

One more thing, which I never told anyone, but I know now, after talking to your father, that you will be interested: when I was a boy, I came upon my grandfather bathing in the Magpie Pool. He dressed himself quickly when he saw me, but not before I saw that his chest and arms were covered with tattoos. I was terribly shocked, because tattoos in those days were for sailors, and circus freaks. Not for gentlemen. Perhaps it is different nowadays, as your father has told me you now have one or two decorations of your own. It is the natural order of things for the old not to understand the young, so I will leave it at that.

I can't tell you what it means to me to be able to leave all of this in your hands. You gave great joy to this old man in those hours we spent together at the workbench. I'm sorry things didn't turn out more happily for us.

Live a good life, my darling granddaughter. And may this collection bring you as much joy as it has me.

Your old Grandpa

I felt as though he were standing in the room with me, breathing my air.

Someone once said that you don't ever get over grief; you just learn to live with it. Sometimes when I was alone, the crying would be triggered suddenly and, just as quickly, it would be gone and I would feel unblocked, like a drain.

Gradually the tears stopped and I was able to wipe my face on my sleeve and look at the letter again. I wished it had been longer, that Grandpa had sat down earlier and written more about Henry. Now that it was threatened, I felt a sudden hunger to know more about the house, about the man who had built it and the woman for whom it was intended.

But I took four very important facts from that letter. The first was that Henry had lost his wife and her body was never found, which was the cause of the rumours that he had done away with her. I don't know why, but I imagined theirs was a great love, the kind of love you only read about, and that I certainly have never experienced. I had found only failure, again and again.

The second fact was that he had a temper on him. Third, that he had a cabinet of curiosities which nobody ever saw. And fourth, that he was inked. And that was the fact that sealed my connection with this man, my ancestor, Henry Summers.

✻

I got my first tattoo at the age of seventeen: *Tess,* etched in cursive script into the spongy flesh of my inner forearm. Above it, a horseshoe; below it, *memento mori* — remember you must die. My poor skinny mother, clad in cashmere and gold, never forgave me for that first tattoo. She called it morbid, and insisted I cover it whenever

I was near her, but I knew it for what it was: a reminder that because everything must die, we must make the most of the life we have. She didn't like any of my subsequent tattoos, of course, but it was that first one that disturbed her the most. She just wanted to forget.

It was bad enough, she said, to come upon the dead animals I collected and stored in the freezer at home: a bellbird I'd found floating in the swimming pool; any number of sparrows and mice the cat had brought me. I practised on their bodies to hone my taxidermy skills. She said that death clung to me and she sometimes couldn't bear to look at me.

I got my latest tattoo — my tenth — just before coming here. It was a single magpie, wings outstretched. Roland had bent his long body over my wrist, pulling the skin taut with a rubber-encased thumb and forefinger, while I felt the buzz and sting of the needle over gristle and tendon, and smelt the sharp tang of my own sweat, mixed with the pervasive smell of methylated spirits. If there is one thing that tattooing and taxidermy have in common, it is that smell. Tattooists use meths to sterilise the instruments. Taxidermists use it to dry the last stubborn bits of flesh so they peel cleanly from the bone. Perhaps that smell, so much a part of my childhood, is what keeps me returning again and again to the tattoo parlours.

From Grandpa's letter, it was obvious he didn't know something that I had only recently found out: that tattooing was hugely fashionable among the British aristocracy in the late nineteenth century. Men and women flocked to the tattoo parlours of London, where they lay in comfort to have their skin inked. The Prince of Wales was tattooed in Israel, then again in Japan; he urged his sons to visit the same Japanese tattooist and they obliged.

People often ask me if my tattoos hurt. I have only one answer for them. Of course they fucking hurt. But it's for such a short time, and the results are forever, so the ratio of pleasure to pain is great. You hear people talking about how sweet the pain is, how after a while it becomes a tickle, how it gives them a rush. I just feel the pain and do it anyway. The worst is when it's close to bone, like the bluebirds on my chest, or where nerve-endings collect like blossoms beneath the skin. Unsuspecting girls get tattoos on their buttocks, but the pain there is enough to make them vomit. One girl I know passed out when she had her shaved skull inked. After that she grew her hair long and never saw it again anyway.

Roland did most of my work, and he let me rent the flat above his shop for next to nothing. He told me stories about gaggles of bare-midriffed girls who stood at the shop window for half an hour giggling and arguing over flashes before choosing one. They all had the design — something abstract, tribal — engraved on their lower backs one after the other, as though on a factory conveyor belt. A tramp stamp, Roland called it. He didn't like doing spontaneous work, thought such people were most likely to regret their decision and want to get their tattoos removed later in life. He did his share of celtic armbands in the nineties grunge boom but preferred it when people brought him original designs he could adapt, or they gave him an idea of what they wanted and they worked on it together, on paper, for a few weeks, before settling on the ideal image.

I like my tattoos vibrant, with strong block colours, nothing Gothic or heavy metal about them. I either favour Roland's one-offs or old-fashioned flashes such as sailors wore in the early part of the twentieth century: hearts and shamrocks and ribbons. I love the sense of history that comes with those kinds of tattoos, when the only women to wear them were tattooed ladies in a circus. Some of my designs are overtly feminine — flying teacups and bright flowers.

Roland reckoned that his shop had been a tattoo parlour when it was first built in the 1880s. It was right by the port, and every morning I awoke to the groaning machinery of the giant cranes that crouched like praying mantises on the wharf, offloading cargo from ships, or depositing coal and logs that had come by train from the West Coast overnight. In the nineteenth century there would have been no cranes, but the port would have heaved with activity nonetheless, sailors descending on the town's pubs and brothels, looking for a quick flurry of transgression to liven their otherwise monotonous lives. When Roland had stripped off the wallpaper of what was a hardware store when he moved in, he'd found a layer covered with the hand-drawn flashes popular back then, such as ships and anchors, sea monsters and English roses. He kept them behind plastic in a scrapbook and showed them to me once. They were faded and the paper they were drawn on was dark and greasy, but you could make them out all right. I longed to touch them, to smell the paper, which I imagined was impregnated with lantern oil and pipe smoke. But Roland stood over me as I looked and took them off me when I was done, protective. He showed me the signature at the bottom of one. It looked like a squiggle to me, but he insisted it said 'McDonald'.

After the black outline of the magpie, he had started on the shading, and the blood had begun to run. He wiped it away with a cloth as he worked. He finished with white ink. It looked bright, even against my pale, almost blue wrist. The lines were raised and rimmed with red, but they would go down in a few days and I was to rub it with cream twice a day to stop scabs from forming.

'I do know the ritual,' I reminded him as he wrapped it in clingfilm.

'I still have to tell you,' he said. 'One day you might forget and you'll come back complaining when the scabs fall off and the whole thing is ruined.' He grabbed my elbow and pulled my wrist towards his face. 'It's a good one,' he said. 'Why a magpie?'

'One for sorrow,' I said, and paid him.

It took me three trips to carry my groceries to the kitchen and all of my things upstairs. My wrist ached, but the magpie was unharmed. I chose the red room to sleep in, leaving the other five alone. It wasn't the biggest — that was my grandparents' bedroom, with its two sagging single beds — but it was the warmest, with its own fireplace and a northern aspect to catch the winter sun.

I unpacked my laptop and printer and the stacks of files, and put everything on an oak table away from the window. Looking at the novels I was supposed to be analysing, I reassured myself I had done the right thing. Jane Eyre never settled for being Rochester's mistress, just as she wouldn't settle for marrying St John Rivers. She would have lived happily alone if it weren't for the convenient fire that did away with Bertha. I couldn't see that happening to Hugh's wife, and I wouldn't have wished it upon her even if I could.

I hung a few clothes in the wardrobe — a couple of dresses and a heavy coat that I had picked up from the St Vincent de Paul store by the university. When I closed the wardrobe door I caught sight of myself in the full-length mirror: sunken eyes and pale face, the skin of my lips puckered from dehydration. Not a pretty sight. At least I didn't have mascara running down my cheeks from crying — since I'd made the decision to come here I hadn't bothered with the most basic of grooming. The fringe on my straight brunette bob stuck out instead of being blow-dried flat. Dressed entirely in black, I looked as though I had come from a funeral. I pinched my cheeks to tease some blood to the surface, and blew into my cupped hand, checking my unbrushed breath. Not too bad, considering.

The familiar cold of the house was closing in on me. I turned on the ancient panel wall heater with its fake wooden veneer and it ticked and groaned into action. Then I lay down on the bed, pulled the musty eiderdown over me and waited for the day to finish.

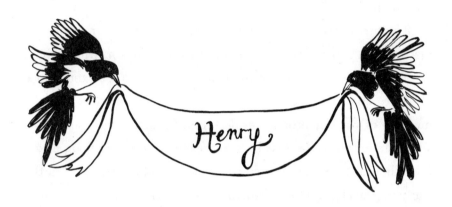

Henry

He is a collector of wonders, of dreams and sometimes nightmares. Of the lesser sulphur-crested cockatoo and the katydid, of turret shells, brittlestars and the *Morpho menelaus*. His collection is full of the treasures he has gathered in his travels. Tribal weapons and fantastic jewels, iridescent snakes, bodies bundled into jars. Animal, vegetable, mineral. He even has a mermaid: dessicated, mummified, the size of his torso. He is not stupid; he knows it is a fake, assembled by some trickster from the remains of a monkey and a fish, but it is enough of a sight to find its way into his wondrous cabinet of curiosities. His Wunderkammer.

He has been collecting nearly his whole life. He has long since forgotten to start a career, anything that his father might deem useful, but what is the point, he thinks, when he is contributing so much to the world's understanding of itself, when his travels bring him both pleasure and knowledge, a sense both of importance and of utter insignificance in the universe?

His cabinet has grown and changed shape, and has spilled over onto his body. He is now the collector of real, womanly mermaids, of dragons and fairies — things never seen before. He is a collector of ink, stitched into his skin.

The first tattoo he acquired in Japan, with the encouragement of his friend and travelling companion, George Norton, who wanted to see first hand the work of the man who had tattooed the Prince of Wales and, more recently, the Prince's sons. Henry carries the memory of the day around inside him, still sharp: the cool of the silk cushions on his back as he stretches himself on the floor, naked from the waist up. Lanterns create a soft glow; he is wrapped in the warm caramel light. Hori Chyo, the master of the craft, grips his arm, stretching the skin as he works. The pain calms him. The explosion of anger he felt — sudden, white-hot, nearly spilling over before he could control himself — when George pushed in front of him and laughed in his face has been dulled by the prick of the needles. Prick, prick, prick, steady, like the beat of a metronome, Chyo swapping his needles as the thickness of the line and the colour dictates. The needles themselves are worthy of collection — intricately carved ivory — and when Chyo turns his back as he finishes, Henry slips one into his pocket, where he will later forget about it and prick his thumb, drawing blood, making the memory fresh. Afterwards, he will flex his arm and the dragon will move. He will stare at it, flexing and flexing while the dragon sways.

⚘

As soon as he disembarks in New Zealand, he sets off to find the port's tattooer. He hesitates outside the studio, checking the address again on the slip of paper. He calls it a studio because this is what they are called in London, but this place is more like a dingy shop. Inside he can barely see in the gloom. A great shape moves and sighs in the corner, like a sea elephant turning on a rock. The air is thick with tobacco smoke and an ember glows in the darkness, flaring suddenly to reveal the shape's face briefly before it sinks back into darkness.

Hello?

The leviathan lumbers to its feet, nods and picks up a lamp. The man holds the light out into the dark space between them. The look on his face is one of surprise, then acceptance — a shrug of the shoulders.

Yes? He spits on the ground.

Sir, I am told this is the place to get a tattoo.

For who?

Well, for me.

The man lurches forward and Henry takes an alarmed step back. The fellow has enormous greying mutton chops, a round belly and a swollen bottom lip, as though he has been in a fight.

Pay by the hour. I'll do one of my own designs — he gestures around the room — or you can give me one of yours and I'll make the best of it. His voice is monotonous, as though he has been standing on a street corner, selling his wares, like oranges, all day.

Henry decides to examine the man's designs. The tattooer lights another lantern and now Henry can see that the mildewed walls are alive with pinned up pages, crinkled with damp. Some of the sketches are basic, just a few lines; others are breathtaking in their intricacy. Maritime images abound — anchors and ships, fish, dolphins and sea monsters. Sailors are obviously the main clientele in this port, where ships arrive daily, depositing their cargo and their inhabitants onto the shore. There are other depictions: flowers, and the faces of beautiful women, who stare out at him. Sweethearts long ago left at home, whether to wait or to marry someone else, who can tell?

He sees butterflies — green ones, yellow ones, papilios and brimstones, though he doubts the wearers care about their names; he sees biblical scenes, Christ's crucifixion and his last supper.

The man is an artist. Any fool can see it. He deserves to be in a London studio, surrounded not by darkness and the smell of sweat and stale tobacco, but by potted palm trees and Persian rugs, electric lights, silk cushions, chaises longues. He could secure the patronage of any number of gentlemen, yes, even of noblemen and ladies. Why, the month he left he saw a tattoo on Lady Wentworth's wrist; she hadn't hidden it, had lifted her bracelet for all to see, a little bluebird of happiness, flying on her skin. This tattooer would do a better job of it — if his work on the skin is as accomplished as his sketches. Henry knows what a skill it is to transfer the art to the body.

What's your name, man? asks Henry.

McDonald, the tattooer says.

You're an artist, do you know that? Not just a tattooer.

The man grunts, laughs, spits. A tattoo*ist*, see. Artist, tattooer. Tattooist.

Yes, says Henry. Shall we begin?

He slips the card with the rose from his pocket. It doesn't matter how widely he travels; England will always be his home.

The man is slow, but meticulous. He wipes away the red ink as it overflows. Each prick builds on the last until Henry's chest sings.

We don't get many like you, says McDonald. He smokes as he works. His instrument looks ungainly, pieces of metal tied together to deliver the ink under the skin, but he wields it like the finest of fountain pens.

Like me?

Gentlemen. That is, we have had one or two, always from London. Never the first time. They've always been bitten by the dragon.

Dragon? I haven't heard that expression.

He chuckles. That's because it's me own. They've had one tattoo, maybe as a trophy, following the fashion, see. They know about the prince and the dragon what he got in Japan. They all want one like that to start with. Only then they want another. Like a fever. They don't usually come back once they've settled in New Zealand though. Not the height of fashion around here. The local gentry would be shocked.

Thank you for the warning. I'm not much interested in fashion these days.

Then why do you do it? McDonald pauses in his work, leaves his wrist balanced, pressing against Henry's sternum.

Why do you? Henry shoots back.

The man chuckles again. It's in me blood. Me father was a sailor and he brought back tattoos from the romantic South Pacific. The most beautiful things I ever saw, the tattoos I mean. I knew I wanted to learn how to do it. To have it done. And to come here.

He spits on the ground. Not quite what I expected, he says, but I guess it's home now. Now it's your turn.

I do it to remember, says Henry.

❦

Later, he puts his hand on his chest, feels the weight of it there on his rose, above his heart. He leaves it there while he stares out the window onto the manicured lawn and garden of a Mr Collins, who has offered to introduce him to local society. He feels cheated. He was led to believe that this country was a wild, untamed place, with strange wildlife and intriguing natives, but this city is nothing but a replica of an English town. He loves England, and wants to return some day, but he did not travel to the other side of the world to live the life of village fêtes and smart shops, groomed grass and flowers. There is no adventure in these things.

He dampens down the flash of anger he feels rising in his chest by placing his other hand on the window, concentrating on its dents and undulations. The hand is knotted with scars. He snatches it away, leaving a starfish print in the mist caused by his own breath. Through it he sees the startling green of the garden after rain, pocked and warped through the glass. That other day, two months ago, when he put his fist through the window, the view had been of manicured lawns and stiff topiary; now it seems little has changed.

He had been attending a party that his father was giving for his sister. He'd had too much wine; the anger had taken hold unexpectedly, as it always does. He feels it physically, running through his body, flickering at the edges of his vision. It is always his body that responds, lashes out, with a fist or a foot, sometimes just his tongue, spewing out words he didn't realise he was capable of.

He hadn't minded the pain — it was nothing he hadn't endured before. His knuckles, roughly stitched, made a pattern he found curiously beautiful; the skin bloomed purple and yellow around the cuts as they healed.

He had found the gaze of Miss Pringle as he stood grasping his wrist with blood trickling into his sleeve, and she had looked away, blushing and furious. His anger had seeped out of him, along with the blood. He could hardly remember what it was that had set him off, but he knew he had lost Miss Pringle for good, and he cared little.

His father called him into his study the next day, holding out a cheque, unable to look at him.

I have decided to fund your next expedition, he said. To New Zealand. You'll continue to get your remittance, as long as you stay there.

He had said no more, but Henry heard the threat in his words. That he would be tolerated no longer. That if he was to have an income, England would no longer be his home.

This then, is all he knows of New Zealand so far. The backward seasons (frost in August!), the murky port, the tattooist, then the short train ride through the tunnel to a town modelled on England, with weeping willows lining the meandering stream (they call it a river but it is a trickle, really) and brand-new wooden buildings among the traditional stone and brick, and oak trees and delightfully proper society, with tea and dancing and church services. Flowers that bloom like manic grins in the gardens of streets named after English counties.

And now, a starfish print on a window and a party in his honour. He must be civil. He will meet important people here, for Mr Collins has invited the director of the museum, who will put him in touch with other collectors and taxidermists. With luck, the director will offer to buy some of his specimens — those he has brought with him and those he will acquire on his travels around the country, through the rugged land that he has yet to see for himself, to believe it even exists.

He moves away from the window as the other guests begin to arrive, announced by a servant. They seem hungry to meet him, to hear news of Home; the ladies in particular strike him as slightly vulgar in their need to know whether they're as fashionable as their London counterparts. He doesn't have the heart to be truthful, so they move away, beaming, after they have extracted their compliments.

He decides to make the best of it and begins to relax after his second brandy is safely in his stomach. He is even starting to enjoy himself when Mr Collins approaches him with a young lady on his arm.

May I introduce my daughter, Dora, says his host.

Miss Collins. Delighted. Henry takes her hand briefly. She wears long gloves — they reach almost to her armpits — and they are cool under his fingers. She is not like the other women, this one. She doesn't bray, or giggle, and he feels her gaze penetrating his chest, where it flickers from his face, as if she knows of the recent tattoo there. Her eyes are dark grey, and her blonde curls look as though they have been subdued rather than coiffed.

And how do you find our little town, Mr Summers? I'm afraid you'll think us rather dull after London society.

Have you been to London? he asks.

Yes. She looks at her father, who finishes for her.

I took Dora there last year, when I met your father. The journey to and fro lasted nearly as long as our entire stay there. It was quite exhausting. Dora loved it, but I confess in my old age I like New Zealand more and more.

Henry surmises that he can't be older than forty-five. Well, he says to Miss Collins, I'm sure you fitted neatly into the society there.

You needn't compliment me, Mr Summers. I have no illusions about being anything other than a simple girl from the colonies.

She glances sideways at her father, who has turned away to talk to someone who has appeared at his elbow. She smiles as though she has got away with some transgression, leans closer and lowers her voice. Forgive me, she says, but you have something just here. She touches her own lip, while her gaze drops to the floor, as if she can't bear to look at his face while he finds the morsel of food.

Thank you, he says. People are so polite about these things. I might have walked about with it for hours.

She blushes. He chastises himself for suggesting she is improper, when he only wants to compliment her. Yes, he realises, of all the women here, she is the one he genuinely *wants* to compliment. But when he goes to apologise, she stops him with a shake of the fingers, as though they are wet and she is flicking water at him. Baptising him.

After Collins has steered her away, he is introduced to Herz, the director of the museum, and they fall deep into conversation about travelling and collecting. Once or twice he glances up to see Dora looking at him but both times she opens her fan and covers her face as she cools herself. The small room has become unbearably warm.

Despite his earlier reservations, the party has proved exceptionally fruitful for him. Herz will arrange for him to travel across the South Island with a man named Schlau, a fellow German currently employed by the museum to mount its considerable collection of animals and native birds. Henry is now gripped by the excitement of the adventures before him; all of the birdlife he has never seen. He feels something akin to bloodlust, a watering in his mouth.

He forgets about Dora until he bumps into her on the stairs as he ascends to his room. She is coming the other way and presses herself against the wall, as though in fright — so different from the confident young lady he met earlier.

Goodnight, he says to her softly, but she only nods at him, keeping her eyes on him as he passes.

The next morning he finds a letter from Mr Collins. The family has been called away to their country estate. He is to make himself at home and to feel free to visit them there. He only needs to send word and a coach will come for him. He tries to remember if he has behaved badly; if he had one too many drinks at the party and said the wrong thing. But he can think of nothing out of order. Perhaps the family really does have to attend to an urgent matter. And now he is freed from politeness and can explore the country at will.

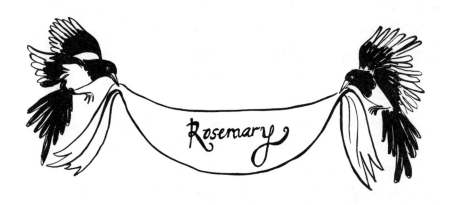

Rosemary

I woke in a panic. A noise had travelled through my dreams, a musical
note, floating up from the front paddock, plucked again and again, a
sound I had heard in my head many times since I had awoken to it
all those years ago. As I lay there, my ears strained to find it, but it
had dissipated. Just my imagination haunting me as usual then, not
a ghost.

The curtains were still open and the night was clear. A shuffle
outside, a moan. Just country noises, I told myself. The house was like
a breathing body; it had always creaked and complained. But I had
never been alone then. There was always someone else to investigate
the sounds if they became unfriendly. I got up and crossed the room
to the window. The night was still and the moon was out. Its light fell
on everything outside: the neglected vegetable patch, the treehouse.

Far off, through the trees, the river. It was as if the house were watching, waiting for something to move, as I was. I heard a sound, like a footstep on the gravel driveway, but only one. I pressed my face closer to the glass to peer to the left, but I would have had to climb out the window to get a look.

That was when it happened. My hand rested on the glass and the window began to hum. I felt it pass through my fingertips, up my arm and down to my toes. The rest of the room began to rock gently, as if the house were a giant that I had disturbed from its sleep, shrugging its body from side to side, and my heart pumped so hard I could feel blood pulsing in my face. It was the sound that disturbed me the most as it travelled across the plains towards me, was all around me for a second, then travelled on through, a low throbbing.

'Letting off steam,' I reminded myself and lay back down on the bed. Even though I knew it was an earthquake, I couldn't get rid of the feeling that the house had caused it somehow.

✿

The last time I saw Grandpa his world had shrunk to his bedroom and the adjoining bathroom. He no longer read his beloved books — they hurt his eyes — but he often fell asleep with the TV or radio blaring. I could hear him at night from my room down the other end of the house. Waking up and unsure of the time, he would turn on the television and fall asleep again while infomercials blinked by, peddling exercise machines and kitchen appliances he would never use.

Sometimes I read to him from his favourite novels, novels by Dickens and Tolstoy, but I suspect he only heard half of what I said; the strain of shouting got too much for me, as did the strain of listening for him.

It amazed me how quickly old age had changed him. He was tiny in his bed, surrounded by plumped up pillows, and his wrists were thin and mottled. In contrast, his ears seemed to have grown and his face was yellowed like cotton sheets left out in the sun too long. It hurt to see him like this, and he knew it. When I sat and held his hand, he had a look of concern on his face that wasn't for his own health, but for me.

'You mustn't worry about me, chook,' he said. 'I've had a long and happy life and all the clichés. You know that, right?'

I nodded.

'I can tell by your face that I look terrible.'

I tried to protest.

'You can't deny it.' His face cracked open in a smile. 'You're just lucky that I've put my teeth in for you. Susan doesn't get that privilege, do you, Susan?'

The nurse didn't look up from where she sat in a chair by the window, doing her crossword. 'That's right, Percy,' she deadpanned. 'You're a monster.'

He chuckled. One of his last pleasures was the banter he had with her, and the two sniped at each other like a married couple. Susan was a squat woman whose children had all left home, so she could devote more than the usual amount of time to him. Grandpa had an alarm that he could activate if he needed her in the night, and she lived only a twenty-minute drive away. But sometimes, on the days when he seemed to be slipping away, she stayed the night in the austere single bed in the next room. She was tireless in her care of Grandpa, but when I tried to tell her how grateful I was, we all were, she shrugged it off and told me she was just doing her job, that she was well paid and satisfied.

It was his greatest joy that I had pursued his hobby of taxidermy;

that it had employed me for a time after I left school, and again when I found myself penniless and alone in London and I took to crafting outlandish creatures and fashion accessories for a curiosity shop in Greenwich. Grandpa asked me again and again for stories of my creations — the hats I adorned with sparrows chirping in their nests, or the brooches I made from tiny mice, their tails replaced with silver chains and their eyes with jewels. I created strange hybrids of animals: cats with pigeon's wings, rabbits with the antlers of a young deer. Grandpa lay basking in my words as I told him about the time my flatmates had come upon me, in my pyjamas, sawing the head off a dead fox on the kitchen floor, and had banded together to have me evicted. There wasn't much blood, but they thought I had murdered it. I had actually found it dead and perfectly intact in the backyard, snout grubby from the neighbourhood rubbish bins. Poisoned, probably.

'I'm glad you see the funny side,' I said as he roared with laughter again. 'I was homeless as well as broke.'

But I always found my feet. I ended up living with the young couple who owned the shop. They had no problems with me bringing home animals to store in the freezer.

'Talk me through it, Rosie,' he said, his eyes closed. 'What did we do with that magpie, that first time?'

'We cut it,' I said. 'Airway to arsehole, just as you told me.'

'And then?'

He was like a child listening to bedtime stories. I told him about the time I worked in the professional studio, right after I left school, mounting hunting trophies mostly for rich American tourists — stags they had paid a fortune to kill. I was fired when I decided to give a wild boar a happy, friendly face instead of the fierce snarl I had been instructed to produce, and I never went back to that kind of taxidermy, where the animals were killed only for the purpose of mounting them. I only used roadkill after that, or donated pets, or even recycled specimens that I restored and gave a new life to, and when I left London to come home after my grandmother died, I started studying for my academic career and never seemed to find the time or space for taxidermy.

❦

In the morning I woke early. Looking around in daylight it was hard to conjure up the eeriness of the earthquake and the still moonlit night. My head was foggy from the dust in the room. I still had my clothes on, but at least I had kicked my shoes off in the night. For the first time in a long time I didn't feel the need to get up for anything. I was used to waking alone; Hugh had stayed the night at my flat only once, after he had returned early from a conference and not told his wife. My flatmate Rita had come across him at the kitchen table, my pink dressing gown straining across his chest, and she had backed from the room, apologising, as if she had found us naked. I hadn't told her about him, but I think she instinctively knew there was something clandestine going on, because that evening she avoided me, and she never mentioned him or asked me about him.

Thirty-three years old and still waking up alone, despite the number of men I'd had relationships with. I had a tattoo for every time I'd been in love and that didn't take into account the other men I'd slept with, or kissed. I didn't really know what had gone wrong. To love so many, and yet none of them lasted. I enjoyed being single, but had never been so for long. I could have seen myself with Hugh, in our cottage in Wales, but as that dream faded, I had nothing to replace it with. Most of the good, interesting men were taken and were starting families, as were some of my friends. I knew that if I stayed with Hugh for as long as he wanted me to, my chance would pass me by altogether. Not that I needed a man to make me happy. Up until then I hadn't thought that I cared whether I had children, but now I wasn't so sure. It was nothing big, nothing conscious, just a feeling that was gradually closing in on me. That I would like at least to have the choice.

I made my way down the stairs, studying the family gallery as I went: snapshots of children and dogs and parties, blown up and framed like paintings; formal studio portraits that my family had organised for my grandparents' fortieth wedding anniversary, with embarrassing hairstyles and clothes that were never to be worn again. That was the last time the wall had been updated, as though the life of the family stopped when I was thirteen. I suppose it did, in a way. Certainly there were no more brightly coloured family gatherings at Magpie Hall after that, just the occasional visit, with my mother always anxious to get away. At least when I visited later, on my own, I could concentrate on Grandpa and not linger over past regrets.

Further down the stairs, black and white photos of my grand-parents and their children, on picnics and at weddings. My father and his brother as boys, smiling under Davy Crockett hats, rifles slung over their shoulders and a bouquet of dead ducks hanging on a stick between them. My aunt, Helene, looking serene and beautiful in a white wedding gown, her husband a good two inches shorter.

Further still the photos became grainy. Stiff portraits of my grandfather as a child, dressed in a smock with a big bow, held by his mother, a hard-faced woman with a Louise Brooks bob, not unlike my own, and flanked by his father, Edward Summers. Daughters were dotted about them; daughters we had long since lost contact with, as they married and drifted away to other parts of the country, or were absorbed into their husbands' families.

In most of the photographs, the house stood in the background, solid and unchanging. That was what I liked about it — it was a constant in everyone's lives. I loved the fact that some of the furniture hadn't changed, that the layout of the rooms was just as it had been when Grandpa was a boy, perhaps even his father before him; that Grandpa had courted Gram in the same way my father had my mother — by bringing her to his massive house in the country and showing her the gardens, the river, the outlandish taxidermy. And the women had fallen in love with it all; the house had become as much a part of them as it was of Henry Summers' direct descendants, although my mother grew more detached from it the more it fell into disrepair.

Finally, at the bottom of the staircase, two very old and faded photographs in heavy oak frames. One showed a large group of women in Victorian jackets and long skirts with straw boaters, standing beside bicycles. I recognised the wide avenues from the park not far from where I grew up, although the trees were much smaller.

I had glanced at the other photo many times on my way past, but had never really stopped to examine it. It was a posed studio portrait of Henry Summers, the collector at work. He was dressed casually, in tweed trousers, with leather boots and leggings. Hatless, he gazed sombrely at the camera. He had a strong nose, slim brows and intense, dark eyes. Like my father and uncle, he carried a rifle, and at his feet sat a dog, with a bird held patiently in its mouth. I couldn't be sure, but it looked like a pukeko, or a takahe. Henry was tall, with long, strong-looking limbs and a confidence born of status and achievement. I couldn't tell when the photo had been taken. Before or after his wife's death? He certainly didn't look scarred by grief. Rather he was a man looking at the horizon and all the challenges and hopes it might bring.

I tried to imagine what kind of a man Henry had been, with his tattoos hiding under his Victorian clothes; what his wife had been like and how she had died; and what riches he had collected, then hidden away. I felt a strange connection to him through the hard-earned assemblage of animals and jars I had inherited, and knowing we shared a love of tattooing only made the feeling more acute. Suddenly I had an urge to know more about Henry and Dora, before the house was scrubbed clean of all their memories, along with Grandpa Percy's. Now, though, I needed to get outside into the light and the air.

I was still wearing the black crêpe vintage dress and tights I had slept in. By the kitchen door, I put on a pair of gumboots and a grey tweed riding jacket. I shoved my hands into the pockets, which were thankfully empty. I don't know how I would have felt to come across the remnants of some departed person — a soiled handkerchief, or a sweet wrapper.

My breath fogged the air and the sound of the loose gumboots drumming on the path enveloped me. The skeletons of the poplar trees lining the front paddock were emerging as the leaves thinned, and a cloud of sparrows rose twittering from them as I passed. Beside them stood the windbreak, a solid wall of macrocarpas. Here the magpies nested, collecting straw and grass to make a home, but also barbed wire and pieces of old glass. Grandpa had showed me one of their nests once and it looked uncomfortable, to say the least.

I stopped to gaze over the paddock towards the river. Grandpa's old nag Jimmy raised his head and gave a steamy snort, then went back to cropping the grass. Two magpie sentries strutted around him. The dark shape of Blossom the mare moved in the background. There was a time when the horses in this paddock would come running when they saw me, looking for treats and jostling each other, but these two had no interest. I hoped that someone was looking after them.

I plucked the wire on the fence, but it made no discernible sound, nothing as haunting and musical as the note I had heard the night before and on that morning all those years ago. For a moment I thought I saw another shape in the distance, smaller than the others; but my pony, the animal on which I had learnt to ride as a child, was long dead. Just another ghost I had worked so hard to forget.

I turned towards the walled garden, where my grandmother would spend most of her days, pottering about with a cigarillo hanging from her mouth, her long grey hair immaculately twisted high on her head. She paid more attention to that hair than to anything else, as though her house could gather dust about her so long as she was well presented in her person. She always wore slacks and gumboots when she gardened, with a paisley shirt buttoned to the top and pearls under the collar. When I was little she sometimes let me come and sit with her while she worked, but she never asked me to help, not since I had pulled out half her herb garden, thinking the oregano and thyme were weeds.

Gram carried herself with elegance no matter what her task. I always felt that she thought we were all a bit beneath her somehow, and it showed when she'd had one too many brandies and we felt the sharpness of her tongue. The only time I really saw her soften was when she thought she was alone with Grandpa. I would see a look pass between them, or a tender touch on the wrist, but she seemed determined to keep the rest of the family from seeing that softer side, as if it might be regarded as a sign of weakness on her part.

The garden was overgrown, brown in some places where flowers had died off without being lovingly dead-headed, and in other places a riot of green weeds, strangling everything in sight. Sunflowers that had once stood bright and taller than I was were slumped and desiccated. Once the B&B was in business, this could all be replanted, but I imagined my aunt and uncle would rather knock down the walls of the garden and turn it into a tennis court or a swimming pool — something easier to maintain and to use as an added attraction for those tourists. I imagined their sweaty bodies pounding the ground where Gram's dahlias had been. I looked inside myself, poking around for some kind of emotion. But Gram had died more than five years ago, of lung cancer unsurprisingly, and any grieving I had done for her was mostly through watching Grandpa adjust to life alone.

I struggled down the path to the gazebo at the end, where I climbed the stairs and sat down on one of the wooden seats. From the raised vantage point, with the jungle of the garden in front of it, the house looked as though it was being reclaimed by nature. At any moment I expected the earth to rise up with a sigh and drag it underground. The tower jutted up against the grey sky. I used to go up there when I was a child and pretend to be Rapunzel, or some other princess locked up there. From the tower I could keep an eye on everyone and everything — the other kids, Gram in the garden, the horses sheltering under the trees from the sun or the wind or both, Grandpa, wherever he might be. But I had stopped going after the year I turned thirteen.

The long grass shook and a figure burst out from the undergrowth. The world tilted for a moment while I placed myself back in the garden and remembered I was not the only person on earth.

'Jesus, you scared me!' I hadn't seen Sam the farmhand for two years, and then we'd only waved to each other in passing as he rode the back of the ute up the hill to the shearing sheds.

'Sorry,' Sam said, and looked at the ground in front of me. 'I brought you these.' He held out a blue ice-cream container, but seemed wary of approaching to actually put it in my hands. So I stood and moved the few steps to him. A clutch of eggs tilted the container — six of them, brown and white, one speckled.

'Oh, thanks.' I took them from him.

'Yeah, I was going to bring you a rabbit, but Josh said you're a vegetarian.'

'I am. How'd you get the rabbit?'

'Got caught in a possum trap. It's fresh, though. Only happened this morning.' He narrowed his eyes, suspicious that a vegetarian would be taking an interest in a carcass. 'Why do you ask?'

'Are you going to eat it?'

'Nah. I'm not much of a cook. I can skin it all right, but all those bones. Yuck. I'll give it to the dogs.'

'Bring it anyway, if you want. Maybe I'll stuff it.'

'Oh, right. Yeah, Josh mentioned that too. Taking after the old man, then? Funny hobby for a girl. Specially a vego one.'

'Did you want to sit down?' I gestured to the seat, then sat down myself. Sam stood there, scuffing the toe of his gumboot on the bricks. His hair stood up almost straight on his head, fixed there no doubt by sweat and lanolin from the sheep. His Swanndri was big on him, and came down to his knees, a baggy plaid dress.

'Nah, I'd better be getting back. You look like something out of an old story book sitting there.'

'Which one?'

'Dunno. *The Secret Garden*, maybe? You're all old-fashioned looking with that haircut. And that dress! Great with the gumboots. If I didn't know better, I'd have thought you were a ghost come to show me another world.'

'Maybe I am,' I said.

Sam took out a tobacco pouch and stood silently rolling a cigarette.

'Thought you had to get back?' I asked.

'Yeah,' he said lazily, and turned around as he lit the cigarette. 'See ya.'

'See ya. Thanks for the eggs.' I watched his hunched shoulders as he walked away. He glided through the overgrown garden as if he were part of it.

I cradled the container of eggs in one arm and lightly touched them. Still warm.

❦

Bags of food were strewn over the kitchen benches where I had left them the day before. Looking at the eggs reminded me that I hadn't eaten since I arrived. The room was cold and empty. Mrs Grainger, the housekeeper, would have had a fire going by now, and been moving around as if on wheels, baking this, cooking that, the kettle freshly boiled. She looked after Grandpa well, gave the house a warmth and friendliness that he needed. I wondered sometimes if Mrs G wasn't more like a wife to Grandpa than Gram was. Certainly after Gram died the housekeeper was a huge comfort. I suspected that towards the end she might have been more to him than that, although the one time I brought it up with my family they had looked horrified. When he became ill, he wouldn't let her look after him any more than he would let us — that wasn't what she was paid for, he said. He left her a tidy sum in his will, and she told us she had a fine lot of savings to show for thirty years living in the country with nowhere to spend her money. She had children of her own anyway, to care for her — she was in good hands and I didn't need to worry about her. I was allowed to miss her, though — the buttery smell of porridge cooking on the stove, served not with brown sugar but with maple syrup.

I put the eggs on the wide bench, suddenly starving. After poaching a couple and eating them with fresh bread because I couldn't find the toaster, I put away the rest of the groceries and went back up to my room.

My thesis sat on the desk, taunting me. I was terribly behind schedule, what with Grandpa's illness, and death, and then the realisation that things with Hugh were a mess. I had gathered all my research material and ordered my thoughts, but now the work of putting it on paper had to begin in earnest, beyond the scribblings I had made to date.

I sat at the desk and was going over my notes when I heard a noise downstairs. Instantly I was on my feet, moving towards the staircase, much bolder than I had been in the middle of the night.

'Hello?' a male voice called from the kitchen.

'Coming!' I wasn't really frightened, but I decided to lock the door after whoever it was had left.

Sam stood in the middle of the room with a sack in his hand. He looked as though he had no intention of coming any further than that, which I appreciated. He had removed his gumboots at the door and his big toe poked through one of his thick grey socks.

'Sorry,' he said, unnecessarily, but again it made me warm to him. 'I've got that rabbit you were after.' He held out the sack and I took it from him.

'Thanks.'

We stood looking at each other a moment, before he started to back away and turn.

'Cool,' he said. 'Well, I'll leave you to it.'

It was my turn to apologise. 'I'm just doing some work.' I swung the sack. 'Thanks, though.'

'Sure.' He moved to the door, and turned back to face me. 'I was sorry about your granddad. We all were. He was real nice.'

'Thanks. Yes, he was.'

'What's going to happen to the farm? Now that he's gone?'

'Don't you know?' I was surprised nobody had told him.

'Know what?'

'It's being sold. The family's selling up. I thought Joshua would have told you.' But perhaps Joshua didn't know either and I had really put my foot in it.

Sam just looked at me, and I could see him processing the information. He breathed out through his teeth.

'Fucking fantastic.' He picked up his gumboots and walked outside without putting them on, slamming the door behind him.

✻

When I opened the big deep freeze to put the sack inside, it felt as though I was lifting the lid on a coffin. Nobody had emptied the freezer since Grandpa had died. Packages of meat and bags of vegetables were piled inside, along with unlabelled containers of liquid and what looked like stewed fruit. I went to close it again when a couple of items caught my eye — clear plastic bags containing whole animals. It was difficult to see exactly what they were without defrosting them, but they were small and furred — stoats perhaps. A larger, darker mound could have been a possum, although I knew that most of the trapped possums were sent off to my uncle, whose company dealt in possum fur.

As I passed through the hallway I glanced into the living room. There was something missing from the side table — the huia. I looked at the spot where it had been and tried to think whether I had done something with it, but I couldn't remember. The chair was where I had left it after retrieving the bird from the high shelf, and when I looked up, there it was, back on its perch.

Someone was playing games with me. Sam? He looked as though he hadn't ventured any further than the kitchen. But if not Sam, then who? I felt uneasy then, as though someone might be watching me from somewhere in the house.

'Hello?' My voice was absorbed by the carpet and the drapes, and nobody answered. Then I remembered my decision earlier, and I returned to the kitchen to lock the back door. Sam was nowhere to be seen. If someone was in the house, I had just locked them in with me. But that was a risk I was going to have to take. There was no cellphone reception out here, but as far as I knew the landline hadn't yet been disconnected. I still knew how to dial for help.

Back up in my room, I shook off thoughts of an intruder. Maybe it had just been Sam, thinking I had tried to put the bird back on the shelf but couldn't reach. He probably thought he was doing me a favour. I picked up my notes again and tried to conjure up the world of Heathcliff and Catherine, to let my thoughts emerge from the fog. But then I thought about the rabbit Sam had brought me. I wondered how big it was. Was it male or female? What condition would the coat be in? It had been so long since I had mounted anything — not since my mid-twenties. I thought of the menagerie room and all the equipment there, lying idle. Would I still remember how to do it? If I switched off my mind, would my hands guide me through the process again, after all these years? There was only one way to find out.

Henry

He skinned a tiger once. It took five men to do the job. Henry made the incision while four wiry native assistants stretched the animal's limbs taut. Their faces were blank as they leaned back, straining.

The tiger smelled of dust and urine and strong sunlight. Henry worked slowly, careful not to cut too deeply. The sun was so strong he thought it might singe the hairs on the back of his neck.

The knife, newly sharpened, sliced through the skin as if through sand; he shuffled backwards on his knees. By the time he had cut to the anus, his arm ached. He must have pierced a musk gland — the air was suddenly filled with an acrid stench; his breath was thick with it.

The smell made him uneasy. Even in death the animal was exerting its territorial nature, as though it were still weakly alive. But he checked the face, the head flung back, slack tongue lolling from open jaws, like a piece of old ham.

After he had cut from throat to tail, he worked laterally on the front limbs, paw to paw. The beast now lay supine, crucified. The flesh below the lappets was knotty and dark; it reminded him of a woman's most private place. It glistened, made a sucking sound as it lifted away. And now he could skin the animal. It took all his strength. Slowly, slowly, the skin lifted away in one piece, while his assistants grunted and pulled at the bones. It was the largest animal he had ever skinned and as he worked a bizarre thought came into his head: If only my father could see me now. Filthy, clothes streaked with blood and dirt and stinking of musk, wrestling with the pelt of this magnificent beast, far from the drawing rooms where its like ended up, for a pretty penny.

When its belly and legs had been stripped, with much care taken to preserve the contour of the feet, the men heaved the carcass over so they could draw the skin forward over its head. The head took delicate manipulation, and time slowed with his breath as he bent close to the beast with his knife, slitting the skin around the eyes and the conches of the ears, so close to the skull, working deliberately until at last the skin was free.

The most difficult job now completed, they stripped the bones and left the meat in the dust, then carried the skin away to be salted, dried and shipped home anointed in turpentine.

He knew the skin was not the tiger. It could never contain its true essence, the sensuality of each flickering muscle. But it was the closest Henry could get to possession of the animal, to a tactile reminder of their relationship, hunter and hunted, beast and master. With this skin, the tiger would be with him always.

The museum stands on the edge of the botanic gardens: a miniature Kew, with fountains and ponds, and well-fed ducks parading their perimeters. It is Gothic in its architecture, built of solemn grey stone. It is cool inside, cold even; his fingers feel stiff in Herz's grasp when he is welcomed. As he gives the tour, the head of the museum explains to Henry that the whole collection has been built on the bones of the moa, the huge flightless bird that died out before any European could sight it. Henry is confused for a moment, thinks Herz is being literal and that beneath the museum lie bones and feathers, knitted together in the earth as foundations, but what he means is that one discovery in a swamp yielded enough bones of the extinct bird to enable the museum to trade for the rest of its collection.

He is impressed with this little museum. The moa in particular fascinates him: as he stands and looks at the skeleton towering over him, his fingers itch with the desire to find the bones for his own collection. Skeletons dominate the middle of the room, but glass cases around its perimeter house native birds such as he has never seen before: the molten green of the kea parrot; the unusual proportions of the kiwi, with its reed-thin beak useful for nudging out insects from holes in logs and its useless wings that sit on its sides like twigs. And yet its feet are solid, its egg impossibly large. Another bird, the size of a small cat and just as sleek, catches his eye: it is black, with white-tipped tail feathers and a beak that curves like a rainbow. The huia. Oh yes, he has much to find in this country, and he is eager to get started.

After he has left the museum, on a whim he takes a stroll through the gardens, where couples walk arm in arm and the fat ducks congregate around an old man sitting on a bench. For a moment he can imagine himself in Hyde Park, or Kensington Gardens, and he doffs his hat to a carriage full of unchaperoned ladies as they trot by. On the stream a punt slips past silently with a couple trailing hands in the chilly water. His mood is lighter today — he even feels kindly towards the bright spring flowers. He knows he will soon be leaving them and this English town behind him, so he takes a moment to appreciate the gaudy beauty of the tulips and daffodils.

Up ahead a cloud of cyclists stops before it reaches him and the riders dismount. As he approaches, the cloud separates into individuals; he guesses there are fifteen of them in total, all women. They stand now, gripping the handles of their bicycles with gloved hands, casually leaning their hips against them and talking among themselves. They are all dressed in a similar manner, with boaters and blouses or jackets with voluminous leg o' mutton sleeves. Most wear heavy skirts, but a few are clad in loose trousers.

Let them, he thinks, for who would wear a skirt on a bicycle? Uncomfortable and probably a little breezy, too, dragging on the ground, or getting caught in the bicycle's chain. It is not as though a bicycle can be ridden side-saddle. But he can see the looks on the faces of other men as they pass, from mild irritation on some, to downright shock on others. Henry isn't sure whether it is the sight of women unaccompanied, or in trousers, or on bicycles that disturbs them the most.

Their tête-à-tête over, the women remount and set off in the direction of town. As they pass, Henry's gaze alights on the face of the closest to him: Dora Collins.

Miss Collins! he calls, but when she turns her head to look at him her handlebars begin to wobble, and she neither smiles nor greets him before she turns back to concentrate on her journey.

He follows them, walking briskly along the dusky streets to keep them in his sights. When they disappear from view, he continues in the hope they will stop again. He finds himself in the large square in front of the cathedral, and spots his target — the women have parked their bicycles in a great heap on the ground and are unfurling a banner. He waits, hidden, until they have assembled themselves. Two women stretch the banner between them and hold it high: Women's International Temperance Union. The rest have donned sashes and, with much twittering, are distributing handfuls of paper between themselves. They fall silent as one woman addresses them briefly. Her back is towards him so Henry cannot hear what she is saying, but the women stare intently at her, nodding furiously in agreement at her words. No doubt she is preaching the dangers of alcohol, urging them to empty their husbands' liquor cabinets for the good of humanity. Henry has little patience with such women. It is not alcohol that is the problem, he thinks, it is the men who drink it.

He is about to turn away, disappointed in Miss Collins, when the women begin to approach the curious spectators who have gathered, thrusting pieces of paper into their hands. Henry waits to see what the reaction will be. Some of the men politely hand the tracts back; one makes a show of tearing his in two and walking away, the pieces drifting forlornly to the ground before the red-faced messenger picks them up. Still others stand and listen, nodding, but Henry suspects it is to humour the wives attached to their arms, who glance at their husbands as if for permission to react.

His curiosity gets the better of him, and he drifts towards the small crowd. He scans the faces until he sees Dora in conversation with an elderly woman who is shaking her head. Dora appears to be pleading with her, and as Henry approaches the old woman puts a hand up, shakes her head and turns away.

Miss Collins, he says. Dora looks up, then down, and takes a step back, looking cornered.

Do I make you uncomfortable? he asks.

She resigns herself to talking to him and stands her ground, looking up at him defiantly. An unruly blonde curl falls in her eyes and she blinks and brushes it away with a gloved hand.

Not at all, Mr Summers. How pleasant to see you again. Her voice betrays her lie.

May I ask what it is you are peddling? he asks her.

I am not *peddling* anything, sir. I am petitioning.

For? He holds out his hand and she reluctantly places the tract in it.

For women's suffrage. For our right to vote.

Interesting. He glances down at the printed sheet and reads the heading: *Ten Reasons Why the Women of New Zealand Should Vote*. A few scratchy signatures decorate the paper she holds in the crook of her arm.

So you are not petitioning for temperance then? I misunderstood. I saw the banner.

Well, it is true that one has arisen from the other. Mrs Johnson believes that only when women have the right to vote will the government take steps to abolish the sale of liquor, which is harming families.

Then you don't believe that women should vote *per se*? Just that liquor should be banned and this is the way to do it.

No, I do. She stumbles over her words and hesitates. That is . . . She falters again and stops. To be honest, I am not that interested in the temperance cause. It is the vote that is important to me.

Henry chuckles. It's all right, Miss Collins, I am not here to interrogate you. I wish you well. It is a fine cause — I see no reason why women should not vote. Any man who says otherwise is a brute. Perhaps you will be successful and you can teach your English sisters a thing or two.

Are you mocking me? she asks. Because we are quite serious. Mrs Johnson is very well connected. In Parliament. She *will* be heard.

And who is this Mrs Johnson?

He turns in the direction she is indicating and sees a stout woman in her late thirties holding forth to three younger women.

Yes. I am staying with her at the moment. She and her husband have taken me because Father has had to go to the country unexpectedly.

But why did you not go with him, I wonder?

She sighs. I begged him not to make me. He agreed reluctantly, but only for a little while. I am to join him there at the end of the next week.

Miss Collins, forgive me, says Henry, but you seem to be very displeased to see me. I thought that we had become friends when we met yesterday, but I am very sorry if I have offended you somehow. You appear to have quite changed your attitude to me.

Mr Summers, may I be blunt?

But of course.

When I saw you on the stairs last night I smelled you before you appeared. The odour of brandy was overwhelming. You stumbled on the stairs, quite embarrassing yourself. And me. While I am not passionate about the temperance cause, that kind of behaviour is enough to make me change my mind.

And your father, leaving so unexpectedly . . .

Oh, you needn't worry, she says. I did not mention it to him. He likes a drink himself. Now if you will excuse me, I have work to do.

She gives the tiniest of nods and turns her back on him.

Henry finds himself rooted to the spot. He forgets for a moment where he is, what his business is supposed to be. Then he smiles. An Englishwoman would never dare speak to a gentleman in such a way. He thinks he may be beginning to like this country after all.

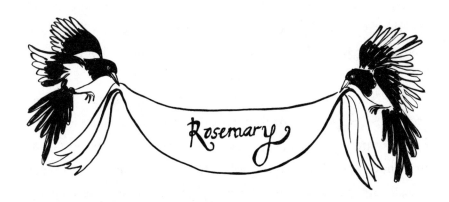

Rosemary

When I think back to childhood holidays at Magpie Hall, the colours are saturated, like the Super-8 films that Grandpa was always shooting. I see myself from the outside, a skinny kid with a page-boy haircut and crooked front teeth, a scattering of freckles, grinning widely at the camera. Charlie follows me around like a toy on a string. In another memory — or perhaps it is a movie — we ride our ponies bareback into the river, looks of concentration on our faces. When I think of those days, they are always silent, with only the ticking of the projector as a soundtrack, and everything is slightly sped up: when we wave for the camera our hands are blurs.

Magpie Hall was a crowded place then, filled with children in swimsuits skidding across the lawn on plastic slides, and birthday parties with pointed hats and kazoos. Parents in shorts and jandals, holding big bottles of beer. Picnics and horse rides, cavorting dogs and bonfires. We often made family treks up to the limestone caves over the hill. We were warned about playing in them because of the danger of falling rocks, and we imagined they were filled with buried treasure. My grandfather was always there in those days, skirting the edges with his movie camera, recording, never being recorded. Perhaps he had looked at everything through that lens to stop himself experiencing it first hand, so his memories were always sugary and colour bloated, the lows and grey spots edited out. I know I would like to remember my life like that.

The summer of the magpie, when Grandpa started to teach me taxidermy, was one of the times that brought change; when the colours started to soften, no longer crayon bright. I spent most of my time indoors, seeking out the dark corners in the house and throwing myself into the new craft. Learning to mount animals brought out in me a passion I couldn't explain. I knew it had something to do with the time a yellowhammer got caught in the chicken coop. I cornered it in one of the laying-boxes with the idea of catching it and releasing it. My intentions were benign but I felt the quivering a cat feels when its prey is in its sights, the involuntary shudder that runs through its body. I caught the bird in one hand and when I pulled it out and opened my fist it lay there with its tiny claws curled like unopened flowers and its eyes closed. It had died of fright in my hands.

I buried the bird in the garden, shooing the cats away, and all I could think about was that I had caused its death when I was only trying to help. That my intense desire to be close to it — to have it *love* me somehow — had in the end caused its demise.

Had I known then how to mount it, I probably would have carried that bird around with me forever, but I hadn't even told Grandpa what had happened; I was too ashamed.

One summer, when I was eleven, I asked him to tell me about the strange bird in the living room, the one with the curved beak and the red wattle and white-tipped tail feathers.

Grandpa went into the library and pulled out a dusty fat book — *A History of the Birds of New Zealand*, it was called, by a man called Walter Buller. It was filled with richly textured drawings and paintings of pairs of birds, all looking as though they were watching and listening. He found the right page and held it out to me.

'The huia,' he said. 'The reason you haven't seen one, not even in a zoo, is that they are extinct.'

'Like the dinosaurs?'

'That's right. Except it's our fault that they're extinct.'

'Yours and mine?' Confusion and guilt flittered and were gone.

'No, humankind. You see, when the settlers came to New Zealand, they brought collectors — men who would catch and kill birds and stuff them, like we do.'

'But we don't kill things just to stuff them.'

'No. But these men took native birds back to England with them, and some of them ended up in museums there, and here, and some in private collections. This man, Buller, who wrote this book, he even said once that because the huia was nearly extinct, he had to try and catch and kill as many as possible before they died out.'

Even I could see the faulty logic in that. 'But that's stupid.'

'Yes, but we have to remember that it was a different time then. They thought differently about conservation. To them, it was all in the name of science. They believed they were doing very important work, and they were, in a way. But the nail in the coffin for the poor huia was when a Maori chief gave a highly prized huia feather to the visiting Prince of Wales, which he put on his hat. Then, everybody wanted one of those feathers and the huia became very expensive, so anyone who killed one could make a lot of money. Which they did. The last ones died at the beginning of the century.'

I looked at the huia on top of the bookcase and suddenly felt ashamed.

'So where did that one come from?'

Grandpa sighed. 'That was caught by your great-great-grandfather, my grandpa. But just remember, things were different back then. He wasn't to know that they would die out. And I for one am glad that he caught just one, so that we will always have it in the family to remind us of how fragile life is. And to always remember the huia. He made sure it would live forever. I like to think he had a bit more of a conscience than most collectors.'

For three years, in every stretch of school holidays, Grandpa and I worked on the animals. We spent all our spare time together, and I stopped riding so that my pony grew fat on spring grass. When I look back now I can't help wonder if things might have been different if I had only paid her more attention, ridden her more often; if Grandpa hadn't been so busy with me he would have taken more notice of what everyone else was doing. After Tess died, Grandpa blamed himself, I think, for not keeping a closer eye on her. People stopped visiting so much after that; kids grew up and moved on, of course, but it was difficult to get comfortable there again. I convinced myself that I was more interested in boys than horses, and that I wanted to spend my summers with my friends, not in some huge house stuffing animals, with only an old man and some dogs for company. I missed it, really, but it just wasn't the same.

❦

I stood in the red room at the end of the following day, looking out through the tall arched windows at the shadows as they stretched themselves over the paddocks. The sun burned on the horizon through the trees. As I felt the walls breathe around me, I imagined Grandpa out there as he would have liked to be remembered: in his favourite grey jersey and gumboots, bent over to gather walnuts from the tree under the window, looking up only to throw one at me, laughing his false-toothed, throaty laugh.

I had an overwhelming sense of calm when I listened to the house, when I stood in its shadows and its bright spots. I felt his presence in every room. Once the architects and the builders had finished with it, he would be dead. And the menagerie room had more of him in it than any other room. The previous night, skinning the rabbit and laying it to rest with a salt coat to dry it out, I had felt him around me, breathing in my ear and guiding my hands. I had talked to him as I worked, explaining to him the myriad reasons I had come, assuring him that I wasn't the one who wanted to renovate the house and cast him out forever.

With nobody to collect them, the walnuts were gathering in drifts on the grass, already dampening with the coming dusk. Further on, Sam was making his way slowly up the gravel road on a quad bike. He must have seen me because he stopped and waved. On a whim, I opened the window and leaned out as far as I could.

'Hey!' I yelled. 'What time do you knock off?'

'Soon!' he shouted back.

'Come over for a drink!'

He gave me the thumbs up and revved his engine. In seconds he had disappeared up the road, two dogs loping after him. In the distance, smoke poured from the chimneys of the cottages, adding to the haze.

I went back to my desk and looked with satisfaction at the work I had done. I had gone off on a tangent but had been reluctant to stop writing and was surprised when I looked up to find the room darkening. I had done enough for one day. I printed out the new pages and just had time to have a shower and dress before the front door bell rang.

'I tried the kitchen door but it was locked.' Sam frowned, as though I had slighted him personally.

'Yeah, sorry about that. Just taking precautions.'

He sniggered. 'City girl. Nobody locks their houses out here.'

'Well, maybe they should.' I felt a blush bloom on my cheeks.

'Okay, sorry.' His hair was wet and he smelled of deodorant. His Swanndri had been replaced by a fleece and he wore sneakers instead of gumboots.

We sat down at the round kitchen table in the bay window. I poured him a beer from the bottle of Lion Red in the fridge and myself a glass of the red wine I had found in the pantry.

Sam and I made idle chit-chat as the shadows deepened, then disappeared with the last of the light. With the sun now gone, the sky moved from light blue to gold to pink. While the room grew darker around us, we made no move to turn the lights on. Behind him, I could see the magpies take a last turn of the lawn, and it was as though they were watching the house, waiting for something. The room was quiet in our pauses, with only the steady hum of the freezer undercutting the silence.

We finished our drinks, poured seconds. We discovered unimportant facts about each other: he had worked there for three years and was now Josh's right-hand man, with more responsibility, but more freedom, too. He had a chipped tooth from a small accident with the quad bike and when he wasn't speaking the tip of his tongue appeared between his lips as it explored the gap. I told him I was there to work on my thesis, but he didn't ask me about the subject, so I went on to say that I wanted to spend some time here before the house was renovated, to remember it as it was with Grandpa in it.

'I can understand you wanting to do that,' he said. 'Change is hard.'

I asked him if he had spoken to Josh about the farm being sold, and whether Josh had known.

'Yeah, he knew. Not happy about it, neither.'

'What did he say?'

'Nothing much.'

Something in his face made me think otherwise, that in fact the manager had had plenty to say. After all, he had started as a farmhand twenty-odd years ago, and worked here most of his adult life; his children were growing up here. What would become of them once the farm was sold? I was dreading bumping into Josh, seeing his accusatory stare. I had no doubt that he would somehow think it was all my fault.

'Guess I'll be out of a job soon.' The darkness I had seen the day before returned to Sam's face.

'Not necessarily,' I said. 'Whoever buys it might still keep all the staff on.'

'Yeah, whatever.' He drained his half-full glass. 'I'm young. Don't wanna stay here forever.'

'How old are you, anyway?'

'Twenty-four.'

I smiled and refilled his glass without saying anything. He was beginning to get drunk — two pink patches had appeared on his unshaven cheeks — and so was I. He no longer sat forward in his chair, shoulders tight, but leaned back and regarded me lazily, as if he was waiting to see where the evening took him.

'Look, I'm going to make some dinner.' I stood up from the table. 'Do you want some?'

He nodded and I busied myself around the kitchen bench, making pasta with a simple jar of shop-bought sauce. Once again, I had forgotten to eat all day. The light had drained completely from the hills behind the house, but the sky was still a deep indigo. I was aware as I worked of Sam staring at me, but when I met his eye he looked out the window, or around the room, pretending to be interested in Gram's old teapot collection gathering dust on the mantelpiece above the range.

We both ate hungrily. The wine had gone to my head on an empty stomach. Sam held his fork solidly and twirled spaghetti as if stirring a cauldron. We barely spoke until the meal was finished.

'Not bad for no meat.' Sam tipped his chair back and put his hands behind his head. 'Couldn't do it every meal, though. I'd starve.'

'Sure, you would,' I said. I picked up the bowls and dropped them in the sink. 'Hey, do want to see your rabbit? I've started bringing her back to life.'

'A she, was it? I didn't look.'

'A beautiful she.' I nodded my head in the direction of the hallway. He followed close behind. I wondered how much time he'd spent in the house, if he'd ever been upstairs, how well he knew Grandpa. Something stopped me from asking, though; I didn't want him to think it was an invitation.

He let out a long low whistle when I opened the door to the menagerie room.

'So I take it you've never seen this collection?'

'No. Man, I'd heard about it, but this is awesome.' He stalked about the room, reaching out and touching things as he went. Then he stopped and looked at me. 'Sorry, is it okay if I touch?'

'It's fine,' I said. 'It's not a museum. Yet.'

'What do you mean, yet?'

'Nothing, it doesn't matter. Anyway, this is all mine now.'

'True that? Well, I guess you're the girl who likes to stuff animals.'

'Mount — the correct term is mount. The girl who likes to *mount* animals.'

He let out a great guffaw then, and I joined him. 'Whatever turns you on, I suppose,' he said.

The room was dark and the looming shapes of the animals watched us as we talked. The rabbit skin lay drying out under the window where I had left it the night before. The salt looked like ice crystals. I turned a lamp on and Sam put his face up close and examined it. 'Nice job,' he said. He stroked the fur. 'Soft. Isn't it weird for you, stuffing — sorry, mounting it — when you won't eat the meat?'

'It's hard to explain. I have my reasons, but it would take all night to tell you.'

He smiled. 'Maybe later, then.'

As he looked around, riveted to the spot, I remembered the birds in the living room.

'By the way, did you move the huia? Back up onto the shelf?'

'Huia? Where?' He turned a circle, scanning the room. 'Aren't they extinct? I'd like to see one of those.'

'Not here — in the other room. I thought maybe you did it when you brought the rabbit inside.'

'Nah. Why?'

'Well, someone did. That freaks me out a bit. Someone's been in the house.'

He didn't look particularly alarmed on my behalf. 'Don't worry about it. It was probably just Elsie or —'

'Who's Elsie?'

'Josh's missus. She's hard case, that one. Bit of a nag. Josh is scared of her, I reckon. Or it could have been Josh. Someone probably just making things tidy for you. You're not the only one who loves this house, you know.'

What a strange thing to say, I thought, but I let it slide.

'Okay, I'm probably just being paranoid. City girl, you know.'

'Probably.' He didn't seem interested in continuing the subject. 'Do you reckon you could stuff a human?' The room was becoming unbearably cold, but Sam didn't appear to notice.

'You could try. It wouldn't look very nice, though. No fur. It'd just look all leathery and strange.'

'Hmm. Worth trying though, I suppose. To achieve immortality.'

'I guess you could say that . . . Actually, you'd be better off donating your body to plastination.'

'What's that?'

'It's like embalming. There's a place in Germany that does it. I thought I might end up there. Why not? I do it to animals, why not let someone do it to me?'

'And then what? You'll be on show?'

'That's right. I'll be exhibited.'

'Naked?' He raised an eyebrow.

'Who knows? Maybe.'

'I'd like to see that.' He moved closer to me.

'Would you now.'

What was I thinking? I wasn't thinking. Well, actually, I was. I wanted to obliterate all thoughts of Hugh in the way I had always obliterated thoughts of love gone bad. With sex. With a warm, hard body, so different from the pillowy flesh of my last lover. With someone I knew I wouldn't develop any feelings for.

Sam brought his body up close to me but leaned back to read my face. I smiled an encouragement and he needed little. His lips were rough and hot and the hand on the back of my neck was callused. I put my hands under his top and felt the smooth down on the small of his back. It was as if we both knew we would end up here, ever since we saw each other in the garden.

'You're sure you're all right with this?' he asked.

'Mm, yes.' I nodded and he took it as a signal to go further, and fast.

His lips trembled on mine as he fumbled with the buttons on my blouse. He pulled away for a moment to see what he was doing.

'Holy . . .' He stopped and stared at the tattoo on my chest — a bluebird hovering above each breast, a ribbon floating between them. 'That is some tat.' He continued unbuttoning my top and it fell from my shoulders.

'Jesus, girl, how many have you got?'

I was shirtless now, sitting on the workbench where he had lifted me as though I were a paper doll. I still wore my bra, but he had the chance to stare at most of my tattoos, including the new one of the magpie, still raised and pink. He walked around the table to look at my back. His were just another pair of eyes in the crowded room. I found myself staring straight at an ancient fox with its teeth bared.

I sat up straighter. It was a ritual I had been through many times before with men: the surprise, the fascination, then ultimately, the renewed sexual fervour. But never in such a strange setting.

'Ten,' I said. 'So far. One for every murder committed.'

He laughed uncertainly as he came a full circle back to me. His finger traced the dahlia on my left shoulder and moved down to the mermaid on my right arm. My white skin goosebumped in the icy room.

'Come on,' he said suddenly, and lifted my blouse back onto my shoulders. 'Let's get you into the living room and get the fire going. You're freezing.'

With the heat of the moment gone, I found my teeth beginning to chatter and I nodded and lowered myself to the floor.

I followed him into the living room and sat on one of the shabby couches while he expertly built a fire. The springs of the couch dug into my thighs and an odour of dog enveloped me. I didn't mind. I sank into the familiar feeling and the smells and pulled the old crocheted blanket off the back to wrap myself in while I waited for the room to warm up.

I thought of Hugh at home with his wife. The children tucked up in bed, the two of them curled up on a couch with glasses of wine, maybe books. The comfortable silence only years of togetherness can bring. I looked at Sam's back as he crouched by the fireplace, poking the virgin flames with a piece of kindling, and for a moment imagined a life with him in the country. He would go out to farm the land while I stayed behind and looked after the children, passed on the Summers art of taxidermy. Maybe even in this house, if I could find some way to persuade my family to let us live here. I could resurrect Gram's garden, grow vegetables.

It was preposterous, of course. I did this with every man I had a glimmer of romance with — slept with them, married them and divorced them all in one night.

'So why the tats? You seem like such a nice girl.' Sam had finished with the fire and was sitting back on his heels and warming his hands.

'What, a girl can't be nice and have tattoos?'

'I don't know. I always thought only biker chicks had them. You've got that sweet little haircut and that pretty face and tattoos. Seems strange to me.'

'Not that strange. Plenty of girls have tattoos.'

'Yeah, maybe one on their ankle or just above their arse, not all over their arms and chest.'

'Well, you learn something new every day, don't you, country boy?'

'Yeah, all right. Got anything more to drink?'

'Hang on a sec.' I rose and crossed the room to Grandpa's liquor cabinet. It held a healthy supply of gin and brandy, and there at the back, an old bottle of Chivas Regal.

'This'll do,' I said. I unscrewed the lid and took a swig. It burned sweetly.

Sam moved back to sit beside me on the couch and took the bottle.

'That magpie you've got there on your wrist. Can I see?'

I uncovered it for him.

'Looks fresh. Which murder is that for?' He touched it, a little too hard.

I didn't say anything, but took my hand away. It throbbed lightly from his fingertip's touch.

'It's your Grandpa, right? One for sorrow.'

'You're pretty perceptive, aren't you?'

His face darkened and he drank from the bottle. 'For a farmhand, you mean. Go on, say it.'

'I didn't mean that.'

'I'm not stupid, you know. I read books. Probably more than you with your fancy education. Go on, ask me how many I've read.'

I sighed. I didn't want to be drawn into this.

'Thousands,' he said, and drank again.

I didn't know how to respond without sounding patronising, so I said nothing. I took the bottle.

'Yeah, yeah, I'm getting drunk. Not far to drive home. Only three people I know have died driving pissed, anyway.' He laughed.

'Are you serious? Jesus.'

He was still laughing, as if the idea of losing his friends was the most hilarious thing in the world. His laughter had the manic edge of a mean drunk. He stopped when he saw I was actually shocked, which had probably been his intention. He wore the look I had seen on his face the day before, when he had stormed from the house.

'You've got no fuckin' idea what it's like out here in the country. You and your prissy mates have got taxis in the city. You've got your pretty little theatres and art gallery openings. We've got the pub. Or parties. Which are usually miles away from home.'

I held tightly on to the bottle of whisky. 'I'm sorry.' I laid a calming hand on his arm and he stared at it.

'You should ask Josh about it some time,' he said. 'Living out here for so long — what, twenty years? I'm sure it's driven him mad. I think getting married and having kids might have saved him. It gets bloody lonely out here.'

I didn't want to talk about Josh. 'So you don't think you'll last much longer?'

'I dunno. What else would I do?'

I relinquished the bottle and he took another swig and stared into the fire.

'I do know what it's like, you know,' I said. 'Losing people.'

'Ah shit, sorry. Josh told me about . . . well, you know.'

'Josh did?' I wondered how much he had said, how much he had admitted to his employee. I didn't feel like finding out.

'Let's play a game for a bit,' he said. 'Let's play for one night that I'm not a drop-kick from the country and you're not a stuck-up rich bitch from the city.'

I laughed. 'What are we then?'

'I don't know. Equals.'

'You don't think we're equals?'

'You don't.'

'That's not true.'

'Look, just play along, okay?' He took my hand and, in a sweet gesture, raised my fingers to his lips.

The room was finally beginning to warm up. I shrugged the crocheted blanket off.

'Will you do something for me?' asked Sam.

'Depends.'

'Will you take off your clothes so I can look at you? At your tattoos?'

I suppose it was part of the game we were meant to be playing — at least, that's what I told myself. I don't think I really wanted to get naked in front of this man. But still at the back of my mind was the image of Hugh and his wife, and the moment I saw my ex-lover's face, I knew what I was about to do.

I kicked off my shoes and slid out of my tights. I declined to make it a strip-tease for him. My skirt came down next, then, one by one, I loosened the buttons of my shirt, until I stood before him in my underwear.

I felt his gaze on my body as I revolved slowly in the firelight. I felt the warmth of the flames as I turned towards them, the coolness when my body fell into the shadow, like the earth rotating around the sun. The only sound was the bristling of the pine logs and our breathing. He read me, as I had been read before, laying myself bare for a near stranger. When he asked me for the story of each tattoo, I refused him. Finally, he stopped asking.

The house moaned and shook off the ghostly music playing through my dreams. A grey light fingered the edges of the curtains. The eiderdown had fallen to the floor in the night but I was warm: the body beside me burned like a furnace.

Hungover. Thirsty. I looked over at Sam, at the tattoo on his shoulder blade that he had proudly showed me the night before — his badge of honour, his connection to me. It was ugly and inexpertly done, a symbol he could neither translate for me or explain what it meant to him personally. The lines were already blurring, the black had faded to green, and he didn't seem to care. He shrugged when I mentioned its colour and mangled shape and said he couldn't see it anyway, so what did it matter?

At least the muscles beneath the skin were nice to look at, so unlike Hugh's soft moonscape of a back. I felt sick. I missed that back. What was I doing?

I turned over and faced away from him. Something was nagging me about the situation I found myself in. Not déjà vu exactly, but I knew I wasn't the first of the Summers to take the 'help' to bed. It didn't feel good. History was beginning to repeat itself in unexpected ways.

Sam stirred, reached for me and pulled my slight body into the pocket between his torso and raised knees. I may as well have been a hot water bottle.

'What time is it?' he murmured into my hair.

'It's seven.'

'Shit.' He released me and rolled out of bed. 'I gotta go.' He dressed speedily, then peered down at me.

'You okay?'

'Not well. Too much whisky.'

'I'll get you some water.'

He disappeared then came back with a large glass, which he set down on the bedside table. He sat beside me.

'Drink up. You'll feel better. I'll come by later and see how you are.'

This was what I was afraid of. 'No. Sam, don't, okay? I'll be fine.'

His body went rigid.

'I get it.' He stood up and turned in the doorway. 'Thanks for the fuck, Lady fucking Chatterley.' I heard his feet pounding down the stairs and the front door slam behind him.

Henry

He sends word to Mr Collins that he is to set off on a collecting expedition and will join him at his country house at a later date. The German, Schlau, has made the trip many times and will be his guide. Henry knows he has found the perfect travelling companion: Schlau barely speaks, seems almost incapable of human interaction, and yet appears to have a rapport with the natural life of the country. When he calls upon Schlau at the museum a few nights before they are due to leave, he finds the taxidermist on the floor of his workshop, his brow furrowed.

I am worried about what will become of my friends here when I am gone, says the German. I am thinking it may be time for extermination.

Henry moves closer. Schlau sits with his back to the wall as two large green parrots scratch at a pile of dirt on the floor, from which they are extracting morsels of food. Their feathers are dusted with white as though sprinkled with snow, and a facial disc of whiskers gives them an owl-like appearance. They start when Henry comes closer, but after eyeing him warily, go back to their business.

What are they? asks Henry.

Kakapo is their name. They sleep here in the workshop during the day, over there, in the corner, with their heads beneath their wings. I caught them on my last trip, to observe them, but now I suppose I have found all I need to know. They will be more useful to me dead. They will fetch a good price.

But are you not attached to them at all? They are your pets.

Schlau shrugs. Not really. They are quite tame, I suppose, but they have never shown any particular attachment to me. I am just their food supply. They are not loyal, like my dog.

As if in answer, one of the birds suddenly leaps on the back of the other and scratches at its feathers; both birds let out a scream that is more like that of a hare than a bird. Schlau scrambles to his feet and stands well back, watching with relish. The victim has managed to shrug the other bird off and now they fight, making bounding leaps and tearing at each other with their substantial claws. Finally, one lies down on its back to try and fight off its aggressor, which soon loses interest and goes back to scratching in the dirt. The room is silent again.

Remarkable, says Henry. He feels privileged to witness the interaction of the birds, who seem quite at home in the darkened room.

You see I can't just leave them here, says Schlau. They might kill each other anyhow and when I returned their carcasses would be quite useless to me. No, better that I kill them now and preserve them before we leave. Cover your ears, sir.

And with that, he picks up a gun and as if for treason, with no trial, he shoots his pets dead.

※

They set off on horseback, the town at their back as they cross the plains. As Henry expected, Schlau is silent, reserving all conversation for his dog, Brutus, a black Labrador that bounds happily along beside them. When they stop to rest and eat, Schlau cuddles the dog and whispers in its ear as they eat together. Henry wonders if he would coldly shoot the dog when it had outlived its usefulness; somehow, he thinks not. Schlau explains to Henry how many dogs he trialled, hounds that ate the very birds they were supposed to be retrieving, or ran off without ever being recalled. By all accounts Brutus had earnt his keep a thousand times over by rooting out specimens and retrieving them, and by defending his master against potential attackers. Henry is beginning to feel safer himself — he hadn't considered the perils of their expedition. He knew that the country had no dangerous animals; he hadn't considered the human population.

It is a fine way to travel, he thinks, ambling up the country on horseback. The saddle creaks and the horse is sure-footed, despite the weight it is carrying: a small tent, blankets and groundsheets, a spare pair of sturdy boots for climbing, and other equipment — compass, watch, barometer, knives and chemicals. Henry has packed extra warm clothing, for they will be travelling into high country, and snow caps the mountains. There is still room in his bags for the specimens he intends to collect; he will skin the birds and animals he finds on the spot, to keep their weight and bulk down. His rifle is slung over his shoulder, and different gauges of shot rattle in the bag around his waist.

He loses himself in his thoughts as the sun begins to sink on the first day and the mountains rise about them. Away from civilisation he finally feels the excitement of a new country, in the sheer scale of the place, with the sky huge above him. Much of the land has been cleared for farming, but still sits empty of livestock, and the native bush clings to the base of the mountains. Waterfalls cascade into the dark lake beside them. Birdcalls he does not recognise rise up to greet them. Schlau points out a good camping spot and they turn the horses' heads away from the track.

The night is so clear that, despite the chill, Henry opts to sleep without a tent. Schlau tells him he is mad, but this is the first time Henry has been in an exotic landscape with no fear of man-eating animals or poisonous insects and snakes. He lies on his groundsheet with nothing but a blanket for padding and another for warmth and drapes the canvas of the tent over his body. The fire sparks steadily beside him and he feels the air on his face as he stares up at the sky, at the cloudy constellations, their brightness broken only by the black expanse of the surrounding hills. Some of the stars are unfamiliar and this alone is enough to send him into an ecstatic sleep.

He awakes to a startling cacophony when the light has barely licked the horizon. His face is wet with dew and his muscles stiff. Schlau and Brutus have still not emerged from their shelter, but Henry decides it is time to rise and reignite the fire for a cup of tea and some warmth. He listens to the birdsong, the chiming and the warbling and even a rhythmic clacking. He tries to imagine the birds responsible and hopes that he will soon see them for himself. For some reason he thinks of Dora Collins, standing as he last saw her, upright and defiant, clutching her little petition. He finds he is looking forward to seeing her again.

As he sits drinking tea, a bird emerges from the bush and hops rapidly over the stones towards him. It is a soft grey colour, with an orange wattle and black eye mask, such as a robber might wear, and it eyes him curiously; probably, it has never seen a human being before. Soon it is joined by another, also hopping, but with lowered wings; its mate, thinks Henry, although they look almost identical. The second bird lets out a call, a flute-like sound, and Henry sits very still lest he scare them away.

An explosion makes him jump and spill his hot tea on his lap. He turns to see Schlau letting off his gun a second time and when he looks back at the birds they lie in a heap on the stones. Brutus bounds forward, picks up both birds in his jaws and carries them carefully back to his master.

Forgetting his burning thighs, Henry is gripped by the familiar tightening in his chest. He feels the blood pound in his face. His fists clench involuntarily and he strides towards Schlau, cursing at him. The dog has dropped the birds at the German's feet and now turns on Henry, baring its teeth and crouching low, ready to pounce. A gravelly growl warns Henry not to come any closer.

Damn you, man. Henry's voice is deflated by the dog's warning.

Schlau places his hand on the dog's collar and looks at Henry defiantly.

What is the problem, Mr Summers? We have come to collect specimens. You were just sitting there ogling the birds. Someone had to take action. The kokako is very rare, especially in the South Island, where their wattle is orange, you see? He shows the birds to Henry as if he hasn't seen them already. The more common variety in the north has a blue wattle, Schlau continues. And now the pair is in my collection.

Henry can explain nothing to this man. His hands reach for the ground and scoop up a large river stone. Schlau stiffens and Brutus barks but stands his ground. Henry heaves the rock into the fire. Hot embers spray outwards and land on his bedding, which begins to smoulder. He swears again, sees once more the damage he has caused, and grabs the billy to pour water on the blankets, feeling foolish and impotent. Flames averted, he turns stiffly on his heel and strides to the lake's edge. His thighs are smarting still from the hot tea. He strips off his clothes and throws himself into the icy lake to try and cool his skin and his temper. He stands waist-deep in the water and rubs at his body, runs his hands over the tattoos on his torso.

He had told McDonald that he gets tattooed to remember, and it is times like this that he needs to remember the past; to take himself away from this place for the moment. Why, here, on his arm, is the tiger that he caught himself and skinned; he is sure that Schlau has never handled such a beast. Instead the man makes do with little birds and common mammals such as stoats and weasels, or else he is employed merely as a taxidermist to mount the creatures that *other* men have risked their lives for. He is nothing, this man, this German. He has not felt the African sun on his back, or braved crocodiles and anacondas to collect the most delicate of butterflies in the rainforests of the Amazon. He is merely a tradesman.

Henry's skin is beginning to turn blue with cold, but he does not want to admit it. He turns to look at his guide. Schlau is sitting on a log, smoking a cigarette, watching him. He feels the man looking at his tattoos with curiosity — perhaps he has never seen an illustrated man before. Henry wades out of the water and turns his back, determined not to answer any questions. But the German says nothing, merely busies himself with preparing the skins of the two kokako, and feeding his wretched dog on their carcasses.

They continue their journey into the interior of the South Island but travel shorter distances than they did on that first day — the terrain is ever steeper, and the temperature drops further every night. The clouds descend on them and a fine mist turns overnight to torrential rain. After a shaky start Henry is able to begin his collection at last. He awakes one morning to find two kea, green mountain parrots, boldly tearing a hole in his tent to try and get at the food supplies within. He watches them a while before shooting them. He manages to kill a pair of parson birds — or tui as the natives call them — and a small green bellbird. At night he hears a kiwi calling but his blunders through the darkness yield nothing. He and Schlau barely speak to each other. Henry is irritated at the man's lack of curiosity, yet Schlau stares openly at Henry's body whenever he washes.

Is there something you would like to ask me? Henry demands one morning as Schlau sits cleaning his gun. About my tattoos?

Not really, says Schlau. I have seen more impressive tattoos.

Have you now?

Yes, on the Maoris. I have met great warriors with their faces fully tattooed with the moko. Women too, who tend to tattoo only their chins and lips. But it has more meaning to them. They are not just for adornment such as yours.

What do you know about why I have tattoos? What do you know of what I have suffered for them?

Schlau laughs. Suffered? A few little pricks with a needle? You wait until you see what these Maoris endure, the tools they use. Not needles but chisels. The patterns are carved into their faces as if they were wood. Now that is real pain.

And what would you know about pain? spits Henry.

Nothing, my friend, absolutely nothing. I have seen only the instruments of pain and the magnificent result. These men and women walk taller when they have the moko. This I have seen.

Schlau stands and walks to his horse, which is already saddled and ready to move on. He rummages through his bag and pulls out a small sack tied with string.

You call yourself a collector, do you not? says the German. Well, don't you think these would make a fine addition to your collection?

He passes the cloth bag to Henry, who opens it carefully and extracts the contents. They are manmade artefacts, beautiful examples of craftsmanship — a fine bone fish hook, an adze of jade, with an edge so sharp he cuts his finger. He extracts a long piece of bone with sharp, comb-like teeth embedded in the ends.

Now that, says Schlau, is the tattooing instrument. It is dipped in ink and tapped with a small mallet.

Where did you find them? Henry asks. He thinks of the needle he took from Hori Chyo in Japan, and how this Maori instrument would further enhance his collection.

Oh, I have many such items in my collection, says Schlau. Some of them I have traded with the Maoris. Others I have found in abandoned pa. Burial caves. It hasn't been hard. Do you like bones?

Bones? It depends what creature they have come from. I should like some moa bones for my collection.

What about human? Of a primitive people. I have two mummified bodies, and many bones.

You took them? From these burial sites?

They have proved to be my greatest challenge. I think the joy of the collecting is in the stories we live to tell, don't you?

Henry shifts uncomfortably on his log. Schlau is trying to prove himself, to put himself on a par with Henry. Let him, Henry thinks.

I can see you are itching to tell me how you acquired these remains, sir. Do go on.

Schlau then launches into a convoluted story with many side branches that go nowhere. Henry is surprised — for a man of few words, once he warms up, the German seems to use a lot more than are necessary. Henry finds himself tapping his foot and nodding with impatience every time Schlau starts to wax lyrical about a pretty bird he saw on the way, or when he fills in the background of a character of absolutely no consequence.

This is the essence of the story: Schlau travelled to the top of the North Island not long after he finished mounting the museum's collection in time for its grand opening. There he gained the trust of some local farmers, with whom he stayed, and a tribe of Maoris to whom the farmers introduced him.

They trusted me, you know, says Schlau, because I am not *English*. His voice is suitably scornful.

There he purchased some items for a very good price, but when he started asking questions about a nearby abandoned pa, and whether he might visit it, the Maoris became less charming.

They told me it was tapu. Are you familiar with this word?

Henry isn't, although he guesses, correctly, at its meaning.

It was sacred, not to be touched. They said that anyone who broke tapu would pay a terrible price.

Such as? asks Henry.

Death. Of course, this was in place to stop the superstitious Maoris from going there, but it wasn't going to stop someone like me.

Schlau tried to visit the pa on his own one day, but the Maoris had become suspicious when he had disturbed a flock of river birds, and were patrolling the area. He climbed a tree to hide from them while Brutus lay quietly in the undergrowth below. There he waited until nightfall, because he knew that the Maoris were superstitious about the dark.

From the huts, he gained a number of precious artefacts, which he declared were just lying there, next to the bodies, unprotected. He dragged the skeletal remains, including several skulls and a carved thigh bone, into the forest and hid them, while he deposited the tools and weapons he found in his satchel, intending to dispatch them by river steamer the next day to rid himself of the evidence as soon as possible. He also sawed the carved wooden head of a tattooed chief off the middle post of one of the huts, being careful to let the sawdust fall into the river.

But the next morning he was awoken early by the farmer he was staying with. The chief and a prophet from the nearby village had come by and voiced their suspicion to the embarassed farmer. They asked to look in his bag, but Schlau was prepared for them. He had been told by the farmer in passing of the Maori belief that lizards and sometimes insects acted as guardians of the dead and that they were greatly feared. He had been collecting spiders and centipedes as well as lizards, and he opened the specimen tins in his satchel, letting the contents fall at the feet of the prophet. The creatures crawled over him, causing both men to back away in fear. The furious farmer banished Schlau from the house immediately, but the German was happy with his collection and continued on his way.

And here you see the results, says Schlau. The skulls and the carved leg bone and wooden head fetched a healthy sum, and I have been on the lookout for such opportunities ever since.

Henry is appalled at the man's trickery, but has to admire his gumption. Perhaps he has underestimated him. It is just this kind of sly ambition that makes a successful collector, particularly of manmade artefacts. But Henry's sense of honour is too great. He would be ashamed to have such a story to tell and he tells Schlau as much.

The German shrugs. That is your opinion. He looks with pity at Henry, who can see any respect Schlau had for him drain from his eyes.

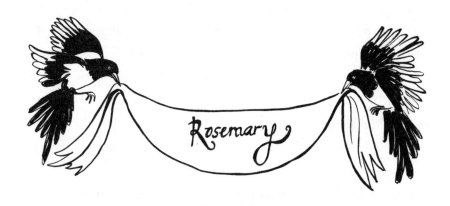

Rosemary

I took a couple of paracetemol tablets and got into the shower. Beyond the dirty window, the rain clouds hung black over the hills. A crack of thunder rolled from one end of the farm to the other, telling me that the weather was here to stay, at least for the day. The shower was falling to pieces; mildew swarmed up the walls and lifted the veneer. There was no fan to pull the moisture away, and the shower itself had only two temperatures, cold and hot, with nothing in between. I was reluctant to admit that this bathroom needed an overhaul: they all did. I don't know how we had let Grandpa live in these freezing, damp conditions for so long. Why hadn't we insisted on his installing some decent, modern heating? He had still used the wetback on the wood-burning stove in the kitchen, to save money it seemed, but why he needed to I didn't know. I wished he'd spent some of his money on himself instead of keeping it out of some misplaced idea that his children needed something to inherit.

Now that Sam was gone, I didn't even want to think about him, let alone line him up to be my next boyfriend. The sex had been all right, but he was clumsy and a little selfish — through youth and inexperience, I supposed. He had moved too fast for me, but I had let him. It was as if I couldn't be bothered telling him to slow down. So many parts of me wanted to sleep with him that the parts that didn't were quickly dampened down. He had asked me how old I was and he was surprised when I told him. 'But your skin is so smooth,' he'd said, as though women over thirty instantly turned into wizened crones. Maybe they did out in the country.

After Hugh, in his forties, Sam's body was so young, with no unnecessary flab and so much change ahead. I suppose trading an older model for a younger gave me a curious sense of satisfaction, and for a moment I could see what motivated middle-aged men to have affairs with their secretaries and to buy sports cars. But Sam was a distraction, nothing more. What I really needed was to be alone, but I'd told myself that so often and every time I had ignored my own advice.

I had been standing under the shower for so long that the cold water announced itself suddenly; I swore as I turned it off. Now I was shivering again, drying myself quickly so I could get my clothes on and warmth back into my bones.

After a quick breakfast, I sat down again at my desk with my coffee and started up my laptop, but the words on the screen blurred and the effort of adding new ones proved too much for my hangover. The day stretched before me — miserable and wet. I considered packing it all up and going back to the city.

But I hadn't finished my business here. I stood up and dawdled from room to room. I glanced into the tight spiral stairwell that led to the tower, but couldn't bring myself to go up. Instead I investigated the smoking room and the library, on the south side of the ground floor, a room with a permanent darkness protecting the thousands of books from the bleaching sun. The lower shelves housed Gram and Grandpa's paperbacks — lines of Catherine Cookson and Jeffrey Archer and the like — and picture books that family had given them as presents over my lifetime, of New Zealand history and birds and animals. There was Buller's *Birds*, just as colourful as I had remembered it, with beautifully preserved plates of the kakapo and the kokako, and the books I had read to Grandpa in those final months. It was in this library that I had first discovered the books that would lead me to where I was today. It wasn't hard, as a young teen, to imagine Magpie Hall in the place of Thornfield Hall and Wuthering Heights, myself always the heroine, dreaming that I too would find a great, passionate love. Perhaps it was in this very room that I had set myself up for perpetual disappointment.

Upstairs, I wandered about the bedrooms, opening dresser drawers, cupboards, not really sure what I was looking for. I wanted to at least cast my eye over everything before my fastidious aunts had it cleared out in a day, their eagle eyes lighting on anything of monetary value and the rest burned or donated to charity. Most of the cupboards were full of sixty years of accumulated stuff: linen, towels, endless stashes of recycled wrapping paper, envelopes. Gram and Grandpa had clearly never thrown anything out since they got married. Every time they bought something new they just stacked the new one in front of everything else: ancient vacuum cleaners, suitcases — one full of nothing but navy-blue pyjamas. In their room, Grandpa's Savile Row suits, barely worn, and a pile of exquisite vintage women's hats, which I carried back to my room.

I tried to straighten some of the clutter, dusting between objects and books, making a start on throwing out newspapers and magazines. Every surface was covered with *things*, whether it was books piled horizontally on mantelpieces or clothes lying over chairs. In the middle of cursing the mess I realised that one day someone would do the same for me and be just as appalled by my accumulation of a lifetime's worth of stuff.

I didn't think of myself as a hoarder, though. I was a collector. Not just of tattoos but of vintage clothes and accessories, antique china, books, shells, birds' nests — the list went on. One wall of my bedroom was devoted to pictures of the tattooed circus ladies of old. They either stared defiantly at the camera while displaying their ink, their faces sometimes beautiful, sometimes plain, or they were depicted by full-colour paintings in posters advertising their extraordinary illustrated bodies and the myths that accompanied them. My whole flat was also stuffed full, every horizontal and vertical surface covered. It encased me, made me feel safe and small. I dreaded to think that one day Roland would close the tattoo parlour and I would have to pack everything up and move it.

My flatmate Rita complained about the clutter, but I knew it was what made her fall in love with the place and move in. She felt more at home in my flat overlooking the port than she had anywhere. She worked two nights a week at a little cabaret bar around the corner in what was built as a movie theatre in the 1930s. The rest of the time she seemed to sleep; what little money she earned she eked out on cigarettes and endless pots of tea. We shared cheap bottles of red wine on Sunday nights and she told me stories in her sing-song voice about the weekend's mishaps and adventures. The cabaret was a favourite haunt for the artists and students who lived around the port and for the swing kids who'd come in from over the hill on a

Wednesday for some social dancing, dressing as their grandparents did during the Second World War. It also attracted sailors from the boats, many of them Russian.

Rita had an abundance of pale skin, and she lolled around the flat draped in a silk kimono that had trouble staying shut. She had just one tattoo, Japanese style, which rolled its way from one shoulder, across her back, to the other, waves that danced with fish and flecks of foam, in rich blues and blacks. She squeezed her ample flesh into corsets for her burlesque act; by day, when she could drag herself out, she dressed like a 1950s diner waitress or a Hitchcock blonde, with high heels and tight woollen suits, her bleached hair immaculately coiffed.

Occasionally Rita brought people back to the flat after one of her shows. She didn't have boyfriends — she 'took lovers'. And these lovers were frequently the transients who came through the port, which suited her fine. Even I had a boyfriend for a week from one of the many that she brought home with the promise of a party, a Russian sailor with a tattoo on his bicep of a heart with a dagger sticking into it and a drop of blood. The name *Tatiana* was written underneath. I asked him about her one morning as we lay in bed and listened to the foghorns calling from the port. 'She *cut* my heart,' he said. The word 'cut' knifed the space between us and he would say nothing more about her.

Mikhail and his friend stopped at the tattoo parlour before they left but Roland refused to give them the Maori design they wanted. When he tried to explain that they had to earn it, they looked at him as if he were deceiving them, although they weren't sure how or why. They left, stopping on the footpath outside to shout something in angry Russian at him. 'Friends of yours?' asked Roland. In truth, I was glad to see the back of Mikhail and after that I avoided Rita's new friends. I changed the sheets and forgot about him.

The damp from the rain began to seep into the house, rising up from the basement and penetrating the walls. I could taste it in the air.

In the upstairs hallway a narrow door opened onto an equally narrow staircase that led to the attic. As children, we were not allowed up there because of the dust and the precarious accumulation of ephemera, but we had sneaked up when we could and invented games of escaping from orphanages and finding treasure. The closest thing to treasure chests were old leather trunks still carrying stickers from the many voyages in my grandparents' and their parents' past, but they contained nothing that could interest a child, just more linen, photographs, junk. Now, looking at all the gathered objects, they lost some of their wonder and became what they were: the lives of my family, stuffed into boxes.

Something was eating at the edges of my memory — a rainy afternoon in the attic, with Charlie. A huge painting of a woman in white, leaning with its face to the wall, as if hiding. A trunk filled with old clothes, carefully wrapped in blue tissue paper, which we raided for dress-ups, Gram shooing us away from it with a gardening fork in her hand. My brother, wearing a top hat, giggling his way down the stairs, while I tripped and fell after him, bruising my hip. Someone else, behind me, picking me up and half-carrying me the rest of the way while Gram thundered down the stairs after us.

I went further into the attic, shuffled some boxes around. Some of them toppled and Christmas decorations, shedding tinsel where they landed, spilled onto the dusty ground. As I moved the boxes, I uncovered piece by jigsaw piece of the large portrait that leaned against the wall. Its heavy gilt frame, the colour of hokey-pokey and rough to touch, was dulled by dust. I sneezed as I picked it up and heaved it closer to the stairwell, where the light was better.

A woman stared out of the painting, the expression on her face demure but with a hint that she might be hiding something. To me, even the placement of her hands looked furtive — they were crossed, her left hand grasping the wrist of her right, in which she held an open fan. Long gloves almost covered her arms. Her white gown, in the late Victorian style, was for the evening, exposing more flesh than would have been seemly during the day, but the fan shielded her, as though she were trying to hide behind it, or at least to project a false modesty. Only the skin on her long neck and pale face was visible. Her hair fell in blonde ringlets around her cheeks.

Could it be Dora, Henry's first wife? Yes, quite possibly. I *wanted* it to be her, and I could see no reason why it wouldn't be. After all, the portrait was in the attic, not on display, as if banished here by a jealous second wife all those years ago.

I opened one of the trunks and felt the excitement, the exquisite sense of potential, that I always get when walking into a vintage clothing store. It was a treasure trove: a fox fur, complete with little paws crossed elegantly; 1940s crêpe dresses with intricate beading, in mourning black and daytime mauve; chemises, petticoats and corsets. Thick silk gloves with pearl buttons.

I knew there was a reason I had been made so small and slight: it was so I could fit into antique clothes. So many of my taller friends had to resort to making their own clothes in the vintage style, whereas I had always been able to wear the real thing.

Towards the bottom of the trunk I found silk. I pulled it out, scrapping with the tissue, and clasped the dress to my body, measuring its tiny waist against mine. Yes, quite possibly, I thought. With some effort, I put it on. It was snug, but it fitted me. I gathered the skirts together and went downstairs to my room, where there was a full-length mirror inside the wardrobe door.

There was no doubt that it was the dress from the painting. Dora and I must have been the same height, but there the similarities ended. My rumpled, bobbed hair was much darker, and the tattoos were vibrant and sharp on my arms — the flowers, the magpie, the horseshoe, the mermaid, the cursive script. The dress was low enough to expose the bluebirds on my chest, the ribbon in their beaks. I put on the gloves. They weren't as long as the ones from the painting, but they came above my elbows. I remembered seeing a fan in my grandmother's dressing table and after I had retrieved it, I stood in front of the mirror again. I assumed Dora's pose and examined the results. The fan covered the bluebirds, and if the gloves had been longer they would have covered the only tattoos visible now on my upper arms. If I had been painted like that, nobody would have known that I had any marks on my body at all.

I stood there for a long time, looking at myself, imagining I was Dora. The room was cold and my skin was goosebumping, making me shiver. I imagined her ghost passing through me, how it must feel, being the ghost of a house that should have been filled with her descendants but where she would instead always be the first wife, the one who never made it . . . at worst, murdered, at best, drowned.

I thought of the women who had come before me, who had died at Magpie Hall. Perhaps I had done the right thing by coming here to try and work on my thesis after all: the house was offering up its ghosts as characters, itself as a setting, and if that couldn't inspire me to finally peel apart and understand those great nineteenth-century novels I had loved for so long, then what could?

The room was getting darker; the rain closed in further. It thrummed on the roof like giant's fingers. I almost didn't hear the car pulling up outside, but there it was, tyres sizzling in the puddles.

As I descended the wide staircase, clad in Dora's dress, I thought of *Rebecca*, of the new Mrs de Winter appearing at the party dressed as the ancestral portrait and unknowingly as the wife she has replaced. I imagined all eyes turned towards me, the look of shock and confusion on Maxim's face. Mrs Danvers, the housekeeper, sneering at me from the door of the west wing.

It was Hugh. He was already out of the car, standing with a newspaper over his head and gazing up at the house when I opened the front door.

'Missy!' He was shouting over the rain. 'What are you doing?'

'Minding my own business. What are you doing?' I swung on the door, half hid my body behind it, neither blocking him entirely nor coming to greet him. I wondered if he had dressed up for me. With his black suit and white shirt, a tie flapping from his pocket, he looked like an undertaker. The suit was rapidly darkening at the shoulders.

'Funeral.'

A second of panic and, to my shame, of hope. 'Whose?'

'An old colleague. You wouldn't know him. It was a long time coming.' He moved away from the barrier of his mud-splattered Japanese car, and put one foot on the steps leading up to the front porch. Mud also marred his otherwise shiny shoes. 'Are you going to invite me in? It's a bit wet out here.'

'What are you doing here, Hugh?'

He walked up onto the porch, out of the rain, fiddling with the wayward tie. His breath whistled in his nose. 'You left so abruptly. Can't we talk about it?'

'I'm working.'

He smiled, suddenly reptilian. 'Sure you are. What's with the fancy dress?'

I sighed. 'Fine. Suit yourself.' I walked back into the house, leaving the door ajar for him. My dress scraped the ground, dragged at my legs. I wandered into the kitchen and poured myself a glass of last night's red wine.

Hugh moved with the sureness of a taller and more handsome man, and stared at me with such concern and affection in his face that tears gathered in my eyes. I turned my back on him and busied myself with the cap on the wine.

He came up behind me and put his hands on my shoulders. 'What's up?' he whispered. I just shook my head and kept my back to him, looking out the window at the stormy day. In the distance I saw a quad bike moving over one of the paddocks. Please God, I thought, don't let it be Sam on his way over.

Hugh had wanted to come to Grandpa's funeral with me. Well, not *with* me, but he wanted to be there for me. I wouldn't let him; it was too risky. I didn't want to see him there and not be able to talk to him or touch him, and I didn't want my parents to see us together and ask questions. They knew who he was — I had spoken about him and pointed him out to them long before the affair began. But he knew how close I had been to Grandpa and I had been touched that he wanted to make some gesture, however small. Even so, his absence, when others in my family had their wives or boyfriends with them, stung me. I knew then that it would always be this way with Hugh, him hovering around some aspects of my life, and it wasn't enough.

I poured him a glass of wine and held it out to him. He took it. A finger snaked out from his free hand to fiddle with the embroidery on the bodice of my dress, but I took a step back.

'Where'd you get it?' he asked. 'You look like the ghost of weddings past.'

'You think this is a wedding dress?'

He shrugged. 'How would I know?'

'I found it, in the attic. I don't know, but I think it belonged to a woman who once lived here. The *first* woman to live here.'

He took a sip of his wine, still staring at the dress — at least, that was probably his excuse. More likely, he was taking the opportunity to look unashamedly at my body.

'I thought you said you were working? Though I suppose this is a bit like work for you. Trying to inhabit your characters, perhaps? Making up Gothic stories about people long dead?'

'You wouldn't understand.' I brushed past him. He followed me.

We sat in the living room, drinking wine in the middle of the day, and it felt as though we were on holiday. We had never been in a building entirely alone — we had met in offices and houses occupied by others who might show up at any time — and I dropped my guard. Hugh made a move towards me, touched my sternum with the back of his fingers, stroking the bluebirds, and the tingling there obliterated all rational thought. He took my glass from my hand, slowly and deliberately placing it on the small table beside him. I closed my eyes and gave in to the warmth. Soon he was kissing me and his hands were on my cheeks, in my hair, and I was telling myself to stop, but I couldn't. I felt a mild disgust that it was not long since I had been here on this couch with Sam. How different the smell of the two men: Sam was all earth and lanolin; Hugh smelt of warm paper, fresh from the photocopier. He was so much more familiar and knew how to touch me, just how I liked it, soft caresses and kisses, building up as my blood turned warmer and I felt it run all through my body.

Our sounds escaped through the house, where there was nobody to hear us and it was so liberating I forgot that he wasn't supposed to be here, not at Magpie Hall, not on my grandparents' couch, not inside me.

Afterwards, I lay with my face on his chest and his lips in my hair. The gloves had come off, but I still wore Dora's dress. It felt right, and yet I knew that it was last place I should be. I gathered myself together, drawing out the moment that I knew I had to end.

'This house is fantastic,' said Hugh. 'I had no idea it was so grand. What kind of madman would build a castle like this in the middle of New Zealand?'

'It's not really a castle. It just has some similarities.'

'Hey, I'm not criticising. I like it, a lot. But it's bloody freezing in here. And look, up there — there are huge damp patches on the ceiling. This is in serious need of renovation. It must be practically unliveable as it is.'

I sat up.

'It's fine as it is,' I said. I hadn't told him about the renovation plans, and yet here he was, on their side.

'But what a waste it would be just to let it crumble into the ground. Don't you think?' He took me by the shoulders and looked at me.

I shook him off. 'You have to go.'

'Yeah, okay. You don't want to talk about it, fine. I'd better be getting back anyway.'

'That's not what I mean. I've left you. You're not supposed to be here.'

'You're serious about it, then.'

'Of course I'm serious. Fuck, Hugh, just give me a bit of respect, okay? You can't just turn up here when you feel like it and expect me to just fall back into your arms.'

He smirked. 'Right.' He put his hands on my waist and tried to pull me back down on top of him.

I thumped him ineffectually on the chest and jumped up. 'God, I'm such an idiot! Just go. Just leave.' As I turned from him, towards the west window, I saw something. A figure, by the window, stepping away. My heart leapt.

'Shit, did you see that?'

Hugh heard the shock in my voice, must have seen my face, because he was on his feet. 'What was it?'

'Someone outside, watching us.' He was moving towards the window and had it open before I could even begin to imagine who it might be. And how long they had been there. I felt sick. I couldn't even say whether it had been a man or a woman. I hadn't had a good look at them, just a sense of a person, a shadow left behind in the air. Before I could say anything, or feel anything, Hugh had climbed out the window and disappeared.

I sat down, crossed my arms over my stomach and leaned forward, closing my body. At least in our fervour we hadn't bothered to take our clothes off completely, apart from my underpants, which lay forlornly on the floor, an insubstantial scrap of nothing. My hand shook slightly as I put them back on.

Hugh came back through the kitchen.

'There's nobody there. Did you get a look at them? Know who it might be?'

I stood, shook my head, frowned. 'I didn't just imagine it, you know.'

'Hey, calm down.' He held out his palms, motioned for me to sit down. 'I'm not saying you did. Although you might have been reading too many novels. A *Turn of the Screw* moment, perhaps.'

I hated to admit that he was right about that, so I said nothing.

'Well, look.' He sat down on the couch and put his arm around me, rubbing. 'Whoever it was isn't there now, and there weren't any obvious footprints outside or anything. You'd think there'd be something in this rain, but maybe they washed away.'

I couldn't tell from his voice whether he was humouring me or not. I was beginning to feel silly. Perhaps I had seen a lock of my own hair out of the corner of my eye. Or a bird flying past. A magpie.

He stopped rubbing and held me tighter. 'There was something, though. Don't panic.'

Another lurch in my stomach.

'There's a dead possum on the kitchen doorstep. That does seem a bit odd.'

I was quiet for a moment, trying to grasp what it might mean, and how to say it to Hugh. 'Do you think someone's left it there?' For some reason, I was whispering.

'Don't be ridiculous. Why would anyone do that? It was probably sick, and died there. Or a dog killed it.'

I couldn't bring up the fact that Sam had brought me a dead rabbit without explaining him. Hugh had once said that I collect men like tattoos, and I wouldn't give him the satisfaction.

The question that plagued me was this: Was it a taxidermy gift or something less friendly? For my sanity, I had to believe it was the former, but I hardly knew Sam, and I didn't know what he was capable of. For a moment I considered asking Hugh to stay, but the idea that I needed him to protect me was repellent. And he would no doubt have to get back to his family, so any comfort would be short-lived.

'You're probably right,' I said. 'And maybe I *did* imagine someone at the window. Sorry. I guess I'm a bit uptight. We shouldn't have done that, it's not helping things.'

'Come back with me,' he said suddenly, grabbing my arms, pinning them to my sides. 'I'll drop you home. It's too isolated out here. You'll go crazy.' He smiled. '*More* crazy.'

I shrugged him off. 'Fuck you. You're the stalker who followed me out here. Who's the crazy one?'

His smile vanished. 'Suit yourself. I was worried about you, that's all.'

'Bullshit. You just wanted to have sex. If you really cared about me we wouldn't be in this mess.'

'It's not a mess.'

'Oh, no, sorry.' My voice was bitter. 'Not for you. It's quite tidy and convenient, isn't it? Well, I for one can't keep doing this to your wife and kids.'

'Honestly, Rosemary, you go on and on like you're this martyr, when you know perfectly well that you're involved with a married man. You walked into this with your eyes open, and you keep blaming it all on me. So why do you keep doing it?'

'That's just what I'm trying to figure out. On my own.' It took all my willpower and moral strength, what was left of it, to push him towards the door.

Henry

It is raining the day he arrives at Redstream, the Collins estate, a comfortably sized wooden house surrounded by rolling hills. The carriage takes him up a long avenue lined with young oaks and for a moment he imagines himself in Herefordshire; the landscape is pasture and farmland, with no sign of the dramatic native bush he has been exploring. He had expected to be away longer, but the cold weather forced him and Schlau to turn back to town after only two weeks. There will be plenty of time to explore when the spring deepens and the temperatures rise. He was not sorry to see the back of Schlau, but the guide had surprised him by clasping his hand warmly and wishing him all the best.

Henry tries to dampen down his disappointment in this pastoral landscape: instead of interesting indigenous birds, he is greeted by the flecces of dirty sheep; closer to the house, horses graze in a meadow and a train of ducklings follows its mother. Only some rocky cliffs in the distance add interest to the view — limestone by the pale colour, he anticipates — and he imagines the fossils and bones that might be waiting there to be discovered.

Well-tended gardens surround the house, early rhododendrons providing flashes of colour amid the greenery. As the carriage pulls up, Mr Collins himself emerges from inside, accompanied by two servants, who collect Henry's luggage. Collins, apparently more excited than usual, walks forward with his hand thrust out.

Your crates, sir, he says. They have arrived from England. I have had to fight my conscience not to open them and find out what wonders you have brought with you!

Henry is confused. But other than those I brought with me, I did not send for any crates, he says.

Mr Collins's smile drops and he looks uncertain. But . . . I assure you, Mr Summers, they were addressed to you, in my care. Might not your father have arranged to send them?

Of course, thinks Henry. His father. How had he been so blind? All this time he has been telling himself he is here to collect specimens to take back to England, where he will resume his life. But what had his father said to him that day? *You will continue to receive your remittance, as long as you stay there.* This delivery is a reminder that he has made no empty threats.

❦

He stands at the window of his room, which affords him a view of the house entrance and the long driveway. He excused himself early with a headache. He had to be alone, to douse his face and hair with cool water from his basin.

As he looks out across the countryside he thinks: Could I live here? Could I really make a life here?

It is preposterous. Of course he couldn't. So removed from the Royal Society, from Europe and from his friends. He is not built for the colonial life, to settle far away and live out his days dreaming of Home. How will he travel, beyond the surrounding Pacific? It is out of the question.

And yet. How is he to live? His father provides him with a very handsome income. How would he survive without it? He sees a vision of himself, reduced to living the life of someone like Schlau, mounting animals for inferior museums and trying desperately to sell specimens and artefacts he has sunk to the depths of immorality to acquire. He has enough of a collection to provide him with a good income for a little while, but after that has gone, then what? The collector in him strains against such a thought — if he sells his collection, he will no longer be able to look at his treasures, remember the dangers he encountered to seek them out. He will be left only with a dwindling pocket of coins. Only his tattoos will remind him, for they at least cannot be taken away.

A horse approaches the house at a canter. The female rider, sitting astride, pulls to a sudden halt and leaps off her mount. Even from here Henry can see that Dora's cheeks are flushed from the exertion and exhilaration of her ride; he notices that her skirts — split to resemble trousers — are wet, as though she has been riding her horse through the nearby river. A servant approaches to lead the horse away but she dismisses him with a wave of her hand, takes the reins herself and walks with the animal in the direction of the stables. She wipes at her brow. Henry loses sight of her as she passes beneath his window and around the house.

His spirits lift at the sight of her, but he is also overcome with a sudden tiredness from his long journey. He lies down on a comfortable bed and promptly falls asleep.

⁂

At dinner, he enquires after Dora, but it seems that he and Mr and Mrs Collins are to eat alone. It is a sad table, thinks Henry, despite the jollity of Mr Collins. He gathers that he has only recently married his wife, a timid woman in her thirties with a face resembling a sparrow's. Dora is his only child and she never knew her mother, who died during childbirth. Henry supposes that the new Mrs Collins is young enough to provide her husband with some more children, but he doesn't imagine they will make handsome offspring together. Collins is stout and balding, with a tendency to crinkle his face like a cabbage when he smiles. Dora's mother must have provided the good looks of the family.

The talk turns to Henry's crates and what they might contain. Henry finds himself replying to questions automatically; he can dredge up stories of his adventures appropriate for any company and in the Collinses he has a captive audience, but he finds himself yawning before pudding is served. He is eager to find out what his father has sent to him; no doubt he just packed up the contents of Henry's study — his cabinet of curiosities — or perhaps he has included only the cream of the collection, in which case Henry will have an excuse to return. But it can wait until morning.

And have you decided how long you plan to stay in New Zealand? Mr Collins asks. Henry thinks he is fishing for information, perhaps even for a scandal; the whole business with the crates and Henry's reaction has no doubt set his gossip fire alight.

I'm not sure, Henry says, and takes another gulp of wine. His head is beginning to feel warmer with the alcohol, and he finds himself glad that Dora is not here to see him.

What if I were to stay here? What would you suggest a man in my position do with himself?

Collins beams at him and rubs his hands together. *Well*, he says. Where to begin? I can't sing the praises of our little community enough. I grew up, as you know, in Surrey and spent much of my youth in London. I was drawn here by all the talk of the 'wool kings' of the South Island, and the fantastic wealth they were accumulating. And I can tell you sir, I was not disappointed. There is money to be made here, if that is what you — here he hesitates, to find the polite word — *desire*.

Not *need*, Henry notices.

Collins continues. With the society that has been built here we have everything we want. All the money we need, and all the comforts. Servants, good food, fine clothes. A peaceful country life with plenty of social activity, and a positively energetic life in the city, with balls, opera, theatre, even a racecourse — and any manner of entertainment that a gentleman could wish for.

He flicks a sideways look at his wife but she seems to not have noticed his implication; indeed Henry is not sure if he has grasped it himself, though he thinks he knows what his host means. He has already helped himself to the services available to gentlemen, in a dimly lit wooden house in one of those streets named after an English county.

In short, sir, Collins continues, one can build a splendid life here, perhaps even more splendid than in England if one invests one's money wisely, in the right kind of station. We have built a new version of England. I know that we all talk of Home and how we long to return, but I have heard of men going back there to live out their final years and yearning for the life here instead. They die dreaming of New Zealand.

While all the vulgar talk of money is distasteful to Henry — he has been raised to take the existence of money for granted and never to speak of it — Collins has given him plenty to think about. He retires for the evening. When he lies in bed, the semblance of a plan begins to formulate in his head. For if he could escape his father, create independent wealth for himself, he could stay here for a few years then release himself back into the wilds of the world, a free man in every sense.

⁂

Collins has had the crates assembled in the library on the south side of the house, where it is cool and dark. He hovers around, hoping to glimpse each treasure as it emerges, but Henry asks if he can be alone. As long as the crates are unopened, his life has not taken a turn for the worse. His collection is the one thing in the world that gives him a reason for living. To have it here, in New Zealand, feels like the sealing of this country's status as his new home. It is not a moment Henry wishes to rush into.

He sits in the gloom for a long time, staring at the wooden containers — his life, reduced to a few boxes sitting on the rug in a foreign country. The room is encased in bookshelves; the books have uniform leather covers, no doubt bought by the yard to give the appearance of a learned household. He wonders if anyone even reads out here.

Finally he stands and moves around the crates, hammer in hand. The first plank makes a groaning sound and flecks of sawdust fall to the carpet. This crate is well packed at least. His cases of insects and small reptiles have all been included and it is with some difficulty that he pulls them out. He opens each drawer slowly, to check the state of the specimens and to enjoy them. Here is the rare *Cithaerias aurorina*, with its transparent wings and their spots of bright pink. He remembers how he twisted his ankle on a tree root and the pain didn't register until he had the butterfly in his net. Here are his lizards — those big enough to mount but small enough to fit in the drawers. Any smaller and he would preserve them in jars. Arachnids both poisonous and harmless, hard-shelled coleoptera, suspended with outstretched legs, seemingly ready to crawl out and make New Zealand their new home. Everything is perfectly intact.

In another crate, one of his jars has broken and the sickening odour of formaldehyde greets him as he opens it. He lifts the clammy body of the adder and lays it on the floorboards next to the rug, then carefully unwraps the remaining jars, which he lines up on the floor beside him. He finds his squid, more lizards, and his more gruesome curiosities: the foetus and the baby's feet, the other body parts. In the soft light of the library they almost look beautiful. He has never felt squeamish about them; he finds them fascinating, and was more than pleased when he persuaded his surgeon friend to obtain them for his collection.

He starts as the door to the library suddenly opens. He places his body between the jars and the doorway and glances back at the intruder. Dora Collins is halfway into the room before she even notices he is there.

Oh, forgive me, she says. I didn't know you were in here. She shows him the books she has in her hand; three of them, all bound in the same leather as the others. I was just returning these. I can come back.

No, please, Henry says. Do come in. He hastily packs the human specimens back into the crate and closes it.

Dora walks around the edge of the room to the far side, facing him always, as though scared to turn her back. She is dressed in simple white muslin, and it gives her a freshness, emphasising her youth, as does the wildness of her blonde hair.

Please ignore me, she says, and finally turns her back to retrieve the library ladder, which she places and mounts.

May I help you? asks Henry.

No thank you. It is quite stable. She steps up three or four rungs and replaces the books in the gaps they have left.

Henry continues with his job, aware of Dora stealing glances at him as she moves about the shelves, browsing for her next book. He discovers quickly that his prized possession, the tiger skin, is missing. He lets out a sigh. Perhaps it would have been easy enough to miss on the floor, but he suspects his father coveted it for himself, and now all the sweat and pride Henry poured into it is lost. It is a final insult. At least he still has his tattoo as a reminder.

The false mermaid is there, hideous though it is, and Henry leaves it sitting in the crate. Truth be told, he prefers the one he has on his bicep; it is certainly more pleasant to look at, with its womanly curves, the hint of a breast beneath long golden hair. But he couldn't resist having the hoax in his collection, even if just to celebrate the audacity of some people.

He has forgotten that Dora is in the room until she gives a strangled cry and slips from the ladder into a heap on the floor.

Are you all right? He takes her hand, and she pulls herself up in her own time.

So silly of me, she says. I'm so embarrassed.

But you are unhurt?

Yes, she assures him, although she is limping slightly as she walks to a chair and drops into it. Would you mind . . .? She gestures to the books that have fallen to the floor. He glances at their titles as he hands them back to her: *The Castle of Otranto, The Mysteries of Udolpho, Northanger Abbey*. Sensational nonsense, filled with castles in foreign lands and imprisoned maidens waiting to be rescued.

You like to read novels, I see.

Dora blushes and tries to hide the books in her skirts. They are just a diversion, she says. I do read other things as well. It's just that sometimes . . . sometimes I like to imagine I am somewhere other than New Zealand, with a life that is not all balls and picnics and the same people everywhere one turns. It can be quite suffocating at times. You can understand that, can you not, sir?

Oh, more than you can know. He chuckles.

We are so far from everything, she continues. It takes months to get to London by ship. Not to mention Europe, or other continents, which I can only dream of visiting.

I am fully aware of our geographical constraints, Miss Collins. In fact, I have just been dwelling on them myself.

Oh, but forgive me, she says. You have the world at your disposal I'm sure. You must tell me one day about your travels. Are they wonderful? Did you bring back wonderful things?

She is looking over his shoulder now, hopeful eyes scanning the crates until they alight on something.

Is that a snake? She puts her hand over her mouth. Oh, I long to see a real snake. But it looks so *alive*.

Henry has forgotten the snake, which lies coiled on the floorboards, looking fresh and meaty; its scales glow in the muted light. He is impressed by her curiosity; any of the ladies he knows in London would have screamed and thrown themselves out the door sobbing at the sight of a snake, dead or no.

I'm afraid it may have started to decay, says Henry.

Dora has risen from her chair, her limp forgotten, and has begun to move towards it.

Do not come any closer, please, he says.

She stops, hovering.

Would you like to look at something else? asks Henry.

She nods. Henry can't help thinking that her attitude towards him has changed since he saw her in the square by the cathedral. The fact that she did not appear for dinner seemed to confirm that she was avoiding him, but now she is all eagerness. He wonders if it is to do with his vast array of treasures, or, more likely, with the novels she has returned to the library, and the heroes within them.

Butterflies, he says. Jewels of the jungle. Just wait a moment.

He retrieves his drawers from the first crate and selects the collection of morphos he captured in the Amazon. They glisten behind their glass like sapphires.

Oh they are beautiful, she sighs. I have never seen such a creature. The only butterflies here are plain little things that are strangers to real colour. The Amazon, you say? Was it terribly dangerous?

Well, yes, actually, it was, he concedes. No more than your usual dangers, but they were plentiful enough.

Such as?

Let me see. The insects for one. Snakes. Crocodiles. Man-eating fish.

Dora's eyes seem to grow wider with every description. He continues, warming to his role of gallant adventurer.

The natives weren't always friendly. Then there were diseases. Cholera. Yellow fever. I caught malaria, and it plagues me still. Do not be alarmed, it is not contagious.

And why do you need so many?

I beg your pardon?

The butterflies. You have more than forty specimens here, and they are all the same. Why do you need to kill so many of them? Did you plan to sell them?

Well, I... He thinks for a moment before answering: The purpose of collecting is not to amass great numbers.

It isn't? I don't understand, given the evidence I see before me.

It's hard to explain. It's a hunger. Not for quantity but for different quality. To you, these butterflies all look the same. But I see forty very different creatures. One is not enough because collecting is all about the search for the perfect specimen, the specimen that represents the entire species perfectly.

And any number of these won't do this?

Oh, one might think so at first. And then one sees another that is bigger, or more symmetrical, or brighter, and one realises that the search has in fact only just begun. You will understand for yourself one day, Miss Collins, if you ever find something that you are passionate about collecting. You will not be able to get enough of whatever it is.

I can only hope, Mr Summers, she says, and smiles somewhat enigmatically. But as for these butterflies... I am in love with each and every one, so perhaps I am on my way. Although I would far rather see them flying about in the jungle with my own eyes than see them dead and halfway around the world. But I suppose that is something I really can only dream of.

We can all have what we want, if we set our mind to it, says Henry.

Do you think?

Just then they are interrupted by Mr Collins, who has walked past the slightly open door and pushed his head in.

Dora!

His daughter jumps. He gestures for her to come to him and she obeys. Collins closes the door behind them but Henry can hear him chastising her. Most improper, he hears.

The door opens again a moment later.

I apologise, Mr Summers. I trust my daughter has not been bothering you with her idle chatter. I'm afraid she reads too many novels. I know you wanted to be alone.

It is of no consequence, says Henry. I was just finishing my work anyway.

Collins pours himself into the room. And is it all to your satisfaction?

Mostly, says Henry. Would you like to have a look?

Collins' face breaks into a broad grin. It is just the invitation he has been waiting for.

※

Collins is an impeccable host. He asks few questions about Henry's intentions and seems to enjoy having him there to show off to a string of visitors. Life here is very much as it is in the English countryside: the neighbours call on each other at all times of the week, families and servants often in tow, and expect to be entertained, fed and given beds. They spend their days in the manner of the leisured classes anywhere: with picnics, shooting, game-playing and idle conversation, centring mostly on gossip about what is going on in town.

He has encountered no Maoris, and in this he is disappointed. Schlau has piqued his interest, there is no doubt, and he longs to meet them, to trade with them, to gaze upon their famous moko. It is as though they have been driven from the South Island altogether.

Perhaps in the north he will have more luck.

There is little sign of Redstream being a working farm — for the most part the stock and the workers are kept well away from the daily life of the house, as if the sight of an escaped sheep is likely to send the nearest ladies into fainting fits. Collins sets off on horseback for a few hours each morning, but speaks little of his business on his return: he has managers for every aspect of the running of the farm and its spoils. The only hint that Henry gets of any difficulty is when dinner conversation with neighbours turns to the plague of rabbits threatening to destroy the pastures.

But this is fascinating, says Henry. The rabbits have been introduced from England, have they not? And they have no native predators? So the colonials have upset the natural order of things in this country.

He intends to ignite a conversation about natural history but the gathering sinks into a stony silence around him until someone else changes the subject. Evidently one can complain about the rabbits, but not about the probable cause of the problem. It is ridiculous. Nobody will meet his eye. Nobody, that is, except Dora. She gives him a smile and a nod, as if to say *I agree*. The effect on him is instantaneous. His breathing slows and he feels the blood that had been rushing to his face subside. Amazing, that this woman, that *any* woman, has the ability to calm him with only a glance. He must pay her more attention; undoubtedly there is something special about this girl. He returns the smile and their mutual gaze lingers.

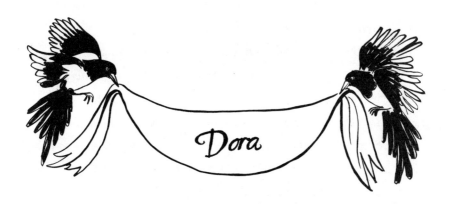

Dora

Dora is startled awake by her bed shuddering across the room. In the fog of sleep she thinks she is back on board the ship that she and her father took from England last year, but within moments she knows this is not so. The earth, which had been shrugging and sighing the evening before, has finally given in to its anger and heaves the wooden house from side to side. It creaks and groans; her washbasin falls from its stand and smashes. She curls into a ball and clutches her knees until it subsides.

The silence that follows seems to last forever. She finds herself wishing for her mother, a mother that she never knew, but it is her father who comes to her, bursting through the door, shouting, Dora Dora, are you hurt, are you all right?

He sits on the bed and she allows herself to be embraced by him as her feet find the freezing floorboards and she realises how cold the room has become in the night, with all her bedclothes shaken off by the earthquake. Her father holds her as he did when she was a little girl until her shivering subsides, while a dark shadow hovers around the door. Her stepmother.

She feels terrible then, that she is keeping secrets from him, but last night, when the last guests had left the ball, he had retired immediately and she and Henry had parted company, with him promising he would speak to her father in the morning.

Last night. At the ball, she watched Henry across the room as what seemed like all the women in the country paraded themselves past him. He spoke to a few of them, charmed them even, and they whispered to each other behind their fans as they walked away. But when it came to dancing he stood resolutely by the wall, observing them all, like a man unsure whether to feast with his eyes or turn away in boredom.

He looked up and saw her, and she did not look away. He had been a guest at her father's house for two weeks now, and she knew enough about him to be sure that he couldn't abide coyness. She had avoided him when he first arrived, she admits it now, but she knows how stupid she had been, how foolish and proud, just because of one night when he had drunk too much. She had been listening too closely to her friend Kate Johnson. It was their encounter in her father's library that made her rethink her opinion of him. After all, none of the men she had met in the neighbourhood or in town had impressed her. They all brayed on about Home, but half of them had never been to England and were happy to live their lives moving between country and town houses with their horsey laughs and their sunburnt foreheads, accumulating money and attending the same parties and races.

Mr Summers was very different from these men. For a start, he only spoke when he had something worthwhile to say. That day in the library she had watched him as he unpacked his wonderful collection, and instead of fidgeting and trying to make polite conversation about the weather with her, as so many of her potential suitors would have done, he ignored her completely. He seemed mesmerised by his work, as if each object he unwrapped transported him back to the time and place of its provenance. She felt infected by him, by his collection: it made her yearn to catch even a small glimpse of what he had seen and done to acquire such treasures. The sight of the adder lying so nakedly on the floorboards — *her* floorboards, in the house she had grown up in — made her want to kneel beside it, pick it up and wrap it around herself like a shawl.

Since that day, they had been spending more and more time together. Her father's initial disapproval relaxed, and he allowed her to take walks with Mr Summers to show him the pocket of bush by the river, where he could crouch beside fallen logs and plunge his little shovel into the loam, looking for insects. Her father implied that she should count herself lucky — back in England, young ladies were expected to be chaperoned at all times.

Mr Summers had accompanied her family on one or two picnics with neighbours, who had quizzed him mercilessly about his life back in England and his travels. He answered politely, and only she could see the vein that popped up in his neck as he spoke, the set of his jaw as he gritted his teeth. But just when she thought he was going to snap, he would find her gaze and it seemed to calm him.

She wondered if he looked upon the ball guests as he did upon a herd of wild animals, hyenas perhaps, gathered at a watering hole to drink and to scavenge what they could. She tried to see the scene through his eyes: Mrs Yates, dressed far too young for her age as usual, yellow feathers in her hair, preening like a cockatoo. Old Mr Dodds in the corner, looking for all the world like a rhinoceros with his jutting forehead, shoving ham and bread into his mouth not looking at anyone. The Whitter sisters standing whispering in their tight circle with large eyes and long, insubstantial limbs, like gazelles in the presence of a lion.

When Mr Summers approached her, she suppressed a smile.

I trust you are enjoying yourself? he asked.

She nodded. As well as can be expected, she said. These balls are all alike; the same people, the same gowns, the same music. Even the same conversation.

And you have been looking at me from over here. Don't think I haven't noticed. Do you think me handsome, is that it?

No, sir, she said.

Miss Collins, you have put a dagger through my heart. He placed his hand there, to prove it.

I can see that all these other ladies think you very handsome. Why do you not go and engage one to dance?

Oh, it is not in my nature to dance. You should know me by now — I am far too serious for such frivolities.

She was about to reply when she noticed the large vase of flowers beside her on a mantelpiece shivering as if it had a fever. Her head felt light for a moment and she reached out a hand to steady herself, catching Mr Summers' arm.

Did you feel that? she asked him, as she took her hand away, embarrassed. A look around the room told her nothing had changed: the dancers continued unaware and people still talked to one another as before.

I did, he confirmed, to her relief. A small tremor. I'm sure it is no cause for alarm.

Still, she was shaken, and the room became unbearably hot at that moment.

Are you all right? he asked. You are quite flushed. Do you need some air?

He escorted her onto the terrace outside, where the spring night was clear and bitingly cold. Everything was still, and the moonlight rested on the chestnut tree, making shapes in the bark. As a child she would lie in its shade for hours, staring at the patterns in the leaves and on the trunk. It was hard to imagine that only moments before, the land was moving of its own accord, however mildly.

You have to admit that this is beautiful countryside, said Henry.

But of course. I grew up here, Mr Collins, and I have had a very happy life.

But you desire something more.

Something of what you have had perhaps, yes.

What if I were to tell you that I desire some of what you have had, and that I propose to stay and make a life here?

I would say that I am very surprised. What she did not say, was that she was also very pleased.

I met a man in the post office the other day, perhaps you know him: a Mr East. He is a schoolmaster here, but like me, he has come from a good family in England and has . . . *decided* to make a life here. He is a very keen botanist and regularly sends his pupils home early so that he can go out collecting. Sometimes he even takes the children with him on nature walks, to teach them about the local flora.

Dora listened, wondering about the purpose of this conversation. She had heard of this Mr East, but never met him — he was a shy man, it was said, and did not attend many social functions, although he was single.

Henry continued. He told me about the collecting opportunities in these parts, not to mention the rest of the country, which I plan to explore by and by. He says there are moa bones to found readily, and the bones of an extinct animal are highly prized, especially in England. He has offered to introduce me to some other enthusiasts in the area, and to lead me in as many expeditions as I would like, to sites quite close to these parts.

His voice became quite high in his excitement. She felt a little cloud of disappointment, for although she was delighted he wished to stay, she was sorry he was not planning adventures further afield. Surely New Zealand could not compare with Africa, or Brazil. She had perhaps been hoping that it was not just the prospect of a few old bones that was making him stay.

And for this, you have decided to give up your life in England?

No, not to give it up. To postpone it. I have made up my mind to buy some land here, to build a house, perhaps, and to stay for as long as it takes.

As long as it takes?

To gain my independence.

Dora was confused.

He sighed and covered his face with his hands. It is complicated, he groaned. I am too ashamed to explain myself any further. But Miss Collins . . .

He surprised her by taking both her hands in his.

Make no mistake, I would like to find a way to make your wishes come true. We could stay here, just for a few years, and then we would be free to explore the world and all its wonders at will.

She felt a tremor run through her body. Mr Summers, she said, what is it you are saying to me?

I am saying that, if I can find myself suitable pastures to call home, I would like you to share them with me. As my wife.

There now, says her father, and he tries to settle her back in bed.

What time is it? she asks. I cannot possibly think of going back to sleep.

It is around half past four, he says. There will be no light for three hours, and you have not had enough sleep.

But what will you do?

I am going to check on the servants, and on our guests. A fine welcome to a new country this must be for Mr Summers!

I am coming with you, she says.

I forbid it. Her father is firm in his resolve, and she sinks back under the bedclothes.

Very well, she says, but I shan't sleep.

When he has gone, she can hear him walking about the house, and talking. She knows that Henry cannot come to her, but the peaceful sounds tell her he is unharmed. Against her predictions, she falls into a light sleep, and when the dawn seeps into her room, she gets up quickly to look out at the surrounding countryside.

The first thing she sees is a fissure that has opened up in the ground not twenty feet from the house. It has travelled through her beloved chestnut tree, and torn it in two.

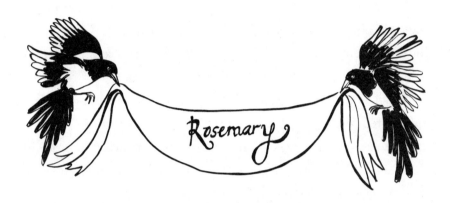

Rosemary

I listened until the engine of Hugh's car was indiscernible from the noise of the rain and the distant roar of the river. I hadn't left the house in two days, and much as I loved it, with Hugh gone its spaces and dark rooms — the relentless cold — were unsettling me. Hugh was right: I had been immersing myself in my material too much, thinking about Henry and Dora, the family ghosts, and now the face at the window, straight out of a horror story.

Even though the rain was still falling, I needed to get out. I wrestled my feet into the gumboots by the back door and put on Grandpa's big oilskin raincoat, which reached almost to my knees.

I'd forgotten about the possum and nearly tripped over it when I opened the door. I couldn't deal with it right then, so I left it there and went out into the stormy afternoon. I ran through mud and puddles, nearly tripping over knotty tufts of grass that had risen in the sludge. I didn't really think about where I was going, but ended up on one of my well-worn paths — over the paddock to the Magpie Pool, from where a path wended its way alongside the river for a good kilometre. We used to ride the horses that way and in the summer always ended by pulling the saddles off and swimming in the pool.

The river had risen, fat and swollen, fed by the torrential rain. I could see how easy it would be to slip and be swept away. One minute you'd be there, the next carried, tumbling, to who knew where. I pictured Dora, an icy hand stretched out, then gone.

I walked upriver, skidding on the slick grass. The rain on my face invigorated me, just as I'd hoped. In the paddocks, sheep huddled under trees, and a crowd of magpies strutted about. A murder of black and white crows. And they looked murderous, fixing me with their shiny eyes. I counted them: seven. As I got closer, they became agitated, walking back and forth, stopping as if to confer with each other, and then breaking apart. Several of them lifted their wings and rose into the air.

I stopped, feeling uneasy. I turned back the way I had come, but it was too late: the magpies made their move. My hood had come down and I felt the wind from their wings on the back of my neck, heard their ugly cackle as they swooped towards me and away. I slipped again on the grass and this time I went down. My arm was an ineffectual shield as one bird became bold and dived at me. A sharp pain on my head drove me to get up and to try and run, but the magpie's claws had become tangled in my sodden hair, and scratched at my scalp. I screamed, more from fright than from pain, but I managed to push at the creature with my hands and it came free. As it prepared to come back for another attack, I heard a loud bang nearby, which echoed in the valley before being absorbed by the sound of the river.

The magpies retreated. I stood up and wiped my face with a muddied hand. I looked around for the source of the noise and saw Sam walking over the paddocks towards me, a shotgun in his hand.

I didn't run to him, just turned my back and waited for him to get to me, feeling idiotic.

'Are you okay?' I felt a hand on my arm as he pulled me around to face him.

'I'm fine. Thanks.' We had to shout over the roar of the river. I looked down at his hand gripping me and he dropped it.

'They can get mean, those buggers. Oh shit.'

He was looking at my hair, so I put my hands up to feel it and they came away smeared with watery blood.

'You've got a bit there.' He pointed at my forehead and I wiped at it ineffectually.

'You're just smearing it around now. Let's get you back to the house and take a look at it. It might not be too bad — heads bleed a lot, that's all. But we should take a look just to make sure.'

I couldn't argue with him. It would be impossible for me to look at my own head. I needed him.

'What are you doing out here with a gun anyway? Jesus, did you try and shoot them while they were attacking me?'

He snorted. 'Of course not. I'm not that stupid. I just fired a warning shot. Punched a hole in the clouds, as my old man used to say. Good for making it rain.'

Despite myself, my stinging scalp, I smiled.

'So what have you been shooting? Possums?'

'Rabbits. They come out when the rain stops. Little bastards. You want some? You could make a rabbit army. Guard you from the magpies.'

I didn't know why I had worried about him being menacing.

He was the picture of joviality. I wouldn't go so far as to say he was my hero, but there was no denying that he had rescued me.

'Thanks for this,' I said.

He picked up my hand and squeezed it, and I let him hold it all the way back to the house, although it felt awkward. We walked around to the back door, where the possum still lay. I said nothing, waiting for Sam to react in some way. He just opened the door and stepped right over it, casually saying, 'Another one of your projects?'

I stopped in the kitchen and studied his face. 'You didn't leave that there?' I asked.

'No,' he said.

'And that wasn't you at the window earlier?'

'Window? What, spying on you?'

I said nothing and my jaw went tight.

He laughed, but it was mirthless. 'Shit, you're serious. What do you think I am? Why would I spy on you when you give it away freely?'

'Forget it,' I said. 'Can you look at my head now?'

He pushed me into a chair at the kitchen table and turned on the light.

'Let's see . . .' His fingers parted my wet hair. 'It doesn't look too bad . . . a few scratches —'

'Ow!' I jerked my head away.

'Sorry. There's a bit of a bigger gash here. Looks like you've been pecked. I don't think it needs a stitch. I'll give it a good clean, though. You never know what nasties they might carry.'

He left me sitting there while he rummaged in the downstairs bathroom. He seemed comfortable in the house, almost as if he'd grown up here. He emerged shortly with cotton wool and disinfectant.

After he had washed the wound, he looked satisfied. He had

taken off his raincoat and without asking went and lit the fire. I said nothing as I watched him, not sure whether to ask him to stay or go.

'Jesus, this house is freezing,' he said. 'Why don't you ever light the fire?'

I shrugged. 'Too much work. Lazy.'

'Your grandfather always had it lit. At least, when he was well. I suppose he didn't need to at the end.'

'Did you visit him here?'

'Sure, sometimes.' He hung his coat over the back of a chair and pushed it towards the fire. I was still wearing mine. The dress looked ruined, smeared with mud and a few drops of pink — blood mixed with rain. What an idiot I was, so anxious to get out I'd probably ruined a family heirloom. I was shivering.

'Look,' I said, 'I've got to go and get changed out of these wet things.'

He looked at my dress. 'I'd say that's wise. What have you got on there? You do wear the strangest things. Is this a city girl thing? You're on a farm now, love. Your wedding dress isn't really going to cut it.'

I didn't answer, just stood there waiting for him to take the hint and go, but he didn't move either, just rocked on his heels, warming his hands by the fire.

'So . . .' I said.

'Got anything to drink?' he asked. 'Any more of that whisky? That'll warm us up.'

I folded my arms. I wanted to take the wet raincoat off but I didn't want him to see the full effect of my outfit. 'I've got work to do. Reading. Thanks anyway. For helping me.'

'What are you reading?' Stalling.

I sighed. '*Jane Eyre*, okay?'

'Mad woman in the attic, eh? That's you, I reckon. Especially with that dress.'

He was pleased at having another chance to impress me but I was becoming bored with the game. I also didn't like the implication that he knew I'd been in the attic. I ignored his question. My silence unsettled him. He shifted from foot to foot in his socks.

'Just go, okay? I can't deal with this right now.'

He grabbed my hand and I wrenched it away.

'Is your boyfriend still here?' he asked. 'Is that what the problem is?' He stood close to me and I finally placed the smell that had been coming off him. Under the stale tobacco, he smelled of clay after rain.

'So you *did* see me with someone. That *was* you, looking in the window. What about the possum? Was that your little gift?' I felt a surge of adrenaline.

'I told you it wasn't. I saw his car pull up. Some guy in a fancy suit. Dressed up for you, did he?'

I didn't like his tone and started to back away.

'Two guys in one day, is that your style? One soft, one rough?' His eyes were red, and I wondered if he'd got stoned before going out to shoot rabbits. I folded my arms and stared at him.

'I'm sorry, okay.' He didn't sound sorry, but at least the threat had gone from his voice. 'I'll go. You don't have to worry about me any more. Have fun with the magpies.' He spun around and marched out the kitchen door, then turned back, holding the possum by the scruff of its neck.

'You should really get this in the freezer before the flies come around.' He tossed it and it landed with a thud in front of me, eyes bulging. He shoved his feet into his gumboots and must have kicked something over when he got outside, which clattered down the steps.

I locked the back door and hung my raincoat on its hook, then paced around the ground floor, making sure all the curtains were drawn shut and the other doors locked. Only when I heard Sam's quad bike start up and roar back up the hill did I sit down and cry. What a fuck-up, I told myself. I never should have invited him over in the first place. I thought about calling Josh, but I didn't want the fact that I'd slept with Sam to get back to my parents, or to have Josh ask me too many questions. Truth was, I was avoiding him too. I hadn't talked to him in years, and I didn't want to have to be the spokesperson for the family, to have him glare at me, judge me, when it wasn't my decision to sell up. I had lasted this long without seeing him, and wanted to keep it that way.

The intense sunsets that had punctuated the last few evenings had retreated under the dreary clouds and night fell suddenly. I sat in the murky kitchen, lit only by the glow of the stove, gathering myself. When the fire began to dim, I stirred my stiff body, dropped another log through the stove door and went upstairs to change into something warm and dry.

Back at my desk I wrote for hours, gripped by a renewed vigour for my writing. I worked wrapped in a heavy blanket to stave off the cold. My hands on the keyboard were freezing. About two in the morning I got up and made myself a sandwich and a cup of tea, as much to warm my stiff fingers as to have a drink. The window above the sink had no blind on it and I tried to stare out into the blackness but saw only myself reflected back, hair wild, with a hobo's rug around my shoulders. I was my own madwoman in the attic. Even in the middle of the night the idea that someone was watching me from outside grew in my head, and as I strained to listen for any tell-tale noises over the hum of the kettle, I flicked off the light to stand in the dark.

Later, when I was spent, and my fingers on the keyboard had locked up uncomfortably, I piled the blankets on the bed and went to sleep with the sound of the rain hammering the windows and roof. Somewhere, the walnut tree tapped against the side of the house. Behind it all, I heard the rush of the river.

All these sounds invaded my dreams, which swirled and spun with images and colours that I couldn't catch onto. I lay in bed listening to the walnut branch, and yet I knew I was still dreaming because the room was filled with outlandish shapes and shadows cast by a light I knew didn't exist. The tapping advanced and receded, and finally came closer, until it reached my window. I thought the sound would drive me mad, so I went to find some way to stop it. The clasp wouldn't budge but, seized by the need to silence the tree, I knocked my elbow through the glass and reached out into the night to grab the branch. Instead, my fingers closed over an ice-cold hand. I tried to draw my arm back, but the hand clung on. A girl's face swam into view before me, but before she spoke, I knew what she was going to say, for I had read this scene many times.

'Let me in, let me in!' the girl sobbed. Her face was pale and her dark eyes squinted against the rain.

'Who are you?' I asked, even though I knew what she was going to answer — Cathy Earnshaw.

'Why, Rosie,' she said, and her grip on my hand tightened, 'don't you remember me? Have you forgotten already?'

I stared at the girl, floating there in her nightdress, and it seemed impossible after all these years. I wrestled with her, trying to make her let go, and then I did the only thing I could: I pulled her towards me and rubbed her wrist across the broken window pane, so that the glass sliced through her skin and the blood ran down into the room, washed by rain.

The girl didn't cry out. She merely pleaded again: 'Let me in, Rosie, it's freezing out here.'

I screamed. I had never felt such intense fear and frustration. I hated myself for what I was doing to her, and as I dragged her wrist back and forth I felt and heard the sawing of bone. 'Let me go! Please!' I cried. Finally the fingers unlocked and she was gone, as if the wind had picked her up and whipped her away. And yet still, when I returned to my bed, I could hear her calling, 'Let me in!'

'Go away!' I shouted. 'I'll never let you, not in twenty years!'

'But it has been twenty years,' she called back. 'I've been a waif for twenty years.'

The knocking on the walls began again in earnest. I yelled, threw my face into the pillow and woke up.

I lay on my back. Sweat pooled between my breasts. I looked at the window but it was intact, and the tapping sound was once again just the walnut tree. I was breathing heavily, and I wished I wasn't alone.

❦

In the morning, I woke with a start to see sunlight spilling through the curtains. I thought for a moment there had been another earthquake, that this was what had disturbed me. But as I lay there, getting my bearings, I heard the front door close with a bang. Voices. Deep. A guttural laugh.

I leapt out of bed and opened the curtains to look outside. The back end of a shiny SUV was visible below my window. I crept to the top of stairs and listened. The voices — two of them, male — drifted up from the direction of the kitchen, but I couldn't quite make them out. I hesitated, unsure what to do — to get out now, or to find out who the casual intruders were. I decided to be brave.

The two men stopped talking and just stared at me when I appeared before them. One of them, short and weathered-looking, flinched a little as though he had seen a ghost. I guess I must have looked unusual, to say the least — still dressed in old-fashioned black clothes, my face drawn from lack of sleep and crying.

The other man, taller, with a sheepskin jacket over a dress shirt and pants, spoke. 'I'm sorry, we didn't know anyone was here. You are?'

'Who are you?'

'Andrew Preston. This is Bill. We've been asked here by the family.' He was looking at me as though I didn't belong, as if I were something that had crawled up from the river and taken shelter in the house. He held a large roll of paper in both hands, and a briefcase was propped beside him on the kitchen bench.

'Well, I'm the family. Can I help you?' It was less a polite offer than an accusation.

'Look, I think there's some kind of misunderstanding here.' He moved towards me. Bill hung back, still eying me warily. 'We're here to look at the house. I'm the architect the family's employed to do the renovations. Bill's here as project manager. We're due to start next week, and just need to take a look around if that's okay . . .' He searched the air for my name.

'Rosemary.' I was stunned — I hadn't realised it was all happening so soon.

'Right. Are you Joe's daughter? Or Brian's?'

'Joe's.'

'I'm sorry, he didn't say you'd be here.'

That was because I hadn't told them I was coming. Any of them.

'It's not a good time now,' I said. 'I'm working. You'll have to come back another day.'

Bill gave an explosive, nervous laugh, then went solemn again.

Andrew turned to look at him, then back at me.

'I don't think you understand,' he said. 'I've come from the city. That's a two-hour drive. I left at dawn to get here.'

'That's not my fault.'

He stared at me, unsure what I was going to do next. I saw him looking at my wrist, at my magpie, and I covered it with my hand.

'Look,' he said eventually, 'I'll just give Joe a call. We'll get this cleared up.' He pulled a mobile phone out of his pocket and I couldn't help but smile as he flicked it open and looked at it. He sighed and looked at Bill. 'You got any reception?' Bill went through the same process and shook his head.

'Got a landline?' asked Andrew.

'Sorry, no,' I said in a sing-song, innocent voice.

It was a stand-off. They glared at me, I glared at them. Finally Andrew started to move towards me. I stood aside as he went through to the hallway. Bill took the opportunity to scan the walls and ceiling, turning to look at the spot where I expected french doors were going to go.

'Right,' he said when he saw me watching him. As if he couldn't help himself, his meaty fist came out of his pocket and knocked on an internal wall as he passed. He joined Andrew in the hall and I herded them towards the front door. I could hear them murmuring to each other.

'Got our work cut out, mate,' said Bill, 'but she should come up nice. All original?'

'Pretty much. Some of these rooms were reconfigured about the 1930s, but those walls'll be coming down. Get some light into the place.' Andrew glanced over his shoulder and lowered his voice even more, but I still heard. 'It's a big job just to make it habitable. Don't know how anyone could live in it like this.'

'I can hear you, you know,' I said. 'And you can just fuck right off.' My voice was rising; I had no control over it. 'You don't know anything about this house. You're just going to come in and *butcher* it with no regard for its history. Just piss off. Go!'

They were at the door now and couldn't open it quickly enough. As they scampered for their four-wheel drive, Andrew flipped his phone open again, and for a moment I thought he might be trying to call the police, though he'd have no more luck out there than inside. He pocketed the phone and roared off, wheels spinning in the gravel.

Henry

Magpie Hall. That is what he will call it, for the black and white birds that lurk inside the ruined corner of the house. It will signify a new beginning, both for the house, and for Henry.

It was the earthquake that brought the house to him. Part of it had fallen down, killing its owner, and the family, which consisted only of married daughters, was selling it for a good price. He wrote to his father and told him of the opportunity: *If you can see your way to making the purchase on my behalf I can assure you that I will not attempt to return to England*. It was a risk, but eventually a letter arrived from his father in which he agreed to the terms.

Now he stands before it: a small house by the standards he is used to in England, with only two storeys, but the rooms are large and there is plenty of space for the two of them and some servants

— after all, he doesn't plan to stay here too long, or to start a family soon.

He wants to surprise her with the additions he has planned. He will rebuild the crumbled part of the house, making it sturdier than ever before, strengthening its walls and chimneys. No earthquake will shatter it again. The brick exterior lends itself perfectly to the Gothic style of architecture he admires, and knowing how much Dora loves Gothic novels, he will make it a miniature castle for her. He will add arched windows and a tower; he closes his eyes, sees turrets and ramparts stretching into the sky. He will create a walled garden for her, with a gazebo, just as his mother has at home, and where he lost himself as a child, hiding from her and collecting beetles and caterpillars for his fledgling collection.

He will retain the staff of the station as they are. He has made enquiries and discovered it is in good hands. The land is returning a profit. But the very best thing about this property is the presence of limestone caves over the crest of the hill. He is sure that with some digging they will yield all manner of curiosities, animal or mineral. Or perhaps human. When he questioned the daughters about them, they shrugged and said they had never even seen them, so who knows how long it is since they have been investigated, if at all.

A river runs through the property, and he has already discovered a perfect bathing place, not far from the house. The daughters have described with nostalgia the many picnics they have had along its banks, and how in stormy weather it swells dramatically. They are never short of water, although the presence of limestone can clog the pipes sometimes and he will have to take proper care of them. A trifle, really.

Yes, he and Dora will be very happy here, he can tell. His engagement to her is not something he had originally planned, but the more time he spends with her the more he discovers that she is the perfect companion for him. He is charmed by her lively and enquiring mind, her hunger for travel and the fact that she can both hold her own in polite society and shoot a rifle (her father insisted she learn, for her protection). He has never come across a woman like her, in London or New Zealand, where the ladies are universally silly and interested only in fashion and gossip. Dora, his Dora, is different. And there is no denying the calming effect she has on him. In her presence, his anger at last appears to be under control.

He'd had too many drinks the night he proposed to her and was perhaps a little carried away by the moment, but after the earthquake, he knew he had no regrets. And the fact that, for the moment, she was the sole heiress of her father's estate did nothing to diminish his ardour.

As he turns to leave, he disturbs the magpies that have gathered to investigate the intruder. They are different from the curious birds with the glossy feathers and long tails he knows from home. These birds are bullish black and white crows, and their presence, he confesses, makes him a little uneasy. But he admires their gumption. They may be sifting through the remains for shiny treasures to take back to their nests, but it is as though they are staking their claim on the house. They remind him of himself. He must remember to shoot one for his collection when he gets the chance.

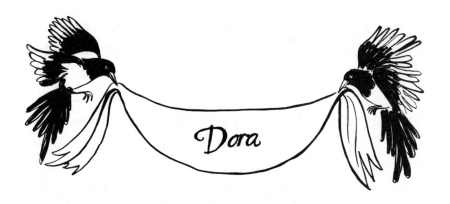

Dora

She wears white silk and orange blossoms in her hair. As they say their vows in front of a gathering of well-wishers, the sun breaks through the clouds and pours through the stained-glass church windows; the patterns dance on her body, colouring her dress.

And later they are finally alone, in the house he has restored for her. There are two bedrooms with an adjoining door, and a large bed in each. One will be hers and one will be his.

He was so proud the day he brought her to inspect the property and its restoration.

Look, my dear, he said, his hand resting lightly on her waist. He pointed out the turrets and the tower. A team of gardeners was planting the walled garden; by summer it would be alive with colour and the hum of insects. He stayed close behind her as she ascended the narrow spiral staicase to the tower and stood by, looking pleased with himself, as she surveyed the view on all sides, feeling the light on her face. The river glinted through the trees.

I love it, she said finally, and she did. She loved the effort he had poured into it on her behalf. The house felt uncannily cold, but she was sure once the fires were lit and the servants had moved back in it would be as warm as a beating heart.

He leaves her in her room to get ready for bed. She sits at the new dressing table and looks at her face, pale in the lamplight. Her hand shakes as she pulls the pins from her hair and watches it fall about her shoulders. Next, she takes her brush and runs it through her curls so they fly away and fan about her face. This mundane routine calms her, as if it were any night. Her maid waits patiently nearby, and when Dora nods, comes over to plait her hair, then helps her take off her wedding dress. It rustles about her ears as it lifts over her head and the loss of its weight makes her body light. Next, the maid unlaces the corset. Dora takes a deep breath and sits down, suddenly dizzy. Thank you, Mary, she says. I can manage now.

She removes her remaining undergarments and lays them on a nearby chair. Her nightgown lies fresh and new on the bed. She pulls it over her head and breathes deeply again; its newness smells like a spring lawn. Then she slides under the covers.

She lies with the sheets pulled up around her ears, listening for signs of her husband. She hears him bump into something, and laugh gently to himself, which makes her smile. If she didn't know better she would think he was drunk, but he has hardly touched a drop all day and night. As she waits, she looks around the room, at the lamplight shadows flirting with the walls. Henry has had the room decorated just for her, with rich burgundy floral wallpaper and heavy velvet drapes over the tall arched windows — only the finest for my bride, he said. A collection of beautiful blue butterflies decorates the wall. All different sizes, their wings catch the light and glow like waterfalls. Her trunks sit by the wardrobe, waiting to be unpacked. Her new home.

A gentle knocking comes from the door between their rooms.

Come, she says, but her voice is a whisper. Come! she says again. The door opens and Henry pokes his head in.

She is relieved at first that he seems as nervous as she is, pacing around the room in a silk jacket, smoking the last of his cigarette. But the smell offends her suddenly and she becomes irritated. He is supposed to be the man; he is supposed to put *her* at ease and guide her on their wedding night.

Please put that thing out, she commands him and he stops pacing and stands erect. He looks at her in surprise then bursts out laughing.

Yes, madam! he says and disappears back into his own room for a moment, before emerging empty-handed. She has broken the ice and feels the irritation subside. They are both smiling now.

He sits on the opposite side of the bed.

Dora, dear, he says. There is something I need to show you.

She bites her lip. A disease, she thinks, a horrible deformity. He is not as other men. He is a eunuch. But all of these thoughts peel away as he opens his jacket, and then the neck of his nightshirt. He pulls it to one side and reveals a picture on his chest — a rose.

What is it? she asks. She leans over the bed towards it. A tattoo?

He nods.

She has never seen one before, only heard of them. May I? She reaches out towards him. The rose feels slightly raised on its stem, but otherwise it is as smooth as if it weren't even there.

You're not angry? he asks.

Angry? No. I think it's . . . I think it's lovely.

She is not lying, not trying to put him at ease. The red blooming against his pale skin is as arresting as a real rose would be, had she come across it in the snow.

That is good, my love. He raises the covers and slides into bed beside her. Because there are more.

He shuffles around beneath the bedclothes, and then his nightshirt is travelling up his body and over his head. He drops it on the ground.

She gasps.

How had she not known about this? A dragon wrapped around his forearm — intricately drawn, breathing hot fire; a mermaid with long golden hair covering her nakedness; an insect she does not recognise, with a long tail and pincers like a crab; a springing tiger. In the golden light they emerge from the shadows of his body as he lies down and turns over for her. She runs her hands over the snake on his back and his skin shivers under her touch.

She hasn't even registered, until now, that he is naked beside her and she pulls her hands away sharply.

She surprises herself by saying, I have never seen anything so beautiful in all my life.

He turns and pulls her to him and she allows herself be encircled by his tattooed arms. He kisses her and kisses her and kisses her.

They don't sleep all night. He is gentle with her, but still the pain is too much this first time. He holds her instead, and they talk until a finger of light tries to pull back the curtains. She asks him about his tattoos, tries to understand how they came to be. He tells her about his first visit to Hori Chyo, in Japan, shows her how the dragon dances when he flexes his forearm.

But you have to hide your body all the time, she says.

It is not hard, he says. I bathe alone. The only people who usually see them are . . . he hesitates.

Women, she thinks. His other women.

The tattooers. But I didn't need to hide them back in England. Many of my friends have tattoos. Even the Prince of Wales and his sons have been tattooed, by the same artist that tattooed my dragon. Once they had tattoos, everyone wanted them. You should see them all, trying to outdo each other. And the ladies, too.

She sits up. The ladies? she repeats.

He laughs. Yes, my dear. They are quite fashionable among the ladies of London society. You will see. I will take you there. There is a famous London beauty, Lady Churchill. She has a snake tattooed around her wrist.

But what if she ever wants to hide it?

She simply wears gloves, or a bracelet. But she has no need to hide it. All those women, they copy each other.

Dora thinks for a moment, stroking the colourful patterns on his arms.

I should like one, she says.

Oh, now, come, my dear, it is not something to be entered into lightly.

But if those ladies have one, why should not I? Do you think we colonials are not sophisticated enough?

Shhh. He strokes her hair, kisses it. Not at all. But it is permanent. If you decide you do not like it after all, there is nothing you can do about it.

But I do like it. I liked your tattoos from the moment I saw them. They are part of you.

What she doesn't say is, *They excite me.* They remind her of how worldly he is, and how domestic she is. As if she somehow does not quite measure up.

They lie there for a while longer, enjoying the warmth of each other's skin. Finally, he speaks.

Very well. If in one month's time you decide that you would still like to be tattooed, I will take you. We shall go together.

And with that, she thinks — never mind the vows — we will be bound until death parts us.

They take the train to the port, as the night falls. Henry does not want to risk being seen; he thinks it will damage her reputation.

It is a short walk over the bridge into the town. On every corner stands a hotel; as they pass she glances in the windows at the dull light and swirling pipe smoke, the dark shapes of sailors and other men moving within. She holds Henry's arm more tightly. A carriage comes close, throwing up mud, but Henry moves them both deftly out of the way. The driver doffs his cap at them and sniggers, showing yellowed teeth in the light of his lamp, then is gone. Dora sees a woman's face pressed to the carriage window, with a look of alarm.

All about them the smells of the place swirl: wood smoke, rancid fish, oil from the lanterns. Men hurry past them with heads down, suspicious bundles under their cloaks — at least, Dora thinks they are suspicious, imagining them to contain dead animals, or body parts. A woman trussed up in velvet and feathers stops a man and murmurs to him, but he pushes her arm away and continues walking while she makes a rooster noise after him. She laughs when she sees Dora and winks.

'Ello, sir, the woman says. Nice to see you again. She calls after them: Got yourself a nice one there, my love! A real gentleman. Knows how to please a lady.

Henry pulls her in closer. Don't listen, he says. She is nothing. She is fooling with you.

They turn a corner into a deserted lane. They pass darkened shopfronts — a butcher, with pig carcasses hanging in the window, a printing shop, a draper with faded bolts of cotton lawn on display — until they come to one that gives off light. There is just one word painted on the window: *Tattoos*.

We have arrived, says Henry. Are you sure about this?

Dora nods and takes the first step towards the door, pushes it open with heavy hands. Her heart is beating so hard she feels the blood pulsing in her face and arms.

The room is deserted. The floor crunches as they walk. A single lantern burns in the far corner, illuminating the nearest shapes drawn on the walls while the rest fade into the darkness.

They had talked earlier about where the tattoo should be placed. Henry suggested her back, a location that was unlikely to be seen by anyone, but Dora wanted to be able to look at it. On her back she would need a mirror to see it and she would never be able to gaze at the actual picture. She likes the idea of the butterfly on her chest, the symmetry of it, but in the end she settles for her leg, to one side, above the knee.

A huge man emerges from the back room, drying his hands. His voice is as rough as the room around them.

You came, then, he says to Henry. And this is the young lady.

My wife, says Henry.

Right you are. The man nods. Come through then, madam.

She is grateful that he is at least respectful.

Have you . . . have you tattooed women before? she asks as she follows him behind a curtain to a well-lit room with a worn bed and an armchair. A table with instruments stands beside.

One or two, McDonald answers. There's one girl — Lucy — she's in the Quirk Brothers' circus. I've done most of hers. She stops by whenever she's in town.

Dora hesitates and looks at Henry. Circus? she asks. Like a freak show?

Henry takes her hand. You won't be on display, he says. You are nothing like that woman. She is tattooed from head to toe, I'm sure. He looks at McDonald, for reassurance.

That's right, he nods. Not her face, mind, but just about everywhere else. Quite a beauty she is too. Now, madam, you just make yourself comfortable on this chair. Did you bring the picture?

It is one of Henry's own paintings of the *Morpho rhetenor* he captured in Brazil. He hands it to McDonald, who looks at it and shakes his head.

Is there a problem? asks Henry.

It's blue, see? Ain't no one invented blue ink that will stay put. It bleeds. Terrible mess. We only got the five colours.

And which are they? Dora asks.

Black of course. Green, brown, red and yellow. You want a yellow butterfly, or a green, fine.

This is an unexpected setback. She had dreamed of the blue butterflies, watched them alighting on her body. She wanted her tattoo to remind her of that love.

Henry takes her hand. There are beautiful yellow and black butterflies. I will show you. You will love them.

She nods, puts aside her disappointment. She's not sure if she wants to go through with it now, but she has come this far. Very well, she agrees.

Very good. And did we decide where we wanted this butterfly?

She can hardly bring herself to say it and she feels herself blushing. She won't look at him. Here, she says, and points through her skirts to her lower thigh.

Very good, he says again. Well, you just get the place ready in your own time.

She sits on the armchair and Henry moves behind her to rest a reassuring hand on her shoulder. She pulls her skirt up gingerly, then rolls down her stocking, exposing the area. Her skin looks very white, like pristine bone china, and she has an urge to pull the stocking back up and float right out of the tattoo shop. But Henry's hand on her shoulder is firm, as if he senses what she is thinking and what she needs to keep her there.

McDonald pulls up a low stool to sit beside her, dips a pen into an inkwell and begins to draw on her leg. He works in feather-light strokes, and by necessity he leans his right arm on her lap. His left hand pulls the skin of her thigh tight, his great palm wrapped around her, as if it is nothing to him to be handling a lady thus. Instead of being offended however, she finds it quite thrilling, this huge bear of a man treating her as if she were a sailor. His hands are unexpectedly clean, apart from a few ink stains — she expected more dirt. He is so close to her that she can smell him, a mixture of pipe tobacco and sweat and alcohol; she is not sure if the latter is from drinking or from sterilising. She does not want a drunkard working on her with sharp needles, but his hands are steady. Only a fine down covers his great bald head and diamonds of perspiration are caught within it. She is feeling quite hot herself and the tattooing has not even begun.

Is that to your satisfaction, madam? He has stopped drawing and is now looking up at her. She glances at where his hands still rest on her leg. The butterfly is rendered beautifully in black lines, as if the man himself were a lepidopterist sketching his latest conquest.

She nods.

Then we will begin.

Henry picks up a stool from nearby and puts it on the other side of her. He sits and takes her hand. He is trying to comfort her, but she feels the sinew in his fingers taut and anxious. He squeezes too hard.

Dear, she says, and extracts her hand with the other. She pats his arm.

McDonald lines up his needles and picks one up. He dips it in a tiny pot of ink.

Are you ready? he asks.

She nods and takes a deep breath. This is not how she imagined it, although she had no clear idea of what receiving a tattoo would be like. Some nights she has dreamed of a man in shirtsleeves and a neat waistcoat with a pocket watch performing the task. Other nights she awoke sweating after she was held down by leering sailors who wanted to do more to her than mark her with a butterfly. She could still feel their callused hands on her ankles and wrists and the searing pain of the needle, as if she were being branded with a hot iron.

Instead, here she is with this curious man, so rough-looking and formidable, and yet polite and gentle, with clean hands.

She had imagined it would be like a deep scratch, that he would drag the needle across her skin like a quill, ripping through her flesh. Instead he plunges the needle into her skin and out again, prick, prick, prick. The pricks are hot little bee stings. It does not hurt as much as she thought it would. He pauses to wipe away the ink that spills and to dip his needle in the pot again.

She lets out the breath she realises she has been holding and turns to Henry.

But it doesn't hurt as much as I thought it would, she tells him.

He takes her hand again, but this time it is more relaxed, even though she is conscious of how damp her palm is in his.

That is good, my love, he says.

Instead of abating however, the pain grows as the area of the tattoo expands. She notices that when McDonald rubs away the ink now, it is coloured red with her blood. But she finds that if she concentrates on the pain rather than trying to ignore it she can transform it into heat, or pressure; she can deaden her own senses at will. Besides, it is a small price to pay for the result — her favourite insect in all the world, and the bond that this will create with her husband. She thinks of their first night together again, of how she ran her hands over his body and how it responded to her touch. She imagines him doing the same to her, running his hands up her thigh and lingering on the delicate wings of her butterfly. She will never regret what she has done.

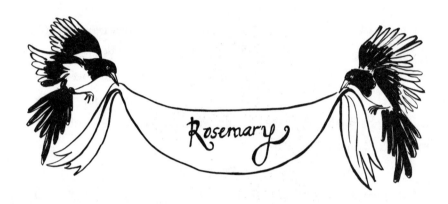

Rosemary

Half an hour after the intruders had left, and I had tried to go back to sleep, the phone rang. The noise filled the house: the old-fashioned mechanical bells of the downstairs phone and the newer, electronic sound coming from my grandparents' bedroom. It was a melancholy sound, the way it kept going and going, and I pictured those two empty single beds with the phone between them, and nobody there to pick it up. I lay there and listened to it ring five, ten, twenty times before it stopped.

I didn't need to answer it to know it would be one of my family calling to berate me. Let them call, I thought. I didn't have to answer. Finally, I relaxed enough to fall asleep. I had intense, loud dreams, with lots of action and purpose, but when I woke up, I couldn't remember them. They played just out of reach, like a piano in another room.

I spent the day with my feet by the heater, working. I amazed myself with the level of concentration I was able to muster. Towards late afternoon, however, I became distracted. The day was still, which was particularly eerie after the storm of the day and night before, and was puncuated only by distant farm noises — a dog barking, or a sheep calling; a distant engine. The sound of the river had once again died down to nothing, and the sun had even managed to stay for most of the day. But as I worked I became aware of a shift in the atmosphere of the house. Magpie Hall was always creaking and groaning, so I didn't worry too much about that, but the noises I started hearing were different somehow. Scraping sounds. Light thumps. Even though I was finally warm enough, I felt cold air on my neck like damp breath.

I got up without making a sound and poked my head out into the hallway. I was pretty sure the noises had come from the other end of the house, so I headed in that direction, past bedrooms and the stairs to the attic. The hallway turned sharply right and took me past what used to be the servants' quarters, once separate from the other rooms but now, with some wall removal, incorporated into the rest of the house. The bedrooms here were tiny, with narrow single beds as bowed as a ship's bottom, where we were made to sleep as children. It was in one of these rooms that I had woken that morning to the mist and the ghostly music coming from the home paddock, like a harp string amplified in the still air. To this day I don't know how she made that soulful note; I have tried and failed to replicate it many times.

The door to the room at the bottom of the tower steps stood slightly ajar. I pushed and it opened to reveal a clean, quiet place with bookshelves and, on the walls, a few insects behind glass. It lacked the chaos and clutter of some of the other rooms. I often wondered, with no proof, whether this was where Henry had kept his cabinet of curiosities. There was something about its awkward size and almost round shape, the way it was hidden away behind a door more suited to a cupboard. Grandpa had talked about hearing Henry pacing and muttering, and this seemed like the most apt place for a madman to ponder his past regrets. Apart from the tower itself, of course, but that wouldn't be the most practical room to house anything precious, with its windows on all sides, its exposure to the sun and the wind.

More sounds, closer now: a light tinkling, a clicking, coming from over my head. My scalp prickled. Rather than backing away, I decided to go up there for the first time in twenty years. Even if I found nothing, the tower would give me a vantage point like no other. From there, I would be able to see Sam, know that he was far away and that the noises were just my imagination. And there might be an earthly explanation — a trapped bird trying to find its way out.

The staircase was a tight, suffocating spiral, with such tiny steps that I had to walk on tiptoes. It was absolutely dark with the door at the top shut. I had to lean my weight against it to open it. I expected to blink in the light but it was gloomy. Blinds covered the windows. It smelt of cold and something else. Smoke. Stale tobacco. As I walked slowly around the column created by the stairwell, my ears started to hum. I closed my eyes and took a few more steps.

She was there again, under the far window. Her back emerged pale in the murky light, her hair piled languidly on top of her head. She was hunched over something; the tension in her back suggested concentration, and she hadn't heard me come in. The bird appeared to hover above her shoulder blades, all curves and dipping wings, waiting to take flight. She was completely silent, and the sound of my breath filled the room. It was only a matter of time before she heard me, and sure enough she sat up straight, alert, and her shoulder began to turn. Soon I would see her face. It was all happening exactly as it had on that day all those years ago. Perhaps she had never left this room, had been waiting all this time for me to come back. I closed my eyes. But as the moment stretched out I felt a sharp, cold wind on the back of my neck and the door to the stairs slammed shut. Instinctively, my head snapped back to see who or what had closed it, and I was just in time to see a curtain shiver and settle. An open window.

When I turned back, she was gone. I froze, looking right and left without turning my head, and called out into the thick air. 'Hello?' The only sound was the curtain stirring in the breeze. I pulled it back to let in some light and to close the window. Although the figure was no longer there, the room was not empty. A telescope was aimed at one of the windows. Against the wall, where she had been, lay a mottled and lumpy-looking single mattress, with a grey army blanket bunched at the end. An ashtray sat to one side of it, overflowing with roll-your-own cigarette stubs, the source of the stale smell. I went over and kicked at the mattress — no way of knowing how long it had been there or when it had last been used. Had someone been here the whole time? Sleeping here? *Living* here? I felt sick, and more scared than I had moments before. Ghosts I could handle — cigarette-smoking intruders I couldn't.

This was too much. Although I didn't feel that my business at Magpie Hall was done, it was time to leave. I had always known that the house was an eerie place, but now I felt truly frightened.

I tried to open the door to the stairs but it was stuck. I pulled harder. I jerked at the handle and felt a stabbing pain in my shoulder from the effort. This was not just a sticky door. This was a *locked* door.

'Help!' I shouted, and hammered on it with my fist, but the only person who would be able to hear me would be the one who had locked it in the first place. Better to stay quiet and find another way out. I looked around for something to bash the door handle, but there was nothing useful up here. I went to the open window and looked out. This particular window faced north, over the river, and I could see it meandering, reduced now to its pre-storm state, a benign stream. The sun was sinking in the west, rimming the clouds with gold. I moved to the western window, where the telescope was positioned. I could make out someone up in one of the paddocks on the hill, riding a quad bike, flanked by dogs. A waterfall of sheep cascaded down the hill in front of it. A quick look through the telescope told me it was Sam, or Josh, I couldn't be sure. Josh, I thought: he was a big man, broader than Sam, a darker, more solid presence. Another person stood by a gate, watching — an androgynous figure in a raincoat and a hat, though my instincts said it was a woman, or a girl. She was short enough to lean on the gate without bending.

Both of them were too far away to hear me if I yelled and they wouldn't be able to see me inside. I knew there was a ladder outside that climbed the side of the tower to a small balcony. It was easy enough to get out there, though I'd never done it before. The father of a childhood friend had slipped from a roof and broken his back and that fact had long kept my curiosity at bay. But today called for decisive action. I pushed the window as far open as it would go and stood on tiptoe to get my leg out, my skirt hitched around my waist. I held tightly to the window frame as I lowered myself down. The ladder was a few feet away and I eased myself around to it, a little at a time, not realising until now just how scared of heights I actually was. My hands were slippery and hot and my chest felt tight with the effort of breathing. Once I had the ladder in my grip I relaxed a little, and prepared myself for the short ascent.

At the tower's balcony I jumped down to safety and crouched to catch my breath. My skirt was immediately soaked by a dirty puddle filled with autumn leaves and I stood up again.

It was magnificent. I couldn't believe I had never been up here. From the top of the tower I felt as though I were a bird soaring over the farm, with a 360-degree outlook and the biting wind swirling around my slight body. But I barely felt the cold; instead I turned and turned and looked out over the roofs of the house, over its chimneys and turrets and to the land of the farm beyond. The land that had been in my family for five generations and was now going to be lost to us forever.

I heard a shuffle and looked left to see a pair of magpies staring at me from one of the chimneys, no doubt surprised to see a human up here. They conferred for a moment, then flew away, leaving me to my fate.

The figures in the distant paddock were still there, but I could see now that it would be futile trying to get their attention. I waved my arms over my head a couple of times, but they were too far away.

There was nothing for it but to find a way down off the roof by myself. The sun had sunk dangerously low now. Soon it would be dark and I didn't want to stay up here all night — the cold would kill me.

I'd never exactly thought of myself as a lucky person. I'd had too much of my share of misery and grief for that. But as I stood there, on that tower, looking in vain for a place on the roof that looked safe to descend, where I wouldn't slip on the tiles and slide to my death, I slowly became aware of a sound that I hardly dared hope for.

I heard it coming from the east, where the wind was blowing from; as I turned towards it the last of the leaves were fleeing the poplars and flying towards the house to gather in its gutters. The deep rumbling faded in and out as a car rounded corners and drove up and down the hills and valleys of the farm.

I stood, waiting. Finally, an old cream Mercedes rolled into view: my brother Charlie. I laughed. I had never felt so much relief, so much tension dissipate at the sight of anyone. I jumped up and down and waved, but he didn't see me; I could picture him hunched over the steering wheel, hands at ten and two, concentrating on avoiding the puddles so his precious classic car would stay as clean as possible. I lost sight of the car as it pulled up in front of the house. I would just have to wait and hope that my voice was loud enough that it wouldn't be whipped away from me by the wind.

The heavy door thudded and I heard his footsteps crunching on the gravel. I took a huge breath and called out to him.

He stopped walking for a second, then resumed. I heard the boot of his car open and close. I called again.

'Charlie!'

He had stopped walking. I heard him, barely. 'Rose?'

I leaned as far over the balcony rail as I dared. 'I'm up here! On the tower!'

He didn't call out again. Instead I heard him walk up the steps to the house. His every movement was so loud, carried to my ears by the wind, but he seemed to be having trouble hearing me. He knocked on the front door.

'Charlie!' I called again. 'I'm up here!'

I could hear his footsteps as he walked down the drive again. And then there he was on the lawn, looking up at me.

'What the hell are you doing up there?'

I laughed. I could have flown down into his arms.

'I'm locked up here. You need to come in and unlock the door to the tower. Please,' I added.

'Okay, but the front door's locked.'

Damn. I had barricaded myself inside the house. I had no idea how he would get in.

'You might have to break a window. Please hurry. I'm freezing up here.'

I crouched down to shelter from the wind and hugged myself, waiting for the sound of breaking glass, but it never came. Five minutes later, his voice came from just below me and made me jump.

'Rose.'

When I got to the bottom of the ladder he reached as far as he could out the window and I took his hand, steadying myself as I crept towards him. He pulled me through the window and I reached up to give him the biggest hug of his life.

'Thank God,' I said into his neck. 'You don't know how glad I am to see you. I thought I was dead.'

'Okay,' he said, bemused. 'You can tell me later what you were doing up there, but you should know — the tower door wasn't locked. In fact, it was slightly open. You weren't stuck up here at all.'

My cheeks began to burn. 'How did you get into the house?'

'That was easy too. The kitchen door was open. Like it always is.'

'But I locked it!'

'I don't think so. Why would you do that?'

I didn't answer.

Charlie got the tall, skinny gene in our family, from our father's side. His lithe body drifted down the stairs to the ground floor while I scuttled behind him.

'What's going on here?' His groomed self looked out of place in the room — he showed up all its ragged edges and dusty corners, its flaking wallpaper. 'Jesus, it's freezing. Why don't you put the heater on or something?'

'You're in a great mood,' I said, but I knew what the problem was. The architect, the phone call that I didn't pick up earlier.

'Well, what do you expect? I don't even know what you're doing here.'

I nodded. 'Okay, you got me. I broke into *your* house and I'm squatting. I'm a dirty squatter.'

He rolled his eyes. 'Don't be like that. You know you can come here any time — it's just as much yours as it is mine.'

'I don't know about that.'

He flopped down onto the couch. A cloud of dog hair and dust rose around him.

'Rosemary.' His voice was pleading. Even when he was telling me off he was so easily offended. He still wanted to be liked, even by his sister, even when she had made some mistakes. So different from Charlie as a child — a pinching, biting, kicking, annoying little brother.

'So what's the problem?' I asked.

'Dad's worried about you. The architect called him this morning and told him you'd been really obstructive. Were you?'

'Maybe a bit.'

'Why? And you still haven't said what you're doing here.'

'I'm working. I'm really behind on my thesis. They were making heaps of noise.'

'Oh, bullshit. He told Dad you acted like a complete nutter. Dad told him to turn around and come back, but he refused. I think you scared him.'

I smiled.

'Not funny. Dad called me, really worried. Asked me if everything was all right, how you're coping.'

'And what did you say?'

'I said I thought you were okay but what would I know? So I jumped in the car to find out for myself.' He paused. 'And to be here if those guys decide to come back over the weekend. Mum and Dad are pretty pissed off. But I didn't think it was a good idea for them to come. Not if you're in one of your moods.'

'My moods.' I had thought them all oblivious to my ups and downs. 'Fine.' I sat down next to him, pushing his bag onto the floor. 'Actually, I'm quite glad you're here. I would have frozen to death up there.'

'Not if you'd gone back inside. You would have seen the open door.'

'Things are weird here, Charlie. Didn't you see the mattress and blanket up there? It's like someone's been squatting here.' I didn't look at him. 'Someone other than me.' I hesitated for a moment, then told him about Sam, about what had happened when Hugh turned up. I didn't spare much detail — I'd always been able to tell my brother anything.

He didn't give me the sympathy I was looking for.

'Jesus Christ, Rosemary. Look at yourself. You're a total fuck-up.' He gestured at my clothes, covered in hair and dirt. 'Always getting yourself into situations.'

I ignored the obvious truth in his words. He went on. 'And how *dare* you throw those two out this morning.'

I stopped him before he could go further. 'I didn't want them here. I hated watching them poke around the place.'

He looked at the ceiling for a moment, as though searching the cornices for patience. He gave a grunt of frustration. Then he stared at me. 'It's *not your decision.*' His voice was low and strong, as though he were disciplining a dog.

'Not my decision. Right.' I nodded. 'And a moment ago you were saying this place is as much mine as yours.'

'Well . . .' He turned his palms up and shrugged.

'Fine. I get it.' I stood and marched from the room, breaking into a run up the stairs.

'Right, walk away,' he called up after me. 'Like you always do!'

❦

It was Friday. I had lost track of the days. Charlie planned to stay the weekend, had taken the day off work to clean up after me, as he kept reminding me. He didn't know when the architect would come back, but I think he was planning to take me with him when he left, just in case. I waited a long time in my room, not working, not doing anything except walking around and looking at the picture of Dora, which I had brought down from the attic and hung on the wall. I heard my brother come up the stairs and bounce up and down a couple of times on the bed with the saggy springs in the room next to mine. He muttered to himself on the other side of the wall.

Luckily Charlie had come with food — I was starting to run low, and the milk I brought with me had soured. He had been thoughtful, too. As much as he loved meat, he had brought only vegetarian food. And plenty of wine.

I finally came down, after he had ignored me for too long, and he had dinner nearly ready. I sat down at the kitchen table while he poured me a glass of red in silence. He had lit the fire in the lounge and the stove in the kitchen, and I felt truly warm for the first time in a week.

'It's good to see you,' I said, not sure how he would react. He looked up from the pot he was stirring and smiled.

'It's been too long.'

I nodded in agreement. 'We haven't even had a chance to talk about everything. The will. Grandpa. What you're going to do.'

'And you. The menagerie.' He laughed, but stopped when I didn't smile.

'Do you miss him?' I asked.

'What kind of a question is that? Of course I do.'

'But you hadn't seen him for ages before he died.'

'I know.' He was fighting the defensive tone, I could tell. 'Well, my life is busy. And it's been hard for us, coming back here. He knew that.'

'He must have. You were still his favourite.'

He snorted. 'You were, I think you'll find.'

'If I was, he would have left me some of the house too.'

'Maybe . . . but then all the other cousins would have to have had a piece. I think leaving you the animals was his way of telling you. Look, when Mum and Dad die, you'll get their share anyway. He knew it would come to you eventually.'

'You're right. I just feel so . . .'

'Powerless?'

I put down my wine and covered my face. I nodded.

He took the pot off the element and came and sat down beside me.

'It's true you were much closer than I was to him. I'm embarrassed about him leaving the house to me. Do you know how much pressure I feel about that? God, the guilt. He wanted me to take over the farm, to have lots of little farm babies.'

'You'll never even have babies.'

'Who says?'

'Well, it's obvious, isn't it?'

'There are ways and means, my little sister. Try and expand that narrow mind of yours a little. Just because I don't want to sleep with women doesn't mean I don't want to be a dad one day.'

'Okay, sorry. But you'd never come and live here. Be a farmer.'

'Why would I? I often wonder if Grandpa wrote that will when I was five or something. Surely a doctor in the family is nothing to be ashamed of?'

'I don't think it was about that. I think it was about the first son of the first son thing. I've been thinking a lot about Henry. The one who started all of this. It's like, once this place is gone, those ties to the past will be severed. Grandpa thought he was great. I'm pretty sure he was too. I wish I knew more about him.' I remembered the letter then, and excused myself to go and get it. Charlie read it while he resumed stirring the risotto.

'Oh,' he said. He put the letter down and said nothing as he served the meal and poured more wine, then sat down.

'Aren't you going to say something?' I had been so excited to show him the letter, with all its revelations about Henry and Dora.

He looked up at me, his body very still. Finally he spoke. 'It's just so . . . sweet. I'm kind of jealous.'

'I'm sorry. That's not why I showed it to you.' I was filled again with resentment at my family for going against Grandpa's wishes, but it wasn't directed at Charlie and I needed him to know that. 'I don't think this has anything to do with you, anyway. Of course you would go along with what the olds want. I doubt they'd have listened to you if you'd argued.'

He just shrugged and started eating.

'I'm just saying, I think we should at least acknowledge that he wanted the family to go on living here. And now that it's going to be changed so much, who's to say they won't want to sell it off the first time it starts to lose money.'

Charlie put down his fork. 'Well, would that be so bad? There'll be enough money to go around everyone then.'

'But it's not just about the money.'

'No, that's true. Mum and Dad hate this place, with good reason, don't you think?'

'It's not the house's fault.'

'Maybe not to you. But anyway, think about it: what a great parting gift — you could buy a house, pursue your academic career, or whatever it is you want to do . . . What *do* you want to do, by the way?'

I shrugged. This was not the time for that conversation. 'But I want to be able to bring my children here. Give them what I had, teach them taxidermy, take them swimming in the Magpie Pool. Maybe even show them how to ride a horse.'

'Really? You'd do that?'

'It's just a thought.'

'Rose, selling the farm is the only way to keep the house. And if the house becomes a burden, then that'll be sold too. I'm afraid you'll have to stop getting so emotional about things and start looking at things practically.'

'Practically? Coldly, you mean. You're telling me to be rational. Well, I'm glad you can separate your emotions. You're right, I can't.' I knew I was lying. There were whole parts of my life I had successfully shut away when I didn't want to deal with them.

'Look.' He stopped and topped up our wine glasses. His voice became low and even, quiet in the big kitchen. 'I don't know if anyone told you, but the farm has actually been losing money hand over fist.

That's the main reason we're selling it. There won't be much left once the debts are paid, and most of that is going into the house. Do you really think Grandpa would have wanted to leave us with such a burden? I don't think he was that stupid.'

I didn't answer. I was too shocked. I hadn't even considered that the farm was losing money. Why hadn't anyone told me? How could this have happened? I hated to think that Grandpa might have run it into the ground. I'd never heard him complaining about the job Joshua was doing as manager, so whose fault was it? But I didn't know the first thing about how a farm is run. All I knew was that there was a lot of land, a lot of sheep and an army of staff to keep it all going smoothly. But now that I thought about it, I had only seen Sam, coming and going on his quad bike. The old bustle was missing — I had felt as much when I first arrived, but had associated it only with the house. Now I realised the stillness had settled over the whole place.

'Let's get out, tomorrow,' I said.

'Go for a drive?'

'No. Let's take the horses out.'

'Are you serious?'

'Yes, I think it'll be good for us.'

He looked sceptical, scared, even. 'How long since they've been ridden? I haven't ridden since I was a kid. I don't think I'll know how.'

'Rubbish, you were a natural.' It was true. Charlie had many times beaten me in races around the paddock, and had taken off on local hunts while I sat at home and sulked about the cruelty of it all. 'We'll go to the caves. Who knows, it might be our last chance. I'll go on my own if you don't come.'

He thought for a moment, sipping his wine. He sighed, as if

resigning himself. 'All right,' he said. 'I think you're mad, but it's probably better you don't go alone. I'll come with you.'

The tension between us had dissipated and we relaxed into our roles as brother and sister, catching up on news and gossip. The sympathy I had been looking for earlier finally arrived: he went through the motions of patting my arm and reassuring me I had made the right decision to extricate myself from Hugh, that someone much more suitable would be just around the corner. He didn't ask me any more about Sam and I didn't volunteer.

Later that night I took him upstairs and showed him Dora's dress, her portrait hanging on the wall of my bedroom.

'Do you think he murdered her?' We sat on my bed, clutching armfuls of silk, looking up at the painting. She seemed at home here, and I wondered if this had been her room, where she slept and dressed and brushed her hair.

'Surely not,' said Charlie. 'That's just far too juicy a skeleton for the family closet. Have you been sitting here making up fantasies again?' He leaned sideways and butted me with his shoulder. 'I think that thesis of yours is going to your head.'

I shrugged. 'Maybe. I would like to know what happened to her though. Don't you hate the way when Grandpa was there we didn't ask him enough? There are so many stories about our family I wish I knew. And now it's too late.'

The house began to sway gently. Charlie grabbed my hand and looked at me with wide eyes. We both cocked our heads, waiting. There was a creak, as though from a wooden sailing ship riding a storm, then the rocking subsided as quickly as it had begun.

'Letting off steam,' said Charlie, and I nodded, my uneasiness returning.

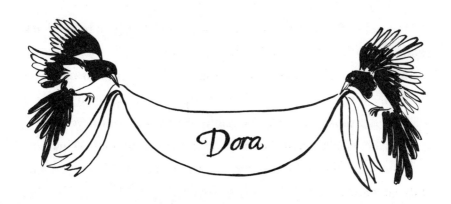

Dora

She knows as soon as she steps through the door that something has changed. The floor is smooth and clean under her feet; a smell of tobacco still lingers, but it is overpowered by the scent of lilac. There is more light but it is softer: the lampshades are made of cool frosted glass. Velvet curtains hang at the windows and over the door to the back; the faded and curling flashes that had been pinned to the wall are gone and now the designs are part of the wallpaper — the walls are vibrant with sailing ships and all that a seaman might desire.

The curtains ruffle, then part. A young man slips out, eyes cast to the floor, and bows.

Is Mr McDonald ready for us? Henry asks.

Yes, sir. That is, he says you should come in and wait. He says the young lady might be interested in something.

The boy disappears again behind the curtain.

But it's changed so, says Dora. Henry takes her hand. Is this your doing? she asks.

I wanted you to experience your tattoos the way you would if you were living in London. In a proper parlour, not in some grubby shop. McDonald was most accommodating once I offered to pay for the refurbishment. Shall we?

He holds the curtain aside for her and she steps into the back room.

McDonald is working — they have come upon him tattooing someone. But it isn't a sailor, as she might have expected — it's a woman. A woman sitting on a straight chair with one arm resting on its back, her cheek against her wrist. Her other hand holds a cigarette. She looks up lazily as Dora enters and their eyes lock. She wears only bloomers and a chemise, the latter opened at the back so that her shoulders and upper chest are bare, like her arms. McDonald is bent over her back, a look of intense concentration on his face as he works. The woman draws deeply on her cigarette and blows the smoke in a stream above her, never once taking her gaze off Dora. Her face is immobile, but Dora can see that the eyes are laughing at her.

She is the most beautiful creature Dora has ever seen. If she forgot herself for the moment she would think she had stumbled into another world. The woman's hair is the colour of treacle and her lips are naturally dark and rose-coloured. Her chest and arms are covered with tattoos, not desultory images collected one by one like Henry's, but jostling against each other so there is no sign of the original creaminess of her skin. Her legs, impossibly long and muscular, are stretched forward, the bloomers hitched up to her thighs, and these too are the canvas for ribbons and butterflies and flowers and figures. It is as if she has on another outfit under her clothing. Dora is drawn further into the room, towards the woman, towards the swirling, tumbling, vibrant patterns; she wants to fall into them. Then she feels a hand on her arm pulling her back.

For Christ's sake, man, says her husband. What do you mean exposing my wife to this?

McDonald stops working and looks up.

I thought she might like to see another lady getting tattooed. His face is calm, betraying nothing, neither regret nor insolence.

Come, Dora, says Henry. We will wait outside.

Dora wants to protest, to say that she doesn't mind. She wants to go forward and touch this woman's skin, to talk to her, but she follows him anyway. She can feel the blood boiling beneath his skin.

Henry, dear —

He raises his hand, palm towards her. When he speaks, his voice is low and deceptively calm.

The nerve of the man, after all I have done for him. To suggest that you have anything in common with that . . . that woman, that *carnival* attraction.

But I am nothing like that woman. We know that. I didn't mind seeing her, not really. I thought her very . . . interesting.

She doesn't say what she is really thinking, that the sight of the woman's long tattooed limbs actually filled her with something like desire, whether for the woman, or to be like her, she is not sure.

They wait in silence for a few minutes, and Dora feels the anger leaving Henry. Finally the boy emerges again, followed closely by the woman, who is now dressed. She wears gloves and her dress is high-necked with a lace collar. She looks perfectly respectable, apart from her boots, which are grimy and worn. Her hat is a little too gaudy to be elegant, with a fake bunch of grapes adorning it, and bright silk flowers.

Dora wants to say something to her, but the words catch in her throat. Henry stares at the ground, but as the woman moves towards the door, Dora sees him glance up, and she thinks she sees a look like hunger in his eye.

In the doorway, the woman turns.

I am sure we will meet again, she says, looking first at Henry, then at Dora. She drops into the slightest of curtseys. Then she is gone, and the tinkling of the bell on the door is the only sign that she was there.

That woman, Dora says to McDonald as he bends over her wrist, working on a snake in green and gold. Is she the one you told us about earlier?

Lucy, the tattooer says. That's her. Quite the beauty, don't you think? Quirk Brothers is coming back this way soon. You should take in a show. It's — he pauses to search for a word, and when it comes she realises he is trying to speak her language, the language of the drawing room, not of the port. It's *diverting*, he says.

Dora says nothing but sinks back into silence, concentrating on distilling the pain of the needles. She is so much more comfortable this time; now she reclines on a chaise longue, with her arm resting on a small table beside it.

Henry has allowed McDonald's apprentice to tattoo him, a small picture of a spider on his leg, and so far the boy is making good progress; husband and wife lie side by side and now and again take each other's free hands. Dora feels a current pass between them — the shared experience creates something that sparks and crackles like electricity. McDonald feels it too — she knows he does. He shifts and sighs in his seat, glancing at their interlocked fingers. If he thinks them strange he says nothing — it is not his place after all; Henry pays him handsomely for his discretion.

They can't take their eyes off each other in the carriage that takes them back into town, to their hotel: Dora feels his gaze burning through her clothing. Henry urges the coachman to drive faster, but this road is perilous over the hills, with tight corners and sheer drops to the crashing ocean below. But all Dora sees out the window is a boundless black, with nothing between them and the great southern icelands but night.

When they finally arrive in town and let themselves into their hotel room, they make love again and again until morning comes, when, finally, they sleep.

❦

One was a curiosity; two were an affirmation. Now she finds herself craving more. She has become addicted to the prick and sting of the needle. She loves the tattoos she has but they are not enough; there will always be a perfect design in the perfect place — she just hasn't found it yet.

Is this what you meant? she asks her husband. About collecting?

He concurs.

It is not just the tattoo itself she yearns for; it is the whole ritual — the way they dress in plain clothes and board the train from town as the light drains from the sky, or order a carriage and drive over sharp hills that slide steeply down into the port. As they walk through the filthy streets of the port they see furtive figures, some with spider-bite eyes as they emerge from the opium dens, or hear the lusty songs of sailors as they spill from the public bar. Henry and Dora have learnt to fade into the shadows, to pass by unnoticed.

Finally they enter the parlour, where McDonald's assistant has tea and cigarettes waiting for them, and they recline on silk pillows.

She no longer has any difficulty choosing the images she wants. She selects treasures from Henry's cabinet and has them tattooed on her body. It is her way of feeling valuable to him, and he encourages her, whispering about the day that he might lose everything and what cannot be taken away from them.

A conch shell from a Pacific island; a clutch of tern and kestrel eggs, speckled like quartz and swathed in cotton, which she unwraps like bonbons; a delicate hummingbird. All these things are transported with care to the port, where McDonald sketches them expertly onto paper, then transfers them to Dora's skin while Henry watches. With every tattoo she feels herself growing closer to him, engraving herself onto his life, his future, his past. Although they do not speak of it, they both know that the tattooed lady they happened upon in McDonald's studio was not an aberration but an inspiration.

She has banished her maid from assisting her unless she is covered up. It is not that she is ashamed of her decoration — on the contrary, the thought of the tattoos beneath her clothing thrills her — it is that they are something private between herself and Henry. Once they move to London she might relax more, allow a glimpse of ink from beneath a glove or a sleeve, but not here. The people in their society would not understand.

As for Henry's collection, she is beginning to know it as if it were her own. He has had a special room built beneath the tower, reached by a discreet door that looks as if it belongs to a cupboard. It houses glass cases and specially built shelves to accommodate treasures of all sizes and shapes. It is separate from his taxidermy workroom, where he stores many of his less exotic animals, and where he mounts the birds he catches, some of which he keeps, others of which he sends to England or to Herz at the museum. A magpie with wings outstretched looks down on the room from a high shelf. Henry is generous with his collection, but his special cabinet is not for sharing with anybody but his wife. Dora thinks she might go blind if she spends too much time in there, staring at the 'mermaid' he fooled her with; a stool made from an elephant's foot; glass jars three deep, with sea creatures so grotesque she can't look past the front layer. The one time she found the courage, Henry stopped her, telling her she would find more joy in his objects of beauty. And there is much beauty here, of course — the shells and the eggs and the figurines hand-made by some distant culture. The butterflies. The tropical parrots and hummingbirds, the birds native to New Zealand. She is dazzled every time she walks in, but she enters only at Henry's invitation.

He disappears regularly with his schoolmaster friend Mr East, up into the hill country for days on end, but she doesn't begrudge him, not when she sees the look on his face as he presents her with the prize he has coveted: the bones of the extinct moa. If she gets lonely when he is away, she only has to imagine the adventures they will have together. She also takes the opportunity to go with her father to town, where she visits her friend Kate Johnson, attends the opera and the theatre.

There is just one thing that detracts from her happy life. The subject of children has arisen only once between them. As they lay in bed and Henry traced ticklish circles over the hummingbird on her belly, describing the jungle he caught it in and how much she would love it when he took her there, she had to ask him.

But what of our children? What will happen to them when we are away?

He stopped caressing her and put his arm behind his head.

Children. He sighed. Children, my dear, will complicate things.

She sat up. Are you saying to me that you don't want children? She had never even considered that marriage could come without offspring; that her duty as a wife was not tied to that of a mother.

I am just saying that we should be very careful. And until we have finished our travels, it would be . . . *expedient* to be childless.

But my poor father! He is longing for a grandson.

He took her hand. It cannot be helped, he said.

That was the end of the conversation and she has not felt that she can bring it up again. Instead she has washed herself carefully every time they make love, and prayed that he will not be disappointed in her. There is no more she can do.

The farm, Henry tells her, is thriving. He employs staff for every aspect of production and management, and only when she rides around the property does she see any of it: he never brings the work into the house, and the workers live far up the hill in specially built stone cottages. Life continues as it always has in the area, through autumn into winter, which freezes the very air of the new house, and out the other side into spring and summer. She longs for the day when Henry agrees it is time to leave it all behind. Only their trips to the port bring her any real excitement, and when Henry announces that he is to take an extended expedition to the North Island in search of the rapidly disappearing huia bird, she despairs of finding any amusement while he is gone.

Take me with you, she says.

Not this time, he says. Maybe next.

She slips, like a ship, into a dark fog. With Henry gone for so long the house is a prison. It echoes with her footsteps as she paces its rooms. He promised, she thinks. He promised that he would rescue her from her mundane life and yet here she is, still here, while he is not, while he travels and has adventures without her. She could tolerate it when his trips were so close to home; after all, she has ridden into the surrounding hills herself before, with her father, when she was younger. But she has never been to the North Island, and although it is not as appealing to her as Africa, or Peru, she would nonetheless like to see it for herself, to see Henry stalking the huia and catching it. If he has fallen back on his promise so soon, what is there to stop him leaving her stranded here while he travels halfway around the world?

She is not home alone for long, but the mood struggles to lift itself. As the carriage slides into town, past parks bright with blooms, she can almost allow the colours to lighten her, before they are gone again. When Kate greets her outside the house, she immediately notices Dora's grey face and thinks something is terribly wrong.

You will think it nothing, says Dora, so please, don't question me. I dare say I will be fine after a night out. It is the house, she says, it is too big and cold to be there alone. And so far from town. I am happy to see you.

She forces a smile and kisses her friend on the cheek.

She doesn't know what compels her to visit the circus. Everybody knows that circuses are not considered respectable, despite their popularity, and managing to persuade Kate to accompany her can only be considered a miracle. Perhaps it is her mood, a certain sense of nihilism that drives her to tempt danger. Or perhaps she is just hoping to see Lucy, the tattooed lady, again.

Dora and Kate huddle together as they move through the throng. There are all sorts here: flower girls clutching irises and daffodils in one arm and holding out a hopeful hand; hawkers thrusting ill-made or shabby wares in their faces; harassed-looking women with hordes of ragged children, running shrieking circles around each other;

gentleman with gaudy women, clearly not their wives, on their arms, who avert their eyes as Dora passes; and one or two respectable-looking couples, no doubt drawn by their curiosity but not looking entirely comfortable.

The great tent stands in the middle of the park like a beacon, beckoning people with its rainbow flags snapping in the breeze. And snaking up to the big top, the paths filled with excited customers.

They collect their tickets and enter the tent. As soon as they are inside, Dora is hit with the smell of animal dung and damp earth, and the air is moist with human bodies. A man holding a cane taps her on the shoulder and beckons to her. With a glance at Kate she follows him and they are led to the front row and shown a seat with a 'reserved' sign on it. She doesn't know whether to be flattered or disturbed; she feels as if they have been put on show.

The benches are hard and uncomfortable, and her buttocks soon begin to lose their feeling. The floor of the circus ring is dying grass, cut to pieces by animal hooves, mixed in with mud and sawdust and excrement, but even in its disappointing state it promises excitement.

I cannot believe we are here, says Kate, looking around her at the chattering crowd, the children who can barely contain their exuberance. I always wanted to go to the circus as a child, but my mother would not let me. I think she was frightened I might run off with it!

I'm glad you are enjoying yourself, says Dora, reassured; if her friend is comfortable here, then she should be as well.

Finally the show begins. At first a series of flea-bitten and melancholy animals are brought out and prodded for the audience's pleasure, including a bear that walks upright and shifts from foot to foot in a grotesque imitation of a dance, while a man drags it around by a chain fixed to its collar. Dora feels loathing towards the audience who cheer disproportionately to the quality of entertainment provided.

But the acrobats take her breath away. They soar on trapezes above her, in glittering costumes, blazing like shooting stars. Their bodies bend and corkscrew as they punch themselves through the air. When the tightrope walker stumbles Dora leaps to her feet, heart hammering in her chest, but he recovers with ease and she sits down, feeling something like disappointment, for she suspects it is all part of the act. As they take their bows, no longer celestial beings, she watches the acrobats' smooth muscled limbs flex, and the make-up on their faces ripple with rivulets of sweat. There are four of them, surely dark-haired brothers, for with their faces painted and their identical costumes, they look like the same man, replicated for the audience by some stroke of magic or trick of the light. They give a shout in a language she does not recognise, hail the audience, then sprint out of the ring into the shadows and she applauds until her palms sting.

The equestrians also do not disappoint. The couple are billed as brother and sister, although Dora suspects this is not true — it is more likely an invention to keep the woman's respectability as she is dressed in limb-freeing attire and is being handled liberally by the man. The two leap between bareback mounts, sometimes with the woman sitting on the man's shoulders, only a thin piece of cotton between her thighs and his face. The horses prance and preen for the audience and as a finale the riders sit astride them, juggling knives.

I don't think I can stand it, Kate confides in her. My poor heart!

Then the lamps are dimmed and a lone figure walks into the ring, swathed in a cloak. The ringmaster calls for silence from the audience, and they quickly quiet down.

Ladies and gentlemen! he calls. Allow me to introduce you to a very special young lady with a tragic tale to tell. Captured by the natives when she was only a girl, she was forced to live with them and endure one of the their most sacred customs — the tattoo!

A spotlight explodes onto the figure, which lifts its head. Dora's stomach leaps. Still draped from neck to floor in a cape, she recognises the glossy black hair and exquisite face of Lucy, the tattooed woman from McDonald's parlour. Her lips have been painted blue and spirals etched on her chin, and for a moment Sophie is shocked, until she remembers that McDonald has no blue ink. These designs have surely been drawn on with a paintbrush.

The ringmaster continues: Luckily for her and for us, she was rescued by a brave soldier, but she must evermore carry around the tattoos inflicted upon her. She has come to like them, after all, they are a part of her now, a dress she can never take off! Ladies and gentlemen . . . I give you . . . Artemisia!

Lucy drops her cloak and steps away from it. The audience gasps and starts to hum, although Dora isn't sure whether it is because of the tattoos that cover her body or the fact that she is dressed so provocatively, in only a corset and short bloomers, exposing her upper chest, neck, arms and legs from above the knee. But the fact that she is tattooed somehow creates modesty — she is clothed in ink. She stands proud and defiant, her hands upturned like an opera singer performing on the finest of stages.

Dora stares openly and greedily. Earlier, in McDonald's establishment, she had been unable to stare. Now, as Lucy moves about the ring, Dora can look at her from every angle, see the flowers intertwined with figures and animals, interlocking like the pieces of a puzzle, from the roses on her ankles to the horse galloping across her back.

Kate shifts in her seat beside her and murmurs, Oh, that poor woman. How frightened she must have been!

But it is just a story, Dora says to her friend. These are not Maori designs, they are clearly European. And they have been made with needles, not with a chisel.

She has said too much. She feels Kate turn to stare at her.

How do you know all of this?

But before Dora can answer, the unthinkable happens. Lucy sees her. Her mask slips and a smile breaks out. A smudge of blue ink marks her teeth. Dora looks away, feels her armpits dampen suddenly, but Lucy keeps advancing.

Dora thinks she might scream. She is terrified that Lucy is about to speak to her. She grabs Kate's hand and pulls her to her feet. The crowd immediately near her falls silent and she can feel their gaze all over her body, piercing the back of her neck, trying to sidle under her clothes.

Dora, what is it? Kate's face is all confusion.

Dora tries to run from the tent, but the aisles are clogged and she must push her body through the crowds, whose hands pull at her and who breathe alcohol and tobacco and disease in her face. But Kate is behind her, holding her steady and together the two women find the exit and tumble into the bright sunlight.

She sinks further. Kate does not ask her to explain what took place at the circus, but nor does she try to cheer her up. Instead, she avoids her, Dora knows she does. When Dora walks into a room, Kate finds some excuse to leave, or refuses to look at her.

Dora takes to her bed, pleading illness, and this gives them both some respite. It is true that she feels unwell. She cannot find the energy to get out of bed, and she stays there while the light moves across her wall and fades away with the day. A maid brings her meals but Dora can manage only a few small bites. She vomits once or twice into her bedpan and the maid removes it without question or concern. When she is alone she opens her nightgown to stare at her tattoos and tries to analyse the state she finds herself in. Why does she feel so low? She has no regrets about the tattoos. She could even show them to Kate. But no, Kate wouldn't understand. Dora cannot be herself, and be accepted by society.

She wants Henry.

A letter from him awaits her when she returns home, exhausted. It is full of wonder about the North Island, the people he has met and the things he has seen. He writes of the pohutukawa tree with its flaming flowers that lift in the wind and fall so the ground is carpeted by crimson snow, reminding him that it is snowing back in England, and how he finds he does not miss it. He speaks of the generosity of the Maori people he has met, who offer him tools and weapons, even the cloaks off their backs, about how he could never dream of deceiving them as his colleague Schlau had done and stealing the bones of their ancestors. He has had the chance to view their magnificent *moko*, their facial tattoos, not just on the men, but on the women too, who have their chins and their lips tattooed. In return he showed them his own, and they were particularly taken by the dragon on his forearm. *Taniwha*, they call it, and they watched in admiration as Henry made it dance for them. They, too, highly prize the huia, for its feathers — black with a bright white tip — and they will show him where they are to be caught. But for now he must post the letter so that it arrives home before he does. He misses her terribly and sometimes regrets his decision to leave her behind, for the journey is not as dangerous as he had at first thought. He longs to gaze upon her body. *She* is his cabinet of curiosities now. He scarcely wants for anything else.

I will bring you a huia, he writes, *to show you how much I love you.*

That night, Dora dreams about the Maori women and their moko. She dreams that they have chosen her to receive it, but she is frightened of the chisel they approach her with. They must hold her down. Even in sleep, Dora feels the tap tap of the chisel on her face, the excruciating pain as it cuts her to the bone.

Despite the summer months, the house is as cold as death. She keeps the fires lit, but the rooms remain gloomy in the unseasonably dark and rainy days. Nobody comes to visit — the neighbours have all gone to town for the festive season — so she reads, and sleeps, and waits.

Finally her father appears and is shocked at the change that has come over her: her hollowed cheeks, her dried skin, her damp eyes.

You must come to stay with me at once, he says. You are not well.

No, Father. I am expecting Henry any day now. I must wait for him.

Well, damn him for leaving you alone like this! I will speak to him when he returns, upon my word I will.

No, really — she reaches out a hand and he clasps it as she faints.

When she comes around, she is in her own bed, so she rolls over and sleeps, but is soon awoken by the doctor.

Her fear, the one she didn't even allow herself to think about, has been realised. She is pregnant. She has little choice in the matter of her father and his wife coming to stay with her. Her father tiptoes around her and whispers as though she is an invalid; he won't even hear of her getting out of bed, even when the days brighten and she begins to feel a little better. She watches him, the pride beneath his concern, the way he holds himself a little taller and absently hums lullabies such as one might sing to a child.

She thinks that her stepmother looks at her with resentment when she brings her soup, and that she spills it on purpose, burning Dora's fingers. She mutters about Dora's blessing, but all Dora wants to say to her is, Take the baby, it is yours. I have no need for it. But she eats her soup in silence.

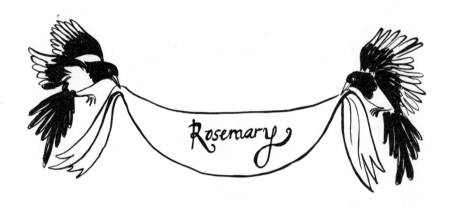

Rosemary

My pony died the August that I was thirteen. A crash and a scream woke me at first, then there was the sound of the horses calling to each other in the mist of dawn, their hooves slapping in the mud. I looked out the window of my little single bedroom and saw their shapes moving in the fog. Then another sound, like music, floating through the air to the house, an eerie note playing over and over. It made no sense.

I ran out as fast as I could, in my pyjamas, with Grandpa close behind, pulling on his coat. I hadn't stopped to put on my gumboots and the gravel of the road spiked my feet, while the cold and damp seeped between my toes. It wasn't until we got to the gate that I saw that Grandpa was carrying his rifle.

My pony Lily — the pony I had learnt to ride on, had cared for and groomed and loved every holiday I had spent there since I was seven years old — lay in a crumpled heap, tangled in a web of wire and fenceposts. Her sides rose and fell in panic. With one leg, she was trying to get up, but instead she kept hitting the wire, again and again, almost rhythmically. It was this action that produced the beautiful and troublesome sound, the note that has played over and over in my head and has invaded my dreams for twenty years. Grandpa and I stood, mesmerised. Then Lily gave an exhausted whinny and gave up. Her back leg was gashed and bleeding; it jutted out an awkward angle. She lifted her chestnut head and glared at us, her eyes rimmed with white.

To this day we don't know why Lily was trying to jump the fence, whether she had slipped on take-off or simply not cleared the height. I wished I could ask the magpies that sauntered around us as we tried to calm her down. The frenzy of her movements caused more damage to her broken body, and eventually Grandpa told me to turn away.

The shot echoed in the close grey valley. The magpies rose, calling out, and for a moment sound upon sound enveloped me, layers of echo in the stillness. I closed my eyes and hugged my cold body. My feet were soaked and numb, hooves of mud. Grandpa gathered me in his arms, keeping my body turned away from the silent horse. His jersey scratched my face. It smelt of lanolin and Gram's cigarillos.

That might have been the end of the matter, except for what happened next. Grandpa gave instructions to Josh, who was just a farmhand then, to get a digger and bury my pony. That afternoon I went for a walk, as I often did, up the hill past the dog kennels so I could look out as the light was leached from the valley. My melancholy gene, Grandpa reckoned, but just as I liked to spy on people from the tower, I liked to look back down over the house and watch people moving about inside, the smoke from the chimneys hanging in the quiet air. I badly needed to remove myself that afternoon.

As I approached the kennels, Josh came from the other direction in the ute. He waved to me as he left the road and started backing up towards where the dogs were now barking, turning circles in their runs in anticipaton. Something made me stop and watch what was going to happen next.

Josh got out of the cab and went around to the back of the truck. He started dragging great heavy lumps of something off it, and throwing them on the ground. The dogs' barks turned to yelps and they threw themselves against the doors to their cages. Once Josh was finished, he let the dogs out, stepping aside while they launched themselves at the lumps, tearing, growling, chewing. Josh stood by, his hand on his hip, his body bent over as though there was a great weight on his shoulders. He slowly looked up and saw me standing there. He gave me a cheerless wave as the dogs tore my pony to shreds and ate her in front of me. The look of satisfaction on his pinched face has always stayed with me.

I refused to eat meat after that. Every time I looked at it I thought of Lily, and the indecent act that had been performed on her body. She didn't deserve it, and neither, I decided, did any other animal. I channelled the same feelings into my taxidermy, visiting acts of respect and kindness on my subjects, bringing them dignity in their death, burying their carcasses and planting trees on top of them. I was nothing if not an idealist.

Later, I heard Grandpa yelling at Josh, threatening to fire him. I listened from my narrow room, which I refused to leave until my mother came and coaxed me away, to leave the farm and return to the city. It would be years before I returned to Magpie Hall, and I never spoke to Josh again.

The horses seemed surprised by the attention but stood placidly as they munched on carrots and we slipped their bridles on. I took Jimmy because he looked as though he could no longer support Charlie's weight; my brother would ride Blossom. Their hooves were beginning to grow over their shoes, but at least they were still shod. I made a mental note to mention to one of the farm staff to get them redone; with Grandpa gone they stood the risk of being severely neglected.

It was one of the misty mornings I had loved as a child. For a moment I imagined myself back in that simpler time, when riding seemed as safe and natural as going for a walk. The horses' breath hung in the cold air and we trudged over dew-heavy grass to the stable to give them a quick groom. By midday the fog would burn off and we would have a fine day. We led them without speaking, listening to the plod of hooves in mud and the jingling of the bits in their mouths. I felt less anxious than I had for days, and at that moment thought of nothing but the task at hand — no Hugh, no Sam, no Grandpa, no intruders. I had forgotten how therapeutic horses could be.

After we'd brushed them and removed the mud and stones from their hooves, we saddled up and headed up the hill by road. We passed the empty dog run. Even though it was Saturday, some farm work just didn't take a holiday. I pictured Sam out there on his bike, whistling and growling in the unintelligible language shepherds use with their dogs.

'Christ, I'd forgotten these muscles even existed,' said Charlie as he stood in his stirrups and stretched. 'We're going to be sore tomorrow.'

I nodded but said nothing. I, too, could feel my thighs weaken with the effort of digging in my knees. My hands tingled with cold and my nose was beginning to run. I wiped it on my sleeve.

The road twisted up the hill, past the limestone cottages. Josh and his family lived in the biggest, and shearers and farmhands used the others. Children's bikes lay scattered in front of Josh's place, but apart from smoke rolling from the chimney, there was no sign of anyone.

'I suppose we should stop and say hello,' said Charlie, starting to turn Blossom's head toward the driveway. 'We could ask them if they've seen anyone prowling around the house, too.'

'Let's not,' I said. 'I haven't talked to them yet and Sam said Josh is pretty unhappy about the way things are going. You could talk to him if you want. Later. I couldn't stand it right now.'

Charlie seemed satisfied and resumed his path. As we passed the house, we saw a face at the kitchen window, looking out at us. A large figure, with unkempt black hair. Charlie waved with his whole arm, a great sunny smile on his face, while I lifted my hand tentatively. Josh's expression remained unchanged. He didn't wave back, and after a moment or two he turned his back and walked away.

'Maybe he didn't see us,' said Charlie.

'Oh, he saw us all right,' I said.

Further up the hill, we left the road and entered one of the paddocks. Charlie urged Blossom into a canter and I followed, worried that old Jimmy might not be able to take the pace. But he pricked his ears forward and took off; I had a hard time reining him in from breaking into a full gallop. Sheep scattered away from us and the wind was luxurious on my burning cheeks. Charlie whooped ahead of me and streaked off. By the time we got to the next gate, I was breathing hard with the effort of staying on and keeping Jimmy under control, but I was exhilarated.

'Oh, yeah!' said Charlie, as he jumped off Blossom to open the gate. 'I can't believe I haven't done that for so long. Where've I been all this time?'

'Too busy being a big-shot city doctor, I expect.'

He shrugged and waited for me to come through the gate before shutting it again and remounting.

'Do you remember the way to the caves?' he asked.

'I think so. A few more paddocks over. Past the church.'

'Wish we had some of Mrs G's bacon and egg pie,' he said. Even I felt nostalgic, despite now being a vegetarian. It was quite a ride. We had only a couple of sandwiches to keep us going.

The fog had lifted by the time we got to the small stone chapel near the top of the hill, but the wind chased thick white clouds across the sky and I could feel it cutting through my jacket into my kidneys. The little building was still standing, leaning slightly on unstable foundations, but the roof had fallen in and what was left of it had become a home for birds and mice. It was a shame, but I liked it like that; it made me think of the English countryside, with all its history. This church would have been built for the first family who owned the house, the people Henry had bought it off after the earthquake, and it would have been attended by them and all the workers and domestic staff they employed. It was probably quite a crowd in those days.

'Can we stop here for a bit?' I asked. Charlie nodded. We dismounted and tied the horses to a fencepost, then went through the little iron gate that barely clung to its hinges. An old-fashioned water pump rusted nearby. Charlie headed for the door of the church, but it was the few stark gravestones that interested me.

They rose up out of the scraggly grass and sheep droppings, small and lichen-covered, with names I didn't recognise — servants long forgotten, perhaps, or ancestors of the original owners. Some stones commemorated the short lives of babies and small children.

One stood apart from the rest, under an apple tree fat with fruit.

This headstone alone was made from marble, and it stood at a slight angle.

Charlie came over and stood next to me as I looked at it.

'Dora Summers,' he said. 'Who's that?'

'You know,' I said, 'Henry's wife. The one who drowned.'

'But I thought her body was lost forever. I thought he murdered her.'

I read out the inscription. '*In Memoriam, Dora Summers, taken tragically*. I think this is just a memorial. I don't think she's actually buried here. See, most of these graves are enclosed. This one just has a headstone.'

'I wonder where Henry is, then? When did they stop burying people here?'

'When the church stopped being used, I suppose. I don't know.'

We stood looking at it a while longer. The clouds threw moving shapes on the ground.

'Grandpa should be here, really, shouldn't he?' I said. 'And Tess.'

'Are you kidding?' said Charlie, taking my arm. 'Mum would never have let them bury her here. Not after what happened.'

'You're right. That was a stupid thing to say. Sorry.'

He squeezed my arm. Tess's name had fluttered up unexpectedly between us, but it seemed that neither of us wanted to grab at it. I broke the silence.

'I'd like to be buried here though. Can you arrange that please?'

I felt him relax beside me. He dropped my arm and stepped away. 'Thought you were donating your body to science. To be stuffed or whatever it was.'

'Ah, so I am. Thanks for the reminder.'

'You know, there is another alternative,' said Charlie. 'You can get your ashes pressed into a diamond. Then your sweetheart can make a ring out of you and wear you forever.'

'A memento mori. I like that. Now all I need is the sweetheart.'

'Well, you don't seem to have a shortage of options.'

I grunted. 'Not viable ones.'

'You're too fussy, that's your trouble. You've read too many romantic novels and you're wasting your time waiting for your Heathcliff.'

'Maybe,' I said. I didn't want to think about it any more.

We left the sad little graveyard behind and crested the ridge that dropped down to the caves. We were not allowed to come here alone as children — Grandpa said the caves were too unstable. One of them had been blocked by falling rocks when he was a child himself. We had seen them just a few times, on family outings, and I could only yearn for the games that we could have played in them. As we approached I had a strange thought: that the caves would make a good hiding place for treasure. The blocked cave had become barred when Grandpa was a boy, which must have been around the time Henry had boxed up his cabinet of curiosities and arranged for it to be sent to the British Museum. Only, it never arrived. Could it have been hidden somewhere on the estate? I had ruled out its being in the house, as Grandpa had found nothing in all the years he lived there. But perhaps the instruction to stay away from the caves was to hide something. Could Grandpa's father have gone against Henry's wishes and hidden the cabinet there, warning his son and subsequent generations away?

Excited, I told Charlie of my theory.

'Jesus, you've got a good imagination,' he said.

The caves lay in the shadow of the limestone cliffs. We tied the horses up, giving them enough headroom to graze.

'Do you remember coming here?' I asked Charlie.

'I do. Grandpa said there used to be moa in this valley. I was convinced I would find one still alive. I was really disappointed when we had to go back and I still hadn't found one.'

'What would you have done with it? Killed it with your slingshot, probably.'

'Yeah, all right. You're never going to let me forget that magpie, are you?'

'Well, it was a terrible thing to do. But it set me on the taxidermy path, so I suppose I should thank you.'

'You're welcome.' He sat down on a rock and lit a cigarette. 'I didn't tell you that I used to come here when I wasn't supposed to, with some of the farm kids. We used to smoke here.' He looked at the end of his cigarette. 'Some things don't change, I guess.'

'I'm not at all surprised.'

'Yeah, well, you and Grandpa were always getting into a huddle over some dead animal. He was too busy to even notice. We used to ride up here and be back at the end of the day and nobody even asked me where I'd been.'

'I'm sorry.'

He shrugged. 'Don't be. I liked it. The Maori kids told me there're rock drawings in these caves, done by their ancestors. We tried to move some of the rocks so we could get into the blocked one, but there were just too many of them. I think they used to be burial caves. They said they were tapu, so we were too scared to dig very deep.'

I was glad now that the cave was inaccessible. I liked the thought of the drawings behind the rock slide being safe from the light and from prying eyes. And if they really were burial caves, I didn't want to disturb whatever was within. I walked a little way into the shallow cavern. It was quiet inside, with only the muffled sound of dripping water and the occasional whistle of the wind catching in the crevices.

'Dora!' I shouted, but there was no answer, only the wind humming to me from outside.

❦

It was late afternoon by the time we got back to the stables, and grey clouds had rolled across the sky to meet us. I felt exhausted, and my legs trembled as I walked around Jimmy, taking off his tack and stowing it away. I gave him a cursory brush, then led him back to the paddock. He lingered as though reluctant to leave, but once Blossom was beside him, they lay down to roll in the dirt. Charlie and I stood watching them, enjoying the moment, before walking around the side of the house.

It wasn't until we were right by the kitchen door that we saw it. I noticed the magpie first, wings splayed in a mockery of flight, head limp on the stalk of its neck. A huge nail had been pounded through its body, right where its tiny heart would be. Blood ran down the white paint, smeared in places, as though the job had been done hastily. I turned to look at Charlie, just in time to see his face as he registered what was in front of him. He stepped back and raised an arm, as if to protect himself.

Moments later I sat crying at the kitchen table, while Charlie sat beside me, shaken but trying to comfort me.

'What have we done to deserve this?' I asked him. Despite my tears, I felt oddly distant from the whole situation. A dead animal nailed to the door was too sinister to be real, the kind of joke Charlie would have played on me when he was a boy. I told him about the possum on the doorstep, how it had appeared just after I had seen the face at the window and how I had talked myself into believing it benign.

'Why didn't you tell me? Jesus, we should have called the police ages ago.'

'Because I didn't know if it was a threat or not. I thought maybe someone had left it there for me as a gift.'

'What kind of a gift?'

'A project, taxidermy. Sam brought me a rabbit the other day and I've already skinned it.'

'You think Sam did this? That bastard.' He stood up. 'He'll get fired for this.'

'I don't know.' I really didn't. Sam seemed the most likely candidate. I'd rejected him and he'd been angry, but I didn't know whether he was capable of something like this.

'I'll call Josh. He'll get him sorted out.'

Resigned, I followed Charlie through to the living room, where the old dial phone perched on a side table. I couldn't avoid the farm manager forever. I sat down on the old familiar couch and pulled the rug over my knees. As I listened to the laboured sound of every number Charlie dialled, I realised there was someone standing in the garden, looking at us. He stood straight and block-shouldered, his arms by his sides, no expression on his face, but his head tilted at such an angle that his thick brows nearly obscured his eyes. He saw me looking at him, but he neither acknowledged me nor changed his position.

'Do you . . . Charlie, do you see who's outside?' I had to know if I was imagining things, yet again.

Charlie replaced the receiver with a clunk. 'I see him all right. Guess there's no need to call him now.'

Henry

Tiny lizards that curl inside his hand like ribbons. Strange, flightless birds with withered wings: the cheeky and bold weka, the shy nocturnal kiwi. The blue-feathered, red-footed swamp hen, or pukeko, that flicked its tail in fright, showing him its white underfeathers before he shot it, and warned the other birds away. Frilly-legged centipedes, and the magnificent giant weta, with its barbed, kicking legs and its feelers stretching many times longer than its own body; it put up a good fight but he got it in the end without damaging it, even though the jar was scarcely big enough to poison it. New Zealand's only native mammal, a mouse-faced bat, proved harder to mount than he had anticipated, but he has done a nice job on making it look fierce, despite its size.

And the huia.

Everything else he packs away, ready to be shipped elsewhere, but the huia he holds in his arms for the last few hours of his journey. He wants to present it to Dora. For it to be the first thing she sees. For her to know that it was all worthwhile, this separation.

A light drizzle falls as the carriage moves up the driveway. Magpie Hall looms pleasingly in the landscape. He never tires of the view of the house as the road crests a small hill and turns a corner, veering away from the river, which is running faster and fatter than usual; it must have been raining while he was away.

He leaps down, the huia safe in his arms.

Dora! he calls, looking up.

Her face appears at the window for a moment, like a ghost, then is gone. She meets him at the bottom of the stairs and he only just has time to put the huia on a side table before she throws herself at him.

Let me look at you, he says. He tries to pull her arms loose from around his neck, but she clings to him like a leech. Her face is hot against his neck, her breath moist. He wants to carry her upstairs. Instead he takes a step back, holding her wrists, and looks at her. She will not return the gaze, however. He is shocked by what he sees: she has lost weight, and her hair is limp, with grease at the roots and a smattering of snowy dandruff. Her eyes are red, as though she has been crying for a week.

Whatever is the matter? he asks, catching her again with his arms as she begins to sob.

She doesn't answer him. He pulls her into the parlour and lowers her into an armchair, where she sits clutching her stomach and squeezing the handkerchief he has given her.

He sits in a hard chair beside her, waiting.

She shakes her head. Nothing is the matter, she says. I just missed you, that is all. She blushes, as though this admission embarrasses her.

He feels a little embarrassed himself.

That can't be it, he says. There must be something more.

She bristles. Do you think me foolish? All that time, and only one letter from you? Did you think of me at all?

He springs up and looks down at her. Her eyes widen and she bites her lip. His shoulders begin to shake. He must leave the room, get away from her: the only way to stop his body convulsing is to ball the force inside him and throw it at something. Or someone.

In the entrance hall he picks up the huia. He looks at it, at his hands holding it, trembling and clenching, and it takes all his strength to put the magnificent bird back on the table and smash his fist into the wall above it.

❋

I'm sorry, says Dora as she bandages his hand. His knuckles are shiny and inflated, the cuts painful. Only himself to blame.

I wasn't angry with you, she continues. I *did* miss you. I don't know what has got into me. I feel better now that you're home, that's all. She squeezes his good hand, smiles, but still the sadness beneath the skin is palpable.

He won't ask her. She will tell him in her time, if that is what she wants.

For now, his own anger has floated away. As usual, he can't even remember what it felt like when it was inside him; he is only glad that he has expelled it. Glad, too, that it is his own body that is damaged, not the huia's or, God forbid, Dora's.

They sit in his room. The fire has been lit and, outside, the dim light is failing further as the day subsides. The green wood crackles and smokes, and he can feel it begin to needle at his eyes, but still, it is comforting. Dora convinced him to come upstairs, to lie down after his journey, and for a moment he was seduced by the idea of a soft bed and oblivion. But now he is too excited about showing her the prize.

She lights the lamp to finish her job, and pulls his hand close to her face to inspect the work.

Yes, that should hold, she says.

Come with me. He stands and takes her hand, pulls her down the stairs. He avoids looking at the dented wallpaper — his hand sustained most of the damage — and presents her with the huia.

At first she looks unsure what to do with it, but then her face begins to glow, and some warmth returns to her eyes.

You found one, she whispers.

For you, he says.

For me, she repeats. She stares at the bird, at its fine curved beak, shaped for nectar-drinking, its deep black feathers. The tail, dipped in bright white paint. It perches on a totara branch, which is in turn attached to a wooden stand, and this is how she holds it, as if too scared to touch the bird itself.

Tell me, she says. Tell me everything.

And so they move into the drawing room, and in front of the fire he tells her the story of its capture. Of how he searched for days for the bird, growing more and more despondent. His guide woke him early one morning with a hand over his mouth, bidding him to be quiet and pointing up into the dense bush, where the huia hopped from branch to branch, hunting insects and seemingly oblivious to the human presence below. But perhaps it was merely unafraid.

Dora, he tells her, I longed to be there a hundred years earlier, when that bush would have been alive with their calls, before they were hunted to near extinction. I would have even found them in the

South Island, but no longer. They are a dying breed. You hold one of the last of the huia in your hands. A female — see the long beak? The males have shorter beaks. But I only wanted one. Just one.

His voice trails away as he relives the moment in his mind. The way he rose quickly and stealthily, reaching for his gun, which he had cleaned and loaded the night before. The way he stalked it, making himself as light as a bubble so not a twig crackled underfoot. He willed his whole body to float over the earth, following the huia's path through the bush. And finally, he brought the gun to his eye. He knew he would have only one shot, and he took it.

It was perfect, he says after he has related this to Dora. The shot was so fine there was hardly any blood. And as you can see, the specimen is perfect.

It *is* perfect, she says.

Later, they lie in bed and watch the light from a single candle dance in a draught. He knows that the gift of the huia pleased her, but there remains a stillness about her, as if any youthfulness she had has been tempered by his absence. He knows she wants to say something to him by the way she keeps sighing, turning to look at him, then turning over again when he meets her gaze.

Finally he props himself on his elbow and takes her chin gently in his fingers.

There is something on your mind, he says.

She pauses before speaking, and when she does her eyes have a nakedness about them that has been hidden since his arrival.

I would like — she begins. No, I *need*, to go back to see McDonald. Soon. Can we do that?

But of course. Do you have something in mind?

My back. It feels empty. I need something there, something . . . splendid.

He doesn't ask her for an explanation, for he knows. He has been through it all himself, felt a hunger that drove him into London just when his father needed him for some business, that compelled him to cover the bare skin on his left bicep.

I will write to him tomorrow, says Henry, and tell him to prepare for our arrival.

Boldly, they have come in the morning this time. By day, the port's buildings show their paint cracked and crusted by salt; the alleyways are damp with puddles of urine from last night's revelry. All activity, however, is focused on the wharves and the ships — from the elevated town streets they can see the dwarfed figures of men scampering over the cargo, hauling it from ship to dock and dock to ship.

McDonald sits bleary-eyed in his shop, waiting for them in a cloud of tobacco smoke. The room smells of alcohol, but Henry knows now to trust that the tattooer is not drunk. McDonald moves stiffly as he leads them through to the back room, muttering about the hour.

You knew we were coming at this time, said Henry, so please close your mouth, sir. It is not our fault if you did not show some restraint last evening.

McDonald chuckles and aims some saliva into the nearby spittoon.

Right you are, sir, he replies. And what do we have here?

Henry puts the box he has been carrying on a nearby table.

It is very precious to us and we have transported it safely thus far, so please be careful with it. He lifts the huia out and places it reverently beside the box.

McDonald lets out a long, low whistle.

That's quite some tweeter! What do you call it then?

It is the huia. From the North Island. I would like you to sketch a design from it and to tattoo Mrs Summers' back. Quite large, that is why we have arrived early.

The thick eyebrows shoot up. Her back is it now? But he says no more, as if suddenly aware it would not be his place to comment.

Beside him, Dora fidgets with her purse and walks tight circles around the room. Her breathing is too fast; Henry is worried that she will make herself faint.

Sit down, he says, too brusquely, and she stops pacing to look at him, startled.

He softens his voice and guides her to a chair. You need to relax or it will only hurt more, he says. Then he addresses McDonald. Where is your boy? Can't you get us some tea? What do we pay you for?

He thinks of the expensive teaset he bought for the establishment, wonders if it remains pristine or has been chipped or broken, or worse, if it is filthy.

He'll be here soon enough, says McDonald as he examines the bird from every angle, trying to find the best place to start his sketching.

Henry doesn't know why he is so nervous. It is not that he disapproves of the work Dora is about to undergo, but he worries for her. She has been so lacklustre; he is concerned she might regret the decision when it is over, or even that she will be left with a half-finished bird on her back for the rest of her life.

If the tattoo does make her happier, as she seems to think, when will the desire to cover her body in ink end? *Where* will it end? Her wrists? Her neck? Her face? Will she be happy only when she has a new tattoo to admire?

But he loves her body the way it is. The tattooing doesn't diminish her beauty; it enhances it. All the more because he is the only person on earth, apart from McDonald, who is able to gaze upon it. For all his fears, it makes him feel as though she belongs to him — the most exquisite curiosity in the world. None of the other collectors has a specimen quite like Dora.

There. McDonald hands the sketch pad to Henry, and Dora huddles into him to look at it. The tattooer has taken some liberties with the positioning of bird, accentuating the curve of its beak by also curving its neck.

I can see it reaching across her back, says McDonald, taking in her shoulder blades. The design will work in with her womanly shape, see.

Dora blushes and looks away, but nods her assent.

How long will it take? she asks.

Not as long as you would think, says McDonald. In fact, I have a surprise for you.

He turns and picks up an instrument. He fiddles with it for a moment and it springs to life with a whizzing sound.

What is it? asks Henry. It looks to him like an automaton, clearly electrified, but it is crudely made with pieces of metal and wood and rubber. McDonald holds it closer and now Henry can see the little nib moving so fast that it is invisible.

The electric tattoo machine, says McDonald proudly. This will revolutionise the tattoo business, mark my words. From now on, everything is going to change.

Dora shudders beside him. I don't know, she says. It doesn't look safe.

McDonald shuts the instrument off and the silence in the room rises to greet them. Oh, it's safe, madam, he says. And it will make the lines finer, and faster. You'll hardly feel the difference except you'll be sitting in the chair for a shorter time and it really will be like drawing on you with a pen. Much more accurate. You'll be pleased with the results.

To prove it, he rolls up the sleeve of his left arm to reveal a ship rendered in intricate detail, like a fine pen and ink drawing. Its sails flicker and blaze in the wind while the waves cream at its bow. There is no denying its superiority.

I'll go first, Henry says, and touches Dora's elbow. Will that help?

She sighs in relief. Yes. Please.

Very well. He settles himself back into the silk cushions. He unties his cravat and unbuttons his shirt, which he pulls back to expose his chest, and takes a cigarette from the silver tray beside him.

Here. He taps his chest, just below the rose that McDonald tattooed when he first arrived. I don't care about England any more. I want you to write her name, just here, above my heart. I want you to write *Dora*.

Very well. McDonald takes a razor and shaves the area, then wipes it clean with alcohol. He dips the needle in ink and the tattoo machine kicks into life with a grunt. Henry grips his thighs and closes his eyes. His pectoral muscles tense in anticipation of an assault. When it comes he gasps, not from pain, but from surprise at the sensation. It doesn't hurt any more or less than the hand-held needle, but it carries a heat with it, and he feels the warmth deposited beneath his skin and spread through his muscles. He opens his eyes and sees Dora, concentrating on his face, reading his every move.

He begins to relax and as he does so, the pain eases. He smiles at his wife.

Yes, he says. You will be fine. It is no worse than before, merely different.

The steady vibration is even pleasant, he fancies, like the steady whirr of a hummingbird's wings as it hovers above a flower to steal its nectar.

Hummingbird, he says to Dora. It's like a hummingbird.

She looks confused but says nothing, only stares at the word emerging on his chest, and so rapidly. It is all over in five minutes. McDonald wipes away a trickle of blood. For such a rough man, his penmanship is most satisfactory, with the D slightly slanted, elegant and bold, running on with a flourish to the smaller O and beyond. The line is cleaner than it would have been before, truer. Most satisfactory.

Dora is smiling now, her face relaxed. He can see the eagerness in her eyes.

Ready? he asks her.

Ready. She sits down.

And you are sure this is what you want? he asks her one last time.

It is, she says. Only, Henry — she turns in her seat and grabs his hand suddenly, fiercely. I am a little scared. Tell me everything will be all right.

Of course it will be, he assures her, but there is something else troubling her, he can feel it in the way her hand grips his, the urgency with which she searches for reassurance.

Everything will be wonderful, he says.

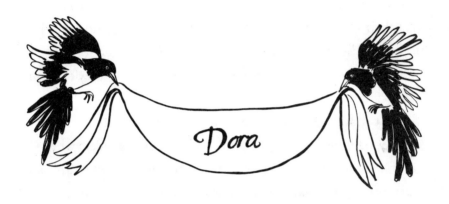

Dora

The huia tattoo took two sessions to complete: first the outline in black, then a return visit a few days later to fill in the colour. She wishes she could see it first hand, but she must look at it through a series of mirrors, so she is never sure whether she is seeing it as it appears, or whether the image is reversed. It is stunning. The huia seems so full of life that it might seek its freedom and fly from her back, and yet it is undeniably stylised. McDonald has taken liberties in the design that only complete the natural beauty of the bird; it moulds to the contours of her shoulder blades and back like a caress.

Although the tattoo is painful, and she cannot sleep on her back, it is worth it. For days she has sloughed off the bad feelings she has been experiencing since Henry's absence and since she learned of her pregnancy. It is as if the ink has given her life; it pulses under her skin, entering her blood and racing to the tips of her fingers. She is in a constant state of excitement, as if something wonderful is about to happen, and every movement she makes seems larger and more meaningful than before. Her head feels light on her shoulders. She wonders if this is what it is like to be drunk.

They stay in town and go to the theatre and to the races. She finds a new vigour for life and every night they make love as if it were their last chance. She wants to return to McDonald, to feel the electric needle singing over her skin, but Henry says no for now, that he must return to the country to oversee his business; they can come back next month.

Next month. As the carriage thunders towards the estate Dora puts her hand on her belly, judging its girth, and wonders when she will start to show the life growing inside. Henry is in an inexplicably bad mood, which happens more and more regularly. He says it is nothing to do with her; that he wakes up feeling black and there is nothing he can do to control it. But when he won't look at her, she can't help but feel slighted. She wonders if he has guessed her condition and is angry with her. She knows that he is growing tired of life at home and longs to get away again, up into the mountains or to the North Island, foraging for treasures. Perhaps he has wearied of her and wants to leave the country altogether, to go back to England, but is kept here by his commitments to the farm.

Pulling up outside Magpie Hall, she feels the life the ink gave her draining away. She loves the house because Henry restored it for her, but it is so cold, so big. It is surely the kind of place people's ghosts cling to when they die, unable to find their way out of its corners and hidden rooms to move on to the next world.

With Henry gone most days, she throws herself into the running of the house. The housekeeper is startled by her interest but tolerates the endless stream of questions about food and fire-lighting schedules, about the household accounts and the industriousness of the maids and the gardeners. Dora knows she works to keep something at bay — the blackness that Henry talks about descends on her also, as though the house has infected them both.

She awakes one morning in April, when the sun has begun rising later and the leaves on the trees are beginning to turn. Henry's arms are wrapped around her and she enjoys the warmth of his body against hers.

He awakes with a hum in her ear.

Good morning, he says, and releases her so he can stretch.

What are you doing today? she asks.

I have just one small meeting, he says, with the overseer. And then I am all yours. Perhaps we could have a picnic, down by the river, if the weather is good.

Dora glances doubtfully at the curtains. Did you not hear the rain on the roof in the night? she says. Honestly, I think you could sleep through an earthquake if it hit us.

She can barely read the clock beside her, which says ten past seven, and the typical morning light is not seeping around the edges of the curtains as it should. She slips out of bed and opens them a crack to look out.

The rain is still coming down in steady sheets — what she thinks of as *wet* rain. If she opened the window she would be able to hear the river.

You're not thinking of going out in this, surely? She pulls the curtain aside from the window and turns to show him.

I'm afraid my business won't wait. Just wrapping up a few things. You'll be pleased when I'm finished, Dora. Then we can go back to town if you wish. We could even book an expedition somewhere. If you like.

Like? She smiles and throws herself back down on the bed. Oh, you have made me *very* happy, Mr Summers.

But later, when Henry has breakfasted and left, she feels her queasiness return. When her maid pulls her corset tight over her chemise she worries that she is squashing the baby inside her and tells her to loosen it. Her navel sticks out more than it used to — surely Henry has noticed? But she has been careful about undressing in the dark recently, and what his eyes haven't seen his hands haven't detected.

How can she possibly travel anywhere remotely dangerous in her condition?

She finds her way to the room under the tower where Henry's collection is housed. In here, she feels as though she is breathing in the whole world — Africa, South America, India, Japan, the South Pacific. The room is getting crowded now and things have been shifted around to accommodate the moa bones, and the new insects and species of birds that have been expertly mounted by her husband. They look down at her — large green parrots with sturdy claws, dainty little fantails clinging to thin branches, and a magpie that glares at her just like the birds that parade around the house and nestle in the chimneys.

She peers though the glass of one of the cases, at the snakes suspended in liquid, at a — yes, she has to look twice to be sure — two-headed kitten hanging in the light. The sight makes her step back. She hadn't realised Henry was quite so morbid, but then again, it is a curiosity, just as the more exotic but single-skulled creatures are. She wonders why she has not noticed it before, and finds herself drawn in to examine the case more closely. She has never minded that Henry has discouraged her from looking in here, contenting herself with gazing up at the bright plumage of the birds, or the fierce eyes of mammals, the sparkling wings of insects framed and hung on the wall. The cases, by contrast, are dingy, with no colour to them. Their contents are pale and fleshy and as she peers closer she begins to make out shapes. A human hand. Her heart beats faster. How disgusting. It looks like a turnip carved for a scarecrow.

She tries the door to the case, expecting to find it locked, but it moves easily under her fingers. She pushes the hand aside and reaches behind it, pulling out the first jar she touches.

No, she says. Her hands begin to shake and the shape inside, which at first she took to be some kind of sea anemone, spins slowly in the glow of the lamp. She is looking at a human baby. Only it is so small, it can never have been born. Its head is large in proportion to its thin body, its eyes huge and veined beneath the skin that covers its sockets.

She feels a churning then, inside, unsure whether the life within her is kicking to be let out, or her own gut is heaving at the sight of the foetus.

But there is more, she knows there is. She brings out another jar — tiny baby's feet — and begins to weep for the child, for its mother. For herself. Her hands move independently, shoving aside eels and pickled stoats, until there, at the back of the case, a face stares out at her — a child's face. She brings it out slowly, with two hands, reads the label: smallpox. The lightly pitted face has been removed from the skull and floats soft and jelly-like, a mask with holes where the eyes should be. A child. Not a curiosity, not something to be coveted and collected and gloated over. *A child.*

The jar slips and smashes on the ground. Liquid splashes over her dress, her feet, and the face flaps like a fish on the ground. She thinks she can feel its cool flesh against her own.

She screams, kicks it away and folds herself into the far corner of the room.

This is the real reason he does not want children. This is what happens to them when they get sick, or die — they become trophies in a cabinet. She must do everything she can to protect the child inside her, and that means staying at home and keeping it safe. Damn Henry and his wild adventures. She puts her head on her knees and sobs.

This is how Henry finds her, only minutes later.

He begins to rush to her but stops when his feet crunch on glass.

What is this? What has happened? He crouches down and stares at the face on the floor, at the wet mess she has made.

It's disgusting, she cries. How could you own such a thing? She expects him to come to her then, to take her in his arms. But he stands, draws himself tall.

You're being ridiculous, he says. It's not as if I murdered it. It is a medical curiosity, nothing more.

But where did you get it?

From a hospital.

He glances at the cabinet, sees it in disarray.

I see you have found my other specimens. I got them all from the hospital. They were just going to be incinerated.

But what about those children's mothers?

They didn't want them! Good God, woman, what has got into you?

They were just babies! she yells. Her shoulders convulse with the effort of holding her tears back.

Henry steps over the mess on the floor. He bends down. She feels his hot breath on her face and recognises the flaming cheeks, the cruel set of his mouth. He grabs her shoulders and hauls her to her feet, then shakes her until she thinks she might vomit on him. He shouts in her face, Pull yourself together! Flecks of spittle fly into her eye.

She pushes him away with all her strength and is astonished at how effective it is. His angry face collapses into surprise as he barrels backwards into the cabinet, which shakes under the impact but does not break or fall.

Dora lifts her skirts and runs for the door, careful to take a giant step to clear the debris on the floor. It is not fear that drives her, but something else — grief, despair, disappointment. She makes for the door because all she knows is that she needs to get out of this house, away from its dark corners and claustrophobic walls.

Outside, the rain still drives from the sky. It washes her face and drenches her hair and clothes, which suck close to her skin as she runs. Towards the river. The distant roar grows louder the closer she gets. She lets herself through the gate of the home paddock, and when her wet fingers fumble with the catch, she leaves it open and keeps running, not looking back to see whether Henry is following her. She thinks she hears her name on the wind, but it is impossible to tell above the clamour of the water. She is upon it now, and stops for a moment to catch her breath. She takes great gulps of the damp air, and the effort hurts her chest.

She turns left to follow the river, walking now, towards the hills. The water churns brown beside her; it has risen so high that she must navigate great puddles in the path. Long grass grabs at her skirts, while rain and damp earth moisten her boots. As she rounds the bend where the young weeping willows are turning amber, a magpie rises slowly into the air, hovers for a second with a squawk, then glides away, following her.

On she trudges, not sure where she is going, knowing only that she needs to be alone. Henry must have lost her, for he would easily have caught up with her by now, and for a second she imagines him engulfing her in his warm arms, shielding her from the rain. From her own foolishness.

She is suddenly conscious of all the sounds around her: of the swoosh of her legs in the grass, and the rhythm of her feet in the mud, the sound of the rain as it is swallowed by the raging stream. Her head is down, listening, and she does not see the ambush waiting for her until she is upon it.

The first magpie has been joined by more. They strut about, surrounding her. She has an urge to turn and run back the way she came, but they are all around her now, staring at her. She stops and waits. Their cacophony drowns out everything else, even the roar of the river. Dora puts her hands over her ears and shouts at them: Stop! Stop! Get out of my way!

But instead they fly towards her. She screams and crouches down, covering her face with her arms, but still they come, pecking at her neck and her back, tangling their claws in her hair. Blindly, Dora stands up, and runs straight into the waiting river.

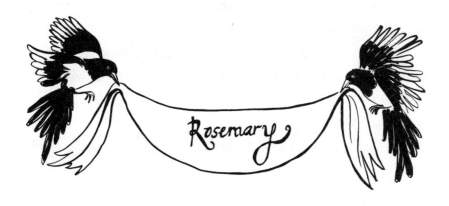

Rosemary

As with all good Gothic novels, this story is full of ghosts. The pages of the books I have been studying reveal them — women long gone, lovers torn apart or reunited in death, the ghosts of dreams and of the imagination, products of too many novels or of an unstable mind. Unreliable narrators.

I never talk about my sister Tess. As much as I can, I try not to think about her, but it is she, not Dora, who is the ghost in this story. She is my Bertha, my Rebecca, my Catherine. She has shaped who I have become in my life, the paths I have chosen. She is there, hovering around the edges of every incident, over every minute of my stay at Magpie Hall — in the attic, in the bedroom, in my dreams, in the tower. Especially in the tower. The time has come to let her out. And to face up to my part in her death.

Perhaps I need to go back further, to the May holidays of the year I turned thirteen. My parents had once again sent us to the country for the two-week break. The winter had arrived early, with sub-zero temperatures overnight and ice on the puddles of mud that we jumped on to hear them crunch underfoot, with hailstorms and dreary, low-lying cloud. Grandpa and I huddled together in the workroom as often as we could, listening to talkback radio with the door shut and the heater on full bore.

I didn't notice then what Charlie got up to, but he was a resourceful child, and stayed out of Gram's way. Of course I now know that he was often away with the farm kids on horseback, skulking around the caves and smoking cigarettes. It was always easy for him to make friends. He pulled them in with his endless banter, his willingness to take risks.

Tess, on the other hand, simmered with boredom. She was soon to turn sixteen and was livid at being left in the clutches of two old people and her younger siblings. She slept until midday and stayed up past midnight, watching horror movies and cop show reruns. She barely spoke to me. Instead she skulked around the house with *Wuthering Heights* in her hand, a wispy, long-bodied girl who was looking more and more like a woman. She was an enigma to me. Back in the city, she ran with a crowd of musicians, played in a band. I knew when she told our parents she was at parties that she was really at a pub, drinking, playing her guitar, falling in love. She was always home by midnight, but I heard the catch on her window as she left an hour later. I watched her and I listened to her, but we hardly spoke.

Tess called me a weirdo. She bad-mouthed Grandpa behind his back, making fun of his false teeth, his untidiness, his obsession with dead animals. She never came into the workroom, and I saw her scuttle past the birds in the living room, averting her eyes, as if afraid they might come alive and fly at her. Grandpa seemed unsure how to talk to her. He and I shared the language of taxidermy, but he and Tess had only a chasm of years between them. It made me mad, the way she talked about him, how her face screwed up as she brushed the dog hair from her clothes. I just wanted her to go, to leave us to our work.

One night, we were gathered in the kitchen for dinner. The dining hall was way too big and formal and too hard to heat. Gram was standing at the kitchen bench, helping Mrs G, when she made an irritated growl at the back of her throat.

'Who's that out there? Percy, there's someone out in the garden. Go and see who it is.' She shook her head, making her pearls rattle. 'Honestly,' she said, 'he's just standing there looking in, like a lost mutt.'

Grandpa went out the door and reappeared a few minutes later with the farmhand, Josh. The old man was shaking his head and talking: '. . . won't hear another word. It's not much warmer in here, but the food will take off the chill.'

Josh hung his head and shrugged.

Gram folded her arms. 'Well, what did you think you were doing out there, boy?'

'Sorry, Mrs Summers. I was passing and I just liked the look of you all there in the kitchen. I didn't mean to snoop.'

Mrs G laid another place at the table and sat him down with a pat on the shoulders. 'Nonsense, Josh,' she said, 'you're most welcome. I expect you haven't had a decent home-cooked meal for a while.'

'Baked beans,' was all he said. He took up more than his share of room at that table; he couldn't help it. Over six feet tall and built like a brick shithouse as Grandpa would have said, out of Gram's hearing, of course. He made me feel small just looking at him and

I shrank into my seat. Having a stranger at the table — a stranger to me, anyway — changed the dynamic and we all ate quietly, apart from Charlie, who tried to impress Josh with some terrible jokes he'd collected from somewhere, jiggling his legs as he ate and talking in funny voices. I groaned inwardly. Josh laughed politely. Tess picked at her peas and tossed some meat on the floor for the dog. She stared openly at Josh. After a while, he began to return the look.

'Who do you live with up there?' she asked suddenly. Startled, Josh was caught with a mouthful of food, which he attempted to swallow before answering.

'Just me and sometimes a couple of the other blokes,' he said. 'Shearers.'

'Don't you get bored up there?' Tess ignored Gram's glares. It was one thing to have the help in her kitchen, interrogating them was another.

'Not really. I guess.'

'Do you have parties?'

Josh looked at Grandpa, as if the old man had laid a trap for him. 'Nah . . . sometimes.' He wiped his black hair away from his forehead, revealing the thick bushes of his eyebrows. 'Just a few beers. Nothing much.'

'It's all right, son,' said Grandpa. 'You're entitled to your fun. Lord knows it's lonely enough up there, and you all work hard. I appreciate it.' He smiled, and I wondered if I was the only one to notice that his false teeth wobbled in his mouth.

After dinner, Grandpa unpacked the game of Trivial Pursuit that we had played so many times we had memorised the answers. 'Will you stay?' he asked Josh.

Gram huffed and left the room, clutching her pack of cigarillos, while Mrs G pottered around with the dishes.

'I'd better be getting back,' Josh said. 'Early start and all that. Thanks, though, Mr Summers, it was real nice.'

'My pleasure,' said Grandpa. 'You know, Josh —'

At the door, Josh turned to look at him as he shoved his feet into his gumboots.

'I'm keeping an eye on you. You're doing a great job. Keep it up. I've got plans for you, son.'

Josh coloured as much as his swarthy cheeks would let him. He nodded his thanks, took a last look at my sister, slouching in her seat, twisting her long dark hair, and he was gone.

'Terrible business,' said Grandpa as he sat down. 'Both his parents dead. He doesn't talk much, but I think he's a good boy.'

Looking back now, I remember being puzzled by Grandpa's referring to Josh as a *boy*. He was in his twenties. Now I see it for what it was — a casual reference to class that someone of Grandpa's status and generation wouldn't have given a second thought.

꙰

The following school holidays, in August, was when it all happened. August was when lambing began, and Grandpa wasn't around much. He took us all out with him one morning, and I remember being surprised that Tess was so willing to go. It was raining and we all donned raincoats and gumboots. Tess's eyeliner ran. Charlie was quiet and a bit pale as we rode the back of the Landrover with the dogs, and for once his running banter was absent. I stood up and held onto the bars, riding the bumps in the road like a surfer, letting the rain fall on my face.

Josh stood over a ewe that was moving weakly, ready to give up. Tess ran over to him as soon as the Landrover stopped and they exchanged a few words before she stepped away and made room for Grandpa, who crouched down beside the distressed animal.

'We're going to lose her,' he said. He moved down her body, to where a purple blob was emerging from her rear end. Charlie stood with his mouth hanging open, then turned and ran back to the truck, which he climbed inside, and refused to look any further. Tess also just stood there, face hidden by the huge hood of her raincoat, fiddling with the silver rings she wore on most of her fingers.

I crouched down beside Grandpa to get as close a look as I could. He grabbed hold of the blob and pulled. With a sucking sound, like mud, the lamb fell onto the grass in a mess of blood and umbilical cord. The ewe gave a last sigh and then was still.

'But what will happen to the lamb?' Tess asked. Her eyes had become red. Josh moved quickly to stand beside her and she leant against his big body. A hand patted her on the back, but when Josh noticed Grandpa looking he stepped away, causing Tess to stumble a moment. The rain kept coming and all I could hear was the sound of it on the hood of my raincoat, incessant.

In the end, the lamb was saved. It was given to a ewe that had lost its own lamb. For a while it was touch and go whether she would accept it, but the desire to mother something must have been too great, and she was soon licking the foster lamb and encouraging it to feed from her.

When it was time to return to the house, Grandpa told Tess to ride in the front with him. I don't know what they talked about, but I could guess. I watched them through the back window. Grandpa did most of the talking. He gesticulated as he spoke. Tess sat hunched in her seat with her arms crossed. She raised her voice at one point, said, 'All *right*! I get it,' and after that, it seemed, nothing more was said. She stared out the window beside her, and Grandpa reached over once to pat her arm. When we pulled up, Tess jumped out and ran straight to her room, where she stayed for the rest of the day while Grandpa drove back up the hill and I continued to work on a stoat that one of the dogs had brought home.

One afternoon a couple of days later, I emerged from the workroom and found the house empty. I walked through the rooms, looking for my family, but the house wasn't giving them up. Even Mrs G wasn't in the kitchen. A quick look outside told me she'd taken her car and must have gone to town, but where was everyone else? Even Tess wasn't in her room or the library, and I had no idea where to start to look for her outside.

The tower was the best place to go to find out. There I could see in one glance whether Charlie was out with the other kids on their horses, and Grandpa up at the paddocks. The rain from the previous days had disappeared, and even though the clouds still hung thick and uncertain, Gram was likely to be tending to the spring flowers that had emerged to brighten the garden.

The staircase to the tower was as muffled and dark as ever, and my small socked feet felt their way on each step, slowly, slowly. I was sure that one day I would slip and fall and be found in a heap at the bottom, so I trod as carefully as I could.

When I opened the door I was surprised to find that all the blinds were down. As I crossed to the nearest window, to let in the dull light, I heard a small sound in the air, a swallow and a breath, barely audible, not even a sigh. I turned towards it.

I saw a pale shape emerging from the shadow, a surprising shape, with blossoming hips and a narrow waist. Long dark hair piled loosely, and below, a picture, drawn onto the skin. A bird, curving with the shoulders, a long arched beak and claws curled around a thin branch. Wings stretched out. Below this, another shape: a large brown hand resting in the small of the back as her body rose and fell, full of concentration. But this shape was no tattoo. It made a tiny movement, a caress.

I stood there for only a few seconds, deciphering what it was I was seeing. I must have made my presence felt, because the figure turned her face towards me, twisting her whole body so I could make out the edge of her bare breast before her eyes found mine. Beyond her, and beneath her, the large shape of Josh, lying as still as possible, trying to make himself invisible.

'Get out, Rosemary,' was all Tess said. 'Get out now.'

❧

I don't know why I was so upset. Whether it was the shock of seeing Tess naked with Josh, or the shock of seeing her with that huge tattoo over her back. Perhaps it was simply the realisation that she wasn't a kid any more. Where my body had only recently begun to change, hers had embraced full-blown womanhood. I began to understand more later, when I picked up the books she had been reading. She was so fully immersed in *Wuthering Heights* that May, that Josh's appearance in the garden, and later at the dinner table, must have seemed to Tess like the delivery of her very own Heathcliff. And just as with those star-crossed lovers, her romance with Josh was not to be allowed, so it was furtive, with stolen moments in the tower while everybody was out. Everybody except me.

She soon came and found me.

'You can't tell,' she said.

I huddled in the corner of my bed, trying to keep the cold from my bones. Tess was warm; I could see it in her flushed cheeks.

'About what?' I asked. 'The tattoo or you and Josh *doing* it?'

She sat heavily on my bed and rolled her eyes to the ceiling. 'You wouldn't understand. You're still just a baby.'

'I'm *not*,' I said. But next to her, that was exactly how I felt. Her eyes were heavy with mascara; each ear had multiple silver rings, like her fingers. I was still cutting my hair short to keep it out of the way and was in staunch denial that the time would soon come to wear a bra. And there was her tattoo. I couldn't imagine ever feeling so sure about anything that I would invite its permanence onto my body. I thought about the way she mocked Grandpa and avoided his stuffed birds, and yet here she was with one on her back. She didn't deserve to be here.

When Grandpa came home, I told him. I will never forget the look he gave me. His face collapsed. All the happiness he carried around with him dissolved in that one moment. Although he said nothing, just listened to what I had to say, he suddenly looked as if he would like to hit me. I backed away quickly and ran upstairs. Tess's shouts echoed up to where I sat, hugging myself and crying. Doors slammed. Footsteps thundered down the hallway and stopped outside my room.

'You're a fucking *bitch*, Rosemary,' she screamed through the door. 'I hate you forever.'

She didn't come down for dinner, and we ate in near silence. Even Charlie was quiet. He looked from one of us to the other. He knew something was up, but he also knew not to ask. At the end, Grandpa wiped his mouth and stood.

'Tess is on the first bus home tomorrow,' he said. 'Who would like to join her?'

Charlie and I sat there without speaking, but my stomach started twisting in knots. *Not me*, I said again and again in my head. Satisfied, Grandpa left the room.

The blame I feel is multi-layered. If I had ridden Lily more often instead of locking myself away trying to bring dead animals to life, then she wouldn't have been so wild on the spring grass; she wouldn't have been spooked in the paddock that morning and tried to jump the fence. If I had just kept my mouth shut, Tess wouldn't have got in trouble with Grandpa and wouldn't have been booked on the morning bus back to the city. She wouldn't have risen at first light to go to Josh, to say goodbye, probably to tell him that she had been betrayed by her little sister.

I try to piece together what I didn't see that morning. I knew Tess spent a restless night. I heard her in the next room, tossing and shuddering up against the wall. Crying. I fell asleep and dreamed of her naked back and the mysterious bird taking flight and diving at me until I retreated down the tower stairs, tripped and fell.

She gets out of bed as soon as the streak of silver appears on the horizon, dresses in woolly layers and pulls a soft hat over her ears. She creeps to the bathroom, only to go to the toilet and to fix her ever-present eyeliner — her pillow is thick with it. She lets herself out the back door, checking that Mrs G isn't up already to light the stove, and chooses a pair of Gram's long gumboots because she doesn't have any of her own. Outside, the mist is thick and the birds in the poplars are starting up their morning sounds. She goes to the stable to grab a bridle, but she has forgotten a carrot to entice one of the horses. They all wait for her to get close before turning around and fleeing with a kick. Only Lily allows her to approach, sweet, gentle Lily, and so it is Lily who has the bridle slipped over her chestnut head, and is led to the stile so Tess can climb onto her bare back. I don't know why Tess doesn't lead her out the gate before mounting her. I can only think that she doesn't want to go that way, that she is worried about the sound of Lily's hooves on the gravel waking everyone. She should know that Grandpa will be getting up around now, that working on a farm is not about sleeping until midday, but about rising with the rooster that has started crowing its head off by the kitchen door.

Does she decide to go out of her way to the gate at the far end of the paddock, by the river? Is this when Lily is startled, takes the bit in her mouth and rushes for the fence? Or is it Tess herself who aims for it, a fence too high for such a little pony, who is accustomed only to jumping small fallen logs? Whatever the reason, Lily attempts the jump, but fails. She collides with the fence, her front legs becoming tangled in the wires, her weight crashing down onto her back legs. And with nothing but Lily's bare hide to cling to, Tess is thrown over her shoulder, where her head connects with a rock.

✻

I know I have told this story before, the one about Lily's death. I know I left out an important detail — the fact of Tess lying on the other side of that fence, dead. But how could I relive it in all its horror, when it was my fault that she was out that morning? It is bad enough that the sound of Lily's hoof on the wire has haunted me all these years, never letting me forget.

I don't know whether Josh ever knew that Tess was due to leave that morning, or that I had revealed their secret. Certainly Grandpa didn't acknowledge that the farmhand might be feeling a loss too, only set him the task of burying Lily while the family gathered together. I saw the grief in Josh's shoulders that afternoon, the slow way he went about his task, the revenge he took on Lily. Or was it me he was taking revenge on, knowing how much I cherished her?

Grandpa blamed himself; I know he did. And when we stopped visiting — I think my mother wanted to punish him somehow — all the life seeped out of Magpie Hall, just as those bright Super-8 films had stopped. I missed it. I missed the house; I missed Grandpa and I missed the taxidermy, which I think is why I drifted back into it when I left school. And I missed Tess, which is why that first tattoo was for her — her name beneath the horseshoe that my mother had found so offensive. I couldn't bring Lily or Tess back to life, the way I had with the magpie that first time, the way I have with countless other creatures, so the tattoo was my way of keeping them both alive. My memento mori. I know that Tess would have approved, just as she would have approved of the way I turned out: the tattoos, the books, the lovers. I have spent my whole life since then trying to make it so.

Henry

Magpies. He has slaughtered every last one of the wretches. He cared little about preserving them, so some are ripped and bloody, while others look as if they have merely closed their eyes and folded their bodies in sleep. But still they come. It doesn't matter how many he shoots, within days new ones will come to take their place, to claim their territory. Usurpers. They were never meant to be here in the first place — just like the rabbits and every other creature that has arrived uninvited by the native birds and animals. They have murder in their hearts.

Dora lies on the high table. Her clothes have dried now, but her hair still has a damp curl about it and her skin is as blue as a robin's egg. He has an urge to cover her in a blanket, to warm her up, to cushion the hard wood beneath her, but he knows that she is best left in this room, with the fire unlit and the door locked. With the cold, he has bought himself some time.

He is unable to drag his gaze away from her. It is as if every shape in his peripheral vision is also turned towards her — every mammal, reptile, bird has its glass eyes fixed on his wife, waiting to see what will happen.

Taking his scissors and, starting at the hem, he begins to cut open her dress. The blades slice easily through the thick cotton, over her legs to her waist, continuing on through the bodice. Here he must apply more pressure to the shears to cut the intricate smocking that gives the dress its shape, but soon he is through and can peel the garment back.

He lifts an arm to cut through the sleeve. The snake around her wrist stands out brightly against her dull skin. He brings her arm to his face and kisses the tattoo, letting his lips linger on the fishy coldness.

He remembers then, the morning when Dora, in a sliver of morning sun, lay on the bed admiring her body openly in front of him.

How beautiful they are, the colours, she said. Will they fade?

Not if you keep them covered, he said. It is sunlight that damages them the most.

And what about when I get old? she asked. Her arms pointed straight out in front of her, her hands caressing the tattoos. Will they sag? Will they wrinkle?

We all must grow old, my love, said Henry, and reached for her lovely flesh. Our bodies change, he said, and these tattoos are part of your body now.

She rolled over on her front and laughed. Then I never want to be old, she said. And when I die, you must keep me on a shelf, just like your birds, and I will be with you always — young and smooth, my tattoos as bright as day.

It pains him to remember. She didn't mean it, of course she didn't. The tattoos belong to Dora and to him, nobody else. He knows that as soon as he reports her death there will be an inquest and her body will become a curiosity for others. Worse: a scandal. He will not be responsible for damaging her name and reputation in this society. He cares little for it himself but this is where she was born, and where her memory will reside. He must think of her poor father, who will be grief-stricken enough when he learns of the death of his only child.

And so his mind is made up. He will tell them of the drowning, yes, of how he watched her being swept away and tried to save her, of how the river had taken her and did not want to give her up. Of how he had tried to go in after her but the river, too swift, carried her away faster than he could run. They will understand, for they have all lost livestock in similar circumstances. Usually the bodies turn up bloated and rotting, snagged on a tree branch or floating in a pool, miles along the river, but there are those that have disappeared without trace. Perhaps the bones are picked clean by eels and sink into the silty river bottom; perhaps they are carried out to sea. This will be Dora's fate.

With some effort, he turns her body over to cut the laces of her corset and remove it. Next, her chemise. The tattoo of the huia springs to life, its reds and blacks in sharp contrast to her bloodless skin. It is a masterpiece. Too good to be buried in the ground. Looking at it brings back a cascade of memories, of stalking and catching the bird, of bringing it home to present to Dora. Of the sound of the electric needle humming against her skin and the sharp smell of her nervous sweat that rose up to meet him when he took her hand. Of her giddy demeanour for days afterwards, as though she were being fed a constant stream of champagne.

He had found her eventually, caught in the shallow water near the ford. He gave up all hope when he saw her face down, immobile, that terrible colour. He sat with her in the freezing river, not believing what he was seeing. Only an hour before she had been warm, her hot breath on him as she shouted. How could she have thought that he had somehow harmed those children, that they were anything more than curiosities? That he had some kind of evil in his heart for collecting them. She was a woman, she simply didn't understand, but to make her run out like that, to have caused this — how could he live with himself? Without her.

He had followed her when she ran out, but not quickly enough. He had called her name through the rain, but if she heard him, she did not stop. If he had been faster, perhaps he could have prevented the magpies attacking her. He saw them swarm over her, watched helplessly as she fell in the water, and again as she was swept past him. By then, her lungs were possibly already filled with water and she was senseless.

He was shivering when he eventually pulled her from the water and lifted her onto his horse. He managed to get her inside the house without anyone seeing and now here he stands, her dress in rags in his hands, her body cool on his workbench.

He turns her over onto her back again and looks at her naked torso, at the hummingbird on her belly. Something is different about her. Despite the fact that she had lost weight when he returned from his trip, he can see now that her stomach is thicker; even as she lies on her back, it rises above her hip bones, soft and full. Could it be? He staggers back, looks around the room for something to cover her with and finds an old sheet he has been tearing up for rags. He throws it over her and allows his hand to fall on her abdomen, imagines the life that might have been growing inside her. His vision blurs with tears. What have I done? he murmurs. He sees her face again, the look of utter despondency as he argued with her about the children's body parts; he should have known then that her feelings were coming from a place deep within her. No wonder she thought him a monster. If only he'd known, he would have made sure that she could never find those jars.

But it is too late. Now she is dead, and the child with her. It is night and he knows he can do no more. He leaves the room, making sure the curtains are shut tight and locking the door behind him.

❧

He sleeps the intermittent sleep of the feverish, one moment cold as the grave, the next hot and slick with sweat. The wind rattles at his window as though someone is trying to get in; he awakes with a start to an empty bed while Dora taps on the glass, moaning to be let in. He staggers over, throws back the curtains and opens the window.

Dora! He shouts into the night, but the only answer he receives is from the wind. He remembers then, her cold, pregnant body lying in his taxidermy room and his chest tightens with horror and regret.

May you not rest in peace, Dora Collins, but haunt me all of my days for what I have done to you!

The wind answers with a low cry.

Dora, he says, quieter this time. His hands linger on the window frame a moment before he pushes it closed and returns the curtains to their place.

He knows what he must do.

❧

There is a service for Dora, in the small chapel up the hill, but there is no body to bury. Her father takes it hard. When he learned of her drowning, he refused to believe she was gone, scoured every section of the river for miles, but he does not suspect what has really happened to her.

When Collins asks him if he knew she was pregnant, he lies and says that he did. How different things might have been. He turns away from her father then, unable to look upon his grief.

They lay a memorial stone for her in the churchyard, a place where her loved ones can grieve, talk to her ghost once it has departed for a better place.

And all the while, Dora lies in Henry's workroom. After it is all over, after the last of the visitors has left (they filled the drawing room and drank sherry only feet from where she lay) Henry can at last be alone with her.

He cannot preserve her body in the full sense of the word; it would be grotesque. With no fur or feathers to cover it, her skin would shrink over her bones like the mummies of Egypt, turn dark and leathery. Her face would become skeletal and ugly, all her beauty erased. But her skin, her beautiful, illustrated skin, that is another story. He can bury her remains, with their child, undetected in the empty grave marked by her memorial stone. But he can save her tattoos, just as she would have wanted, so she will always be with him. He will keep her hidden, and he will guard her for the rest of his life. She will be the queen of his cabinet of curiosities. She will no doubt drive him mad. So be it.

In the cold room, behind the locked door, he takes his finest knife and begins.

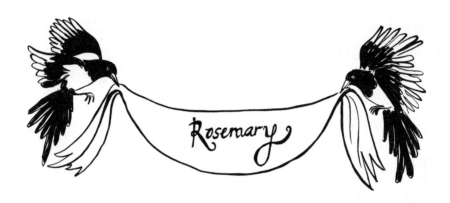

Rosemary

'I'll go and talk to him,' said Charlie, but he lingered by the telephone table, moving his lanky frame from foot to foot.

'No,' I said. 'I'll go. You just stay there and keep an eye on us.' I discarded the comforting old rug and dragged myself off the couch. This was my battle, I realised. I wasn't going to be rescued any more, not by Charlie, or by Sam, or Hugh. This was something I needed to confront on my own.

Josh watched me walk towards him. He rocked on his heels, greeted me with nothing more than a flick of his eyebrows, his cracked lips set in a straight line. I hadn't been this close to him in twenty years. He still held the basic shape of his youth but his face had sucked up the years and the harsh weather and was deeply lined. His dark hair, shot with grey, was still as thick as ever. He was well into his forties by now, and gone was the uncertainty he'd had as the orphan farmhand. This was a man in charge of a large station, and of himself.

I glanced back at the house and saw Charlie sitting on the couch, watching. He looked small suddenly, and I could see the little freckle-faced kid he'd been, waiting for his big sister. I couldn't help thinking that he had let me go so quickly, without any questions. I wondered how much he knew or understood about what had happened to Tess all those years ago. I had never asked him.

'Josh,' I said, when I reached him, keeping my distance.

'Rosemary.'

'Did you see who killed the magpie?'

He smiled, showing straight teeth, with a veneer of nicotine. 'I did see, yes.'

'And do you want to tell me who it was?'

'I think you know.'

'Right.' I folded my arms against the cold. The sun had sunk behind the hills. 'So it's been you all along? Lurking around.'

He spat on the ground suddenly. 'You make it sound so sinister.'

I felt my temper loosen then. 'Well, fuck, Josh. A dead bird nailed to the door? A dead possum on the doorstep? I'd say that's pretty sinister, wouldn't you?'

'Yeah, I suppose so. Look, I was just trying to scare you. It was a joke, really.'

'And what's it all for? I mean, really?'

He wouldn't meet my eyes. Instead, he focused on the roof of the house, the magpies watching us from the chimneys. What he said next came as a complete surprise. He said it so quietly I was unsure at first if I'd heard him correctly.

'I loved your grandfather, you know. He was like a dad to me.'

'You *loved* him?'

He looked at me then, and his face screwed up. 'I was the one who was here for him. You all just left him to that nurse, Susan. I kept him company, every day.' He jabbed himself in the chest with a thumb. '*Me.* Got behind in my work, too, but he was more important than any of that. You just left him here to die alone.'

I felt blood rushing to my head. 'That's not true. How could you say that? I was very close to him.'

'You *were* close to him. He told me all about it. How you two used to stuff animals together. How you just stopped visiting after . . . after she died. You all did. It broke his heart. You know, I used to stand outside and watch you all, one big happy family. That night that I got invited in, that wasn't the first time I'd watched you, and it sure wasn't the last. But after she died, you all just stopped coming. And he started inviting me in, giving me warm clothes to wear, feeding me. Suddenly I wasn't the one outside looking in, any more. You just abandoned it all. You abandoned him.'

'Can't you see how hard it was for us? For my parents? I didn't have much say. But I came back to New Zealand to be near him.'

'But not *very* near. He said that he didn't know you any more. That he wished you were still a little girl so he could talk to you.'

I thought back to the time we spent together just before he died, how he always wanted to reminisce about my childhood, before Tess. How we talked about my taxidermy job in London, but we never talked about my life as it was right then. But what could I talk to him about? My failed love life? My tattoos? How we both blamed ourselves for Tess's death?

'Did he ever talk about her? About Tess?'

Josh hung his head and shook it. 'Nah, not really. It took him a long time to tell me that he was sending her away that day. He blamed himself, that's why. Oh, he was cold about it at first, especially towards me, but when he realised how much I loved her —'

'You loved her.' I couldn't keep the derision from my voice.

He looked at me sharply. 'Yeah, I did, actually.'

'But she was just a kid. She was only sixteen. I mean, come *on*. You were an adult. You should have known better.'

He paused, glaring at me. Then he shrugged. 'I suppose I should of, sure. But I don't know . . . she just had this effect on me. I was hooked on her. Like a drug.'

'Josh, it was twenty years ago. You've got a wife now. A family. Don't they mean anything?'

'Of course they do,' he growled. 'What do you take me for? Tess has nothing to do with them, don't you see? She's been bloody well *haunting* me that girl. I see her, all the time. Ever since Percy died and I found out about you lot wanting to get rid of the place.' He cleared his throat. 'Get rid of me.'

I gulped, suddenly short of air.

'What do you mean, you *see* her?'

'I mean I seen her walking over the hills. Watching me work. I seen her in the tower.'

'The tower. Is that why you've been up there? Have you been sleeping up there or something?'

'Sleeping? Nah. I just go up there sometimes and talk to her. I tell her about your grandad. About all the things he promised me and how your family has come along to fuck it all up.'

'And that mattress. What, is that just some kind of nostalgia trip for you? The scene of your last . . .' I trailed off. I didn't want to say it.

'It was the last place I saw her alive, sure. We were happy. Until you came along.'

'And what's this about Grandpa's promising you things? What kind of things?'

'That the farm would stay as it was. That I'd always have a job. That the house could be as good as mine. I guess he never thought to put all that stuff in his will.'

'Of course he didn't. Don't be ridiculous. This property has been in our family for generations. Why would he leave it to you?'

Josh said nothing.

'You've been in there while I've been staying, haven't you? You moved the huia that day.'

'Just looking after the place. Keeping the clock wound. That kind of thing.'

'Trying to scare me off, you mean.'

He shrugged again. 'Like I said, just jokes.' His voice was anything but jovial and there was no trace of mirth on his face. He was deadly serious.

I had nothing more to say to him. The house would be renovated, the farm would be subdivided and sold, he might or might not keep his job. After news got back to the family of how he'd behaved, most likely not. There was nothing I could do about it. I turned to leave, catching Charlie's eye where he stood in the window, watching us. He gave a flicker of a wave.

'You didn't deserve to be here, alone with Tess. I wanted you gone. I wanted her to myself. That's why I tried to scare you off.'

I stopped, but I didn't turn around.

He went on. 'She was coming to see me that day, wasn't she?'

Still I kept my back to him, looking towards the house, up at the tower. 'How should I know?'

'She was coming to see me to say goodbye, because you'd told on her and she was being sent away.'

When I faced him I was surprised to see tears in his eyes. I tried to keep my voice as calm as possible. 'You've got to let it go now, Josh. I was just a kid. Just like she was.'

'That's bullshit!' he exploded. 'You knew exactly what you were doing. I *knew* it. I knew that very day that it was all your fault.'

'Stop it,' I said. 'It wasn't my fault.' I started to cry, lying to myself, lying to Josh. 'You should have known better! Screwing around with a girl, you were, just a girl!' I threw myself at him, slapping him in the face. He pulled back in surprise, then punched me in the nose.

The light fractured and I fell backwards onto the cold, muddy lawn. My face throbbed with a tight, sharp pain and blood spurted out onto my lap as I sat there. Josh took another step towards me and for a moment I thought he was going to kick me, but I heard feet pounding the grass and from one side something flew towards him, knocking him down. I thought it must be Charlie, but then I felt soft hands pulling me to my feet, and my brother embraced me while Josh fought on the ground with somebody else.

Sam.

Their limbs windmilled as Sam scrambled on top of the much bigger man. Charlie tried to pull me away as they rolled together on the ground, swapping weight and power until finally they came to a stop with Josh pinning the farmhand down. Sam bucked and arched his body, trying to throw him off. It was futile.

'Just quit it!' Josh yelled at him. Sam went limp. He glanced at me, eyes wide, and flicked his head in the direction he had come. I looked. His rifle lay a few metres from where the men now eyeballed each other like dog and sheep. Feeling sick and dizzy, my feet curiously light, I stepped out of Charlie's grasp and picked up the gun. I pointed it at Josh, but I was too scared to put my finger anywhere near the trigger. I prayed that the safety catch was on.

'Get off him,' I said to Josh. His head turned slowly to look at me. He loosened his grip on Sam's wrists, but he looked amused, rather than alarmed.

Charlie, on the other hand, looked terrified. 'Put it down, Rose,' he said. 'What the hell are you doing?'

Freed, Sam turned on his side and scrambled to his feet. He got to me in two strides and placed both hands on the gun, keeping it pointed away from any living thing. 'You okay?' he asked. I nodded. Blood was running into my mouth and stars danced in my vision for a few seconds afterwards.

'This is bullshit,' said Josh, as he rose slowly, knees and hands crusted with mud. He hesitated, looking at me. 'I'm sorry,' he said, then turned and strode away.

We watched his broad back disappearing towards the gravel road, where, in the last of the dim light, I could see his quad bike parked behind a tree. Hidden.

'What were you arguing about?' asked Sam, but Charlie pushed him aside and tilted my face with a finger on my chin.

'No time for that,' he said. 'I think it's broken. Let's get you to the hospital.'

'Yes, Dr Summers.' I looked at Sam. 'Thanks.'

He helped me to the Mercedes and sat with me while Charlie gathered together some warm clothes and a few of my things. As I caught the blood with a towel, it stained the white cotton with Rorschach patterns. It was getting harder for me to see, and when I looked in the rear-view mirror, it was obvious why. The delicate skin around my eyes was turning purple and puffing out like jellyfish. I lay back in the seat and closed my eyes. Colours swirled and pulsed in time to the waves of pain. When Charlie emerged, he shook Sam's hand awkwardly.

'Can you keep an eye on the place, mate?' he asked. 'I'll be back as soon as I can.'

'Are you going to call the cops?' Sam asked.

'I don't know. That's something Rose and I will have to talk about.'

I wound down my window and held out my hand. Sam took it in both of his. Mine was freezing but his were on fire, warming my blood.

'Can you stay? In the house? It needs to be looked after.'

'Sure I can,' he said, and smiled. He squeezed my hand. 'Don't you worry about a thing.'

The Mercedes rumbled into action. Charlie pulled away slowly and I wound the window back up. It was almost dark now. The sky still held stubbornly to its indigo light, but the hills were a solid black. The stark, bare trees were silhouetted, every twig sharp, and the house loomed huge behind us. The magpies watched us go.

I think I knew that would be the last I saw of Magpie Hall in its present state. As I sat under the harsh lights of the hospital emergency room, waiting to be seen by the doctors, I mentally walked through the house and said goodbye to all its rooms. I started in the entrance hall and moved past the great dining hall, with its impossibly long table and matching straight-backed chairs, through to the living room, with its dust and soft, peeling furniture and sagging wallpaper. I moved down the hallway, stopping in the gold-walled smoking room, lined with more insects and butterflies, past the mildewy damp bathroom with its railway-like tiles and stained bath, to the kitchen, the heart of the house. The library was still and quiet as usual, the bookshelves leaning in and enclosing the room. I lingered in the menagerie room, whispering to the animals and the cases full of grotesque specimens that I would be back for them, that they would find a new home. I said goodbye to Grandpa, who looked up from the rabbit we had been working on, and gave a waggle of his false teeth to make me laugh. Up the stairs over black carpet, so thick it had hardly worn in years, and down the passage to the red room, my grandparents' bedroom with frilly bedspreads and faded floral curtains covering the huge arched windows, diminishing them somehow.

And everywhere the clutter that I had failed to finish sorting through. The rest of my family would swoop on it, clear it in time for the renovations. No doubt most of it would end up at the Salvation Army or, worse, the rubbish dump. I glanced into each of the bedrooms, soon to be turned into guest accommodation with ensuite bathrooms and new beds, and finally rounded the end of the hallway, turning a sharp right to the servants' wing, with its stark skinny rooms and cold bathroom. I hesitated at the door to the tower, but pushed in, up the stairs to where the room was bright with light, and the view to the hills was breathtaking. I said goodbye to Gram, dead-heading the roses in the garden, and to young Charlie, taking off up the hill on horseback with the other kids.

Finally I turned away from the window to say goodbye to Tess, who sat on the mattress with a sheet knotted above her breasts, her long smooth legs crossed in front of her. She was smoking a cigarette, one of Josh's rollies, and as I looked at her she blew a stream of smoke into the air around us and picked a piece of tobacco from her tongue.

'You'll be all right?' I asked her, but she said nothing, just smiled and turned her back to me, presenting me with her bird tattoo for the last time.

My nose wasn't broken, but it was close. I looked a sight and they sent me away with a prescription for some strong painkillers, which I took immediately, falling asleep in the car. Charlie drove me back to the city, after some feeble protest on my part that I wanted to go back to Magpie Hall, that I had left all my work there, that I hadn't finished with it. But I knew that I had. Charlie promised to pack up all my things and bring them to me later in the week, along with my poor car.

'You need to rest, anyway,' he said. 'No more work.'

He dropped me off at my little flat above the tattoo studio and I sat for a long time after he left, looking out the window at the lights of the port as workers laboured through the night to load containers onto the tall ships that loomed out of the black sea. It was Saturday night, so I knew Rita wouldn't be home for a long time, and I hoped that she would turn up alone, without any sailors in tow. Shouts and taunts floated up from the street below as people spilled out of the pub on the corner and lingered at the window of Roland's shop. Perhaps in another time the shop would have remained open to catch just such clientele, the flotsam from the ships and other misfits. The odd gentleman.

As the painkillers wore off, I sat up in bed, unable to sleep. I turned on my lamp, which cast a pink glow about the room and up the wall that housed the tattooed women I had collected. I looked at my own tattoos and thought how much more beautiful, more refined, they had become with technology. I had pictured Dora's tattoos as being fine-lined and artistic, but in reality, if she'd had them, they would have been as rough and cartoonish as the ones in the photographs before me, with thick, wobbly lines and an absence of delicate shading and subtle colour changes. I wondered, then, how much of what I had imagined could possible be true. The collector in me had gathered together shiny facts and tried to assemble a nest for Henry and Dora.

I heard Rita come in, clipping across the wooden floors in her heels. She stopped outside my bedroom and knocked softly.

'I saw the light,' she said. 'Mind if I come in?' She held a bottle of red wine in her hand as she sat down on the end of my bed. 'Jesus! What happened to you?'

'How long have you got?' I smiled, and it hurt.

'Wait there.' She put down the bottle and left, coming back a moment later with two glasses. 'Honey,' she said, 'I've got all night if you have.'

She shed her leopard print coat and shook off her shoes.

So I started at the beginning, told her everything that had happened to me at Magpie Hall in the last week. She coaxed out details — she was good like that — and by the end of half an hour she had heard everything there was to know about Sam, and about Hugh.

'I knew there was something going on you weren't proud of,' she said. 'You were so secretive about him. So unlike you. You should've told me. I wouldn't have judged you.'

I shrugged and took another couple of painkillers.

'So which one of those bastards did that to you?' she asked. 'Or did you fall down the tower steps?'

I took a deep breath and told her about Josh, but realised halfway through that I was going to have to tell her about Tess as well, or it wouldn't make any sense.

'Have I ever told you,' I said, knowing the answer, but stalling for time, 'about my sister Tess?'

'Sister? You've got a sister? No, you never said.'

'*Had* a sister,' I said. 'She died. When I was thirteen.' And then I started to cry.

It felt good to confess. I had never discussed it with anyone, the guilt I felt over her death, the part I played in it, not even with my parents or with Charlie. Josh had given me the opportunity and I had turned away from it. Afterwards, I felt spent, drowsy, but that could have been the effect of the wine and the codeine. I lay my head on my pillow and Rita said nothing, just stroked my hair until I fell asleep.

※

The renovations to the house began that week, as if my family were taking advantage of my woozy state to rush in before I could block them further. I don't know what they expected; perhaps they imagined me lying down in protest in front of the trucks as they rolled in. The truth is, I was too tired for any of that, too tired to argue any more.

I wasn't there but I imagined it: the clearing of the clutter, the demolition. Pulling down the wallpaper and sarking to insulate and reline, knocking holes in the kitchen walls to put in french doors. Replacing all the kitchen appliances, installing new bathrooms. Tearing out walls that separated the rooms to make them open-plan and modern. Letting the light in.

I wish I'd seen their faces, their puzzled looks, when they found the contents of Henry's cabinet. They had been there all along, of course, not the cabinet, or the crate it had been packed in — they were long gone — but the curiosities themselves, hiding in the walls wrapped in cloth, like secret offerings. We could only surmise that Grandpa's father had put them all there after Henry died, under the pretext of dividing the house's massive rooms into smaller, cosier spaces. The cabinet of curiosities never made it to the British Museum because Edward Summers had opened it and been aghast at what he found.

The builders had smashed through the walls with a sledgehammer, and what they found caused the work to stop for a considerable amount of time, even though the weather was foul and they'd had to drape the holes in the outer walls in tarpaulin to try and stop the incessant rain and wind from causing too much damage.

Human remains. I suppose that Henry's son had believed the rumours about Dora, that his father had murdered her and hidden the body, and here he was, hiding the evidence, to keep the family's secret safe once and for all. He probably imagined the house would be a constant in everyone's lives for many more years.

I could tell you that what they found were perfectly preserved sheets of human skin, which they at first took to be a series of paintings on parchment: eggs, butterflies, a hummingbird and, most impressively, a huia, delicate and life-like, glowing with the light that fell through the vellum. Only after careful inspection would it be revealed that the ink was embedded under its surface; that it had been tattooed there, not painted. That Henry had kept a beautiful memento mori of his wife, and that he wanted it to be preserved and displayed forever at the world's greatest museum, so that Dora might live on.

But that would be a lie. Oh, there were human remains all right, but the walls of Magpie Hall were full of bones, not delicate parchment. They could have been the bones of a young European woman, and Edward might have thought he was hiding the evidence of a terrible crime, but then that would not explain why there were so many of them, of all different sizes, mixed in with the bones of a large flightless bird, so that they knocked together like percussive instruments. There were skulls, too. Not just one, but several. One no bigger than a child's.

After the police had been called, and experts brought in, it was decreed that they were most likely bones taken from a nearby Maori burial cave sometime in the late nineteenth century, but they were much older than that: probably pre-European contact. They would be returned to the ancestors. The artefacts found with the bodies gave the most clues — adzes and fish hooks made of greenstone, tools and ceremonial weapons — and I would have to tell you that Henry Summers was not the noble gentleman I had made him out to be, and that Grandpa had wished him to be, who shied away from dishonourable collecting. In fact, my ancestor was nothing more than a grave robber, breaking tapu and indiscriminately collecting the remains of women, children and warriors alike. Nobody could pretend otherwise, not after the cabinet curiosities offered up their incontrovertible truth. And perhaps his first wife did drown in the river and her body was never found. Or perhaps he murdered her, as the rumours suggested. We will never know. End of story.

❦

Charlie delivered my car and my work to me a few days after he dropped me off.

'You're looking much better already,' he said.

I touched my nose. Still tender. I looked as though I'd been in a bar brawl and I hadn't left the flat since I arrived. I couldn't bear to face the questions and the looks. Instead I'd stayed in bed, sleeping or talking with Rita as she made pot after pot of tea and blew cigarette smoke all over my room.

Charlie carried my things up the stairs to the lounge. He waved the printed manuscript at me.

'What's this?' he asked. 'I thought you were writing a thesis, not a novel.'

'Did you read it?' I asked.

'I'm sorry, I did. Do you mind?'

I shrugged.

'How did you know all of this about him? About what happened to Dora?'

I hesitated and thought briefly about lying, about saying it was a true and accurate account of a genuine love story that had taken place in our very own family history. That I had found evidence — a diary, photographs. A cabinet of curiosities furnished with human skin.

'I didn't,' I said instead. 'I made it up.'

'Well, that's quite some imagination you've got. You've written the perfect love story. But as if he'd have all those tattoos. A bit of projection on your part, I think.'

'Ah,' I said. 'Now that bit was true. The letter from Grandpa, remember?'

Something about being in the house that week had compelled me to write that story, to believe that Henry and Dora had lived as happy a life together as they could before she died, that she and I shared some kind of profound connection. Call it too many Victorian novels, call it a desire to believe that someone in my family had experienced the kind of love I knew was out there. But even as I wrote it, the house started to lose some of its magic for me, and by the end I had decided that Magpie Hall had been a prison for Dora, and for Henry. Certainly for Tess's ghost. Perhaps even for Grandpa.

It could have been true. Henry had the tattoos after all. It was all there in Grandpa's letter. But when I later found out the truth about his collecting, I realised that the picture of the man I had built crumbled under the slightest of touches. Perhaps it wasn't the fact of his skinned wife that had driven him mad, but the knowledge that he had broken tapu, inviting a curse upon himself and generations to come. Perhaps it is Henry I can blame for my family's misfortune — for all of it.

We didn't go to the police about Josh's assault. In the end we decided that losing his job was punishment enough — the family tossed him aside without a thought, without any consideration of the loyalty he had felt to the farm and to Grandpa. He was offered a plot of land to buy but he declined. I doubt he could have afforded it anyway, as my parents well knew. It was a token gesture. Perhaps if I'd had some say I would have been more lenient on him and fought for his right to stay, just as Grandpa had promised him, but every time I looked in the mirror I knew that was not possible. It was his wife and kids I felt sorry for. I wondered if Tess was still haunting him, but I got the feeling she had done what she came for.

I finished my thesis that winter: depictions of romantic love in Victorian Gothic novels. I wrote holed up in my flat where it was warm, and avoided the university as much as I could. I needed to get the work out of the way so I could move on with my life. There were no more digressions, no more fantasies to write, and the pages about Henry and Dora stayed in a box under my desk.

I went back to Magpie Hall in the spring, when most of the renovations were finished. I couldn't face going alone, so I took Charlie with me. The builders had done a beautiful job, with new windows and walls as smooth as eggshells. The rooms were full of space and sunlight; despite a cold wind outside and the absence of a fire, with proper insulation it was as warm inside as a summer's day. The old carpet, once thick with dust and dog hair, was gone, replaced by wooden floors, stripped back and waxed black, keeping in tune with the style of the house. I surprised myself by wishing we had done it sooner, that we hadn't let Grandpa go on living in such an unhealthy place. Perhaps he would have lived longer if he'd only had more warmth; clearer, drier air.

My family had agreed to let me keep the menagerie room as it was, as a point of interest for visitors, they said, but I think they knew it was a valuable collection and they wanted to keep an eye on it. I didn't mind. In this room at least, I could keep Grandpa's memory alive.

Before I opened the door, Charlie stopped me with a hand on the doorknob.

'They found something else,' he said. 'In the walls. They weren't sure what to do with it all, so they just added it to the collection. Grandpa left you all the animals, so we figured these might as well go to you as well. Unless you've got any other ideas.'

When I stepped into the room, the first thing I noticed was that it was several degrees colder than the rest of the house. Good for preserving the animals, but it only served to illustrate the difference between the old house and the new. The next thing that struck me was the number of birds that were piled up on the workbench, perhaps fifty of them, maybe more.

I don't know why I thought they were magpies. The flash of black and white I suppose; maybe my head was still clouded by the story I had written. But I soon realised what they were. Their red wattles had faded and dried like flower petals, and they had different beaks — the curved for the female and the blunter, less showy one for the male. All their beautiful tail feathers, black with a bright white tip, were intact. They were not small birds, but lying there, they looked so vulnerable. Henry hadn't even bothered to pose each one, to bring it back to life. He had merely swept the huia up out of the bush, like a handful of pebbles, and stuffed them with their wings folded in, their eyes empty and their feet — tagged with luggage labels in Henry's tight script — tucked into their bodies, for easy storage and transportation. They lay there, looking as dead as could be.

I took one bird back home with me — the huia I had loved as a child. The one that had fuelled all our misconceptions about Henry, causing us to believe that he was different from other men of his time; that he respected endangered birds and the rights of Maori to have their dead left undisturbed. The rest of the collection stayed where it belonged, but I knew I didn't want those huia in the house. They would have to go to a museum, and the story would come out. Perhaps it would even make enough of a splash to warrant a small column in the local newspaper, just as the bones had.

I placed the huia on a high shelf in my bedroom, where it would be safe from Rita's drunken guests, and went downstairs to see Roland. I waited while he finished up a job, a man with a shaven head getting his bicep covered with skulls.

'What was the significance of those?' I asked Roland, after the guy had left, clutching his antiseptic cream.

'Said it was for all the mates he'd lost in car accidents. Quite sad, really.'

I thought of Sam. I wondered if he had found work elsewhere. If I'd see him again.

'What have you brought me?' asked Roland.

I showed him the book I was holding, and opened it onto the right page.

'Can you do something like this? Only a bit more stylised?'

He examined the picture. 'Sure. Give me tonight to work on it. Come back tomorrow first thing. I've got nothing on.'

The following morning I put on a vintage 1950s halter dress splashed with flowers to go with the brightness of spring. It showed off my tattoos nicely. I was always given curious looks when I dressed like this: the juxtaposition between the pretty, old-fashioned dress and the sailor tattoos confused some people. Then I fussed about completing the look: curling my fringe under, applying liquid eyeliner to my top lids, flicked out at the sides, red lipstick, and red high heels that clacked down the stairs to the tattoo shop. Roland sat in the only sliver of sun that would penetrate the building all day, and would soon be lost behind the hills. He unfurled his long body when I appeared and pulled out a piece of paper from his pocket. He squinted at it through his little round glasses before handing it over.

'Is this what you had in mind?'

His design had captured perfectly the essence of what I wanted to convey.

'It'll take a couple of visits, at least. I'll start with the outline today, then we'll book you in for the shading.'

I took off my cardigan and lay face down on the padded table, my head in a pillow that smelled of lavender. Roland shaved the area on my back, just above my shoulder blades, then rubbed it with Vaseline. I felt the whisper of paper as he transferred the sketch onto my skin, and I wished that gentle caress was all I would feel. Even after ten tattoos I had never really got used to the pain. Perhaps this would be my last. I couldn't imagine what more I could want or need, or where I would put another.

'Starting now.'

I closed my eyes and pressed my face into the crook of my arm, smelt the sharp tang of sweat that suddenly sprang up. Beside me, Roland would be dipping his needle into the tiny pot of black ink. I heard the hum of the tattoo machine start up and waited for the buzz, for that first scorching sting; I concentrated on my breathing so I wouldn't flinch.

Usually Roland worked silently, to be able to focus, but I preferred it when he talked. It took my mind off the pain, so I was glad when he spoke.

'You know, I have something to tell you.'

I waited for him to go on, breathing in through my nose, out through my mouth until the pain was at a point where I could imagine it turning to heat and dissipating.

The needle shut off as he refilled it. He wiped my back with a cloth.

'I'm shutting up shop. Moving to Wellington.' He started up again and I forgot to breathe. I flinched as the needle went in.

'How come?' I asked.

'Business isn't doing so well. This place is changing. Haven't you noticed? It's all couples now, with kids. All the cafés that are springing up. They're like cold sores, don't you think? It's just not the place for misfits and freaks any more.'

'So what'll happen to the building?'

'Sorry, love.' He stopped working again, patted my shoulder. 'You'll probably have to move out.'

I nodded and kept my face buried. Took a deep breath.

'You okay?' he asked.

'I'll be fine,' I said. I thought of my little flat up there, stuffed with ephemera. It was probably way overdue for a cull anyway. It'd do me good. It would be an impossible task to pack it all up and move somewhere. It was true what Roland said about the port. Rents were hitting ridiculous heights. I'd be lucky to find a room in a house with a whole lot of people for that price.

'I'll be fine,' I repeated, and gave in to the pain.

When he had finished, I stood up, feeling woozy. Roland took my arm to steady me, and led me over to the mirror that took up one wall of the back room. It was surrounded on all sides by photographs of Roland's work — patches of skin, red and raised and freshly inked, shining with Vaseline, including my magpie, which had now moulded to my wrist and become a part of my body.

'You ready?' he asked. I nodded and he held up another mirror behind me, so I could see his work. And there it was, just as I had imagined, curving gently with the contours of my back, the arc of its beak cupping my shoulder blade. The delicate outline of its wattle awaited the colour that would bring the huia to life and make it sing on my body forever.

Acknowledgements

I am grateful to the following people: Julia De Ville, for allowing me to use aspects of her life and work to build my story, and for sharing her knowledge of taxidermy; Mark at Ink Grave, for answering my questions on tattooing and letting me watch him work; Gillian Arrighi, for information on nineteenth-century circuses; Gareth Cordery at Canterbury University, for letting me sit in on his inspiring lectures on the nineteenth-century novel, thereby changing the course of *this* novel forever; the New Zealand Society of Authors and the Lilian Ida Smith Trust; Creative New Zealand for a generous grant and again, along with Canterbury University, for the Ursula Bethell Residency in 2008 — it gave me freedom and space and resources that would not have otherwise been available to me; my editors, Harriet Allan and Anna Rogers, and my wonderful agent Vivien Green; my crew, Kate

Duignan, Katy Robinson and Susan Pearce, for incisive criticism and much love and encouragement; Richard Lewis, Paul Cunningham and Hannah Holborn, all of whom I am yet to meet face to face but who have become trusted early readers; Sharon Blance and Brence Coghill; the Brunette Mafia; Christchurch City Libraries and Under the Red Verandah café for unwittingly providing me with an office away from home; Ros Henry for a sharp editorial eye and again, along with David Elworthy, for helping out tirelessly with family matters so I could write; Thomas Rutherford, for patiently sharing me; lastly, and most importantly, Peter Rutherford, without whom writing this novel really wouldn't have been possible, and to whom it is dedicated.

The Sound of Butterflies

Winner of the NZSA Hubert Church Award for Best First Book of Fiction at the 2007 Montana New Zealand Book Awards, and translated into seven foreign languages.

In 1904, the young lepidopterist Thomas Edgar arrives home from a collecting expedition in the Amazon. His wife Sophie is unprepared for his emaciated state and, even worse, his inability — or unwillingness — to speak.

Sophie's genteel and demure life in Edwardian England contrasts starkly with the decadence of Brazil's rubber boom, as we are taken back to Thomas's arrival in the Amazon and his search for a mythical butterfly. Up the river, via the opulent city of Manaus — where the inhabitants feed their horses champagne and aspire to all things European — Thomas's extraordinary, and increasingly obsessed, journey carries him through the exotic and the erotic to some terrible truths.

Back home, unable to break through Thomas's silence, Sophie is forced to take increasingly drastic measures to discover what has happened. But as she scavenges what she can from Thomas's diaries and boxes of exquisite butterflies, she learns as much about herself as about her husband.

Reviews of The Sound of Butterflies

'Rachael King has written a wonderful novel . . . which sets a new standard for first-time writers in this country.' *Herald on Sunday*

'So lucidly does she write you can easily imagine the sweat dripping down your back and the night noises in the jungle. She knows how to tell a story too . . . The story hums along. I read this book in two days, such was the grip it had on me.' *North & South*

'Not just readable but entertaining, imaginative and funny.' *Sunday Star Times*

'Engaging and tremendously well imagined [and] . . . a ripping yarn. A natural-born writer, King's prose flows as strongly as the Amazon, rich with easy lyricism . . . This is a complete meal of a novel, ambitious and well planned.' *The Australian Literary Review*

'[Rachael King's] mesmerizing combination of narrative, diary pages and letters reveals the true terror that Edgar experienced in the Amazon, where he witnessed one man's inhumanity to his own people . . . a captivating story.' *The Washington Post*

'King's easy narrative moves back and forth from the stultifying social confines of early 20th-century England to the sultry and seductive world of the rainforest . . . Rich and evocative, *The Sound of Butterflies* is an enjoyable debut.' *Financial Times*

'There's a potent array of material here: a love story, exotic settings, sex, travel, colonialism, some disturbing scenes of abasement and brutality, and, at the heart of the book, the mystery of Thomas's silence. Tension builds and as the novel goes on, King's narrative is well paced.' *The Listener*

'With her first novel, Rachael King proves herself one of our most promising writers. Her intelligent gaze snags on quirky details of personality or place or on mostly forgotten history, and spins captivating and provocative stories from them.' *Next Magazine*

'. . . an impressive novel filled with lyrical prose and clearly defined characters. The seductive setting gradually draws the reader into the hot, dangerous world of the Amazonian rainforest . . . The portrait of a man driven mad by his quest for perfection . . . is most convincing and had this reader up until the early hours. I look forward to King's next novel.' *The Christchurch Press*

'*The Sound of Butterflies* fuses Edwardian gentility with obsession, murder, and a glimpse of the giddy excess of the Brazilian rubber boom . . . It's convincing, told in prose as opulent as one of Thomas's specimens.' *The Observer*

'In this debut novel about love, betrayal and devotion, King offers a vibrant portrayal of a jungle inner-world and the characters who roam within it . . . Sensuous descriptions and multidimensional characters carry the novel. Gross displays of wealth, intense bloodlust and the immense beauty and danger of the jungle enrapture, providing a sharp contrast to the tightly-corseted society of early 20th-century England. As Thomas's quest for his perfect butterfly becomes a symbol for flawlessness that does not exist, both he and Sophie must learn to live with their imperfections and adopt a more real, honest love. As lush and captivating as the jungle in which it is set.' *Kirkus Review*